PRAISE FOR CINDY SAMPLE

"Packed with zany characters, humorous situations, and laugh-out-loud narrative. Consider reading this book in one sitting, because once you start, you will be reluctant to put it aside."
—*Midwest Book Review*

"Cindy Sample knows how to weave a story that satisfies and excites. Time literally flew by as I turned the pages… simultaneously harrowing, exciting, tender, and uplifting, a true who-done-it combined with a romance that will warm the heart and sheets."
—*Long and Short Reviews*

"*Dying for a Date* combines the fun of a spunky and smart heroine with an exciting murder mystery. This is an excellent entry to the world of romantic mysteries."
—*San Francisco Book Review*

"Funny, smart with a fast paced plot that keeps you guessing. *Dying for a Date* will keep you laughing, intrigued, and happy that Cindy Sample isn't writing your life story."
—*Fiction Addict*

"Sharp intelligence and flippant wit, turmoil and anxiety, danger and deception…all blend into one smooth and tasty read. I hope this turns into a long running series."
—*Once upon a Romance Reviews*

"A delightful romantic mystery. The plot was entertaining and I was kept guessing the murderer's identity right up until the reveal

D0973187

at the end. I look forward to reading more mysteries in the future from this talented new author."
—*Rebecca's Reads*

"Cindy Sample has an irrepressible sense of humor which is reflected in her writing. Dying for a Date is funny, fast paced and a kick to read. Laurel McKay is a lovable, klutzy protagonist backed by a team of quirky, humorous characters who are going to be a continuing hit with her readers."
—*Mountain Democrat Newspaper*

Other Books in the Laurel McKay series

DYING FOR A DATE

A LAUREL McKAY MYSTERY

Cindy Sample

CINDY SAMPLE

ISBN: 1492367249
ISBN-13: 978-1492367246

DEDICATION

This book is dedicated to my mother, Harriet Bergstrand, the most supportive mother in the world, and my wonderful children, Dawn and Jeff, who have made me a better person and who bear absolutely no resemblance to any characters in the book.

A special dedication in memory of my friend, Jerry Roberts, who departed her family and friends far too soon.

CHAPTER ONE

If I'd known my clothes would be covered in blood by the end of the evening, I probably wouldn't have agonized over my wardrobe selection. But as I prepared for my first date since my divorce, my fashion choice seemed of monumental importance.

Sweaters, slacks, and skirts were strewn across my bedroom, but I still couldn't decide what to wear. After negotiating my curves into a Spanx tummy-control item smaller than my fist, I gazed in dismay at the mess on my barely visible bed.

Too short. Too long. Too boring. Too sleazy.

The bright red numbers on my digital clock glared at me. Less than five minutes to get my butt out of the bedroom and into my car. I zipped up a mid-calf black skirt, buttoned a long-sleeved white blouse and tucked it into the waistband. The mirror above the dresser reflected its disapproval of my selections.

"Nothing looks right," I sighed. "I either look like Betsy Banker or Bimbo Barbie."

"Are you sure you want to go through with this?" Jenna, my sixteen-year-old daughter, slouched against the door. "You're kind of old to start dating again."

Old? Since when was thirty-nine considered over the hill? According to *Cosmo*, thirty-nine was the new twenty-nine.

My teenage critic flopped on my bed, turning the mountain of castoffs into a wrinkled puddle. I didn't need Dr. Phil to tell me that some passive aggressive behavior was going on.

I put my hands on my hips and glared at her. "Look what you did to my clothes."

Jenna slid off the bed with a martyred sigh and disappeared through the doorway. Seconds later a powder blue cashmere sweater sailed across the room and smacked the back of my head.

The loan of the sweater must be Jenna's way of apologizing. Unfortunately it was a gift from her father. No time to ponder the psychological ramifications of wearing an item purchased by my ex-husband for my first date in seventeen years. I slipped the sweater, designed for a smaller frame than mine, over my head and stared at my reflection. Between the tight sweater glued to my chest and the long black skirt on my chunky five-foot-four frame, I'd invented an entirely new look—Bimbo Banker.

I stepped into my new three-inch heels. At least my shoes looked hot. The only reason I was in the middle of a clothing meltdown was that Liz, my best friend, had talked me into joining a dating service called the Love Club—the safe alternative to online dating. As far as I was concerned, there was only one safe alternative.

Not dating.

I flew down the stairs then paused to peek in the family room. Red and gold strobes of light swirled over Jenna's auburn curls. Tucked into a chair, iPod earbuds in place, my daughter attempted to concentrate on her book, *The Joy of Calculus*, while her seven-year-old brother Ben and his best friend battled it out with their Jedi knight laser swords.

A grapefruit-sized lump lodged in my throat as I gazed at my children, re-evaluating my decision to start dating. Was I looking for a partner, or a male role model for my son? If I met someone would it harm the close relationship I had with my daughter? Did I really want to find Mr. Right?

Or just Mr. Every Other Saturday Night? Meaningful questions which I needed to ponder when I had more than thirty seconds to spare.

Fifteen minutes later I walked into Leonardo's, a Tuscan-themed restaurant in El Dorado Hills, an expensive residential enclave located thirty miles east of Sacramento. I'd lost the battle with a stubborn gas nozzle and reeked of gasoline.

I darted into the ladies room to wash the pungent smell from my hands. After tracing lipstick over full, non-collagen-enhanced lips, I peered in the mirror. Another one of those mysterious silver strands had appeared in my copper-streaked bob. I yanked out the wiry culprit, took a deep breath and threw open the door.

The smell of garlic mixed with flowery perfumes greeted me as I click-clacked across the terra cotta tiles to the reception desk. The women milling around the lobby were all taller, slimmer, and better dressed than me. Any minute now the El Dorado Hills fashion police would hand out a fashion citation.

"My name is Laurel McKay," I said to the size zero hostess who was barely larger than the menu she held. "Do you know if Garrett Lindstrom has arrived?"

An arm snaked around my waist. "Laurel, sorry I'm late."

I squirmed away to get a better look at my date. This guy chose me? Garrett was even better looking in person than on his DVD. Over six feet tall, with dark brown hair and designer wire rims—a Clark Kent look-alike clad in a black shirt and slacks.

The hostess led us past a three-piece jazz combo to an intimate corner table. My heart pounded in rhythm with the bass player as I folded the white linen napkin on my lap. Garrett bore an amazing resemblance to the intrepid journalist/superhero. Thoughts of the two of us soaring over city skyscrapers flitted through my brain.

"Do you like to fly?" I asked, still hung up on the Clark Kent likeness.

Garrett looked surprised. "Uh, yeah, I enjoy flying. My accounting practice keeps me busy, so I haven't traveled much. How about you? Taken any exotic vacations recently?"

It took me all of three seconds to contemplate the exotic trips I'd taken in my lifetime. "The kids and I went to Disneyland two years ago."

Garrett gave me a blank look and I mentally slapped myself. Nothing like mentioning Mickey Mouse on a first date to bring the conversation to a crashing halt.

Our waiter appeared before I could embarrass myself further by elaborating on the joys of riding in oversized teacups. He leaned over and lit the small candle on our table. "My name is Aaron. Can I tell you about tonight's specials?"

Garrett winked at me. "I think my date is pretty special, but let's hear about yours."

My cheeks flushed tomato soup-red. It had been years since anyone paid me a compliment. My self-esteem, which had been non-existent since my ex-husband moved out, jumped up a notch.

Once we placed our orders, the silence engulfed us. Silence is never golden in my world. I rushed to fill the gap with anything I could remember from my Accounting 101 class. "Garrett, I'd love to learn about depreciation."

I really needed to find a *Dating for Dummies Guide*.

Ten minutes later when our entrees arrived, he was still discussing depreciation methods. The glow of meeting my superhero dissipated, as Garrett morphed into an IBA—Incredibly Boring Accountant. When he lined up his dining utensils to display the merits of straight-line depreciation, I could see the writing on the spreadsheet. There would be no second date.

I peeked at my watch. If we skipped dessert, I could make it home in time to watch *CSI*. It crossed my mind that I might not be ready for dating if the thought of viewing dead bodies on television was preferable to being out with a live male.

I tuned back in to hear Garrett say, "If you structure it right, it's like getting free money."

Free money? My ears perked up at his statement but my eyes were diverted by the mocha-and-cream confection placed between us. I could always make time for tiramisu.

Once the server cleared our plates and brought the bill, I was ready for the evening to end. Garrett insisted on pulling my chair back for me as I rose from the table. What nice manners...hold on, did his hand graze my right breast?

Nah. Wishful thinking. It had been years since anyone grazed on any part of my anatomy.

The brisk night air felt refreshing after the garlic and basil scents of the restaurant. As we walked through the parking lot, I pawed through my purse. Lipstick, pepper spray, melted gummy bears. No keys and no phone. We approached my car and I peered in the window. The keys dangled from the ignition, right next to the cell phone hanging from the charger.

Some mother I was. Dating was already proving to be too much of a distraction.

"Garrett, my keys are locked inside the car and my phone is in there too. Can I use your cell to call AAA?" I shivered as the cool night air penetrated my lightweight sweater.

He pointed to a large sedan a few spaces away. "It's getting cold. Why don't you make the call from my car?"

Good idea. I slid into the soft leather bench seat of his roomy beige Lincoln Town Car. My date had excellent taste in vehicles. Garrett slipped into the driver's seat and handed me a slim metal phone. I dialed AAA and gave the dispatcher our location. I hung up, turned and...

Thunk.

My head smacked the passenger side door as Garrett thrust himself on top of me. His cell fell out of my hand. My purse flew over the headrest and into the back seat, sending the pepper spray out of reach. My right elbow smashed into the windshield as I struggled to push him off. He grabbed both wrists with a vise-like grip, and covered my face with wet sloppy kisses. The door handle pressed into my back as my superhero transformed into Dr. Evil.

Garrett finally relaxed his hold on my arms and shifted his attention downstream.

Adrenaline surged though my body as anger replaced fear. I grabbed the first thing I could find then raised my right arm.

Crack!

CHAPTER TWO

Blood spurted as the phone connected with Garrett's nose. The back of his head bounced off the driver's side window as he roared out a string of obscenities. Although with his mashed nose, it sounded more like "Puck" and "Pitch" than the usual expletives.

I yanked my purse from the back seat, jumped out of the car and slammed the door. As I raced back to the restaurant, I silently thanked Nokia for designing such an effective weapon.

The hostess looked startled as I rushed past her into the ladies room. I dampened a paper towel, but it was useless on the blood splattered all over the sweater. I threw the towel in the garbage can and leaned against the sink, my hands trembling.

Why had the boring accountant changed into a sex-crazed maniac? Maybe I shouldn't have ordered the tiramisu. Did ordering dessert signify I was willing to be dessert? His behavior didn't seem normal, but when it came to dating I was clueless. I'd married my high school sweetheart, and Garrett was only the second man I'd gone out with in my thirty-nine years.

By the time I returned to the reception area, Garrett's car was gone and the bright yellow AAA truck was idling in the parking lot. In less than five minutes, they unlocked my car and I was on my way home.

I stopped for a red light and then the storm broke. Tears rained down my face and my sweater, enhancing the paisley bloodstains. Between my blurred vision and my heaving chest, I was in no shape to drive. I made a U-turn at the next light and pulled into a McDonald's. Waiting in line behind eight cars for a shot of caffeine gave me time to pull myself together. The mascara running down my tear-streaked cheeks had transformed me into Goth Mom, but at this time of night, the crew had probably seen it all.

The kids were asleep when I arrived home so I didn't have to explain why mottled red splotches adorned my borrowed sweater. I tossed, turned then tossed again all night, finally falling asleep before dawn. The sun blasted me awake around eight. I tied my fluffy pink chenille robe around my waist and padded down the stairs in my matching pink bunny slippers.

"Morning, boys," I mumbled to Ben and Jimmy, sitting cross-legged on the carpet, playing a Nintendo game, "Pillage and Burn." I could tell them a thing or two about pillaging.

My slippers crunched through a trail of Cheerios leading from the family room into our sunny yellow kitchen. My rooster-covered wallpaper usually cheered me up, but this morning I wasn't in the mood to watch roosters strutting. It might be time to redecorate.

After grinding a few extra tablespoons of fresh-roasted beans, I hit the brew button on the coffeemaker then grabbed the Sunday paper. The aroma of Kona coffee wafted through the kitchen as I checked out the advice columnists. No other single woman apparently clobbered her date last night so I wasn't going to receive any professional advice on my encounter.

The shrill ring of the phone interrupted my reverie. I checked Caller ID. Liz.

"What took you so long?" I rested the receiver against my ear as I poured the first drops of steaming coffee into my mug.

"Thought you might want to sleep in." Her British accent was in full throttle as she deepened her voice. "In case you boinked your date."

"How did you find out I bonked him?"

"You had sex with Garrett?" Liz shrieked.

Sex? Oh yeah. I forgot the British definition of *boink* was far different from *bonk*, and did not mean smacking your date with a cell phone.

Liz clucked sympathetically as I recounted each agonizing detail of my encounter. "Well, luv, maybe you were too darn irresistible and he couldn't control himself. Did you wear that luscious lipstick I gave you last week?" Liz owns a full-service spa, and she is dedicated to preserving her youth and mine with all natural products.

"You mean Hottest Hottie Red? Nope, I went with Plain Old Pink."

"Wise move. Otherwise, he might have attacked you before dessert," she commiserated. "I'm sure the next guy you go out with will be a big improvement."

"Nah. I'm done. That was my first and last date. I'm perfectly content to spend the rest of my life alone with my crosswords." And a pound or two of chocolate to get me through those killer puzzles in the Sunday *New York Times*.

"Laurel, you have to get back on that horse."

"Horse?" The closest I'd been to a horse recently was the horse's ass that attacked me last night.

"You know what I mean. You can't quit after one bad date. Don't forget I went out with more than fifty fellas before I met my sweetie. Your wise friend is ordering you to go back to the Love Club. Don't let one rotten apple spoil the apple pie."

My natural inclination was to bury my head in the sand, or better yet, in a book, but Liz did have a point. The agency needed to hear about Garrett's behavior. Not to mention that my bank account had suffered a serious withdrawal when I signed up for the six-month membership. It wouldn't kill me to go out with one more guy.

After agreeing to visit the agency after Ben's soccer game today, I hung up the phone. My daughter slid into the spindle-back chair across from me, her oversize gray sweats covering up a slender and athletic five-foot-eight frame. Most sixteen-year-old girls spend their days at the mall exhibiting an excess of tanned flesh and drooling over gawky, pimply boys. Not Jenna. My math whiz daughter calculates statistics problems as a hobby. When she grows up, she wants to be an astronaut. Or a professional poker player.

"So...how was your date?" Her blue eyes looked anxious as she wound her auburn ponytail around her index finger. Was this the time to have that mother/daughter chat about the perfidy of men? Should I share any details about my oversexed dinner companion?

Someday. But not right now.

"He's not my type," I muttered. I stood and washed my mug in the sink, wishing I could scrub away the memory of the previous evening.

"Maybe you should wait a few more years to date." She stared at her gnawed nail stubs. "You know…like after Ben and I are out of the house."

"How about if I hold off until I'm ready for assisted living. Then when I meet some hottie in a wheelchair, we can roll off into the sunset together."

Jenna chuckled. "Good one, Mom."

I kissed the top of her head and walked into the family room. It was time to get the boys ready for their first soccer game of the season. I detached the duo from their Nintendo controls, ruffling Ben's hair and adding several more cowlicks to his shaggy chestnut mop. As they raced each other up the stairs, I noticed the crest on Ben's royal-blue-and-red pajamas. Superman jammies. Was this a reminder I should stick to pint-size supermen and forget about finding a grown up version?

While I dressed, I reminisced about my high school days. Every Friday night, I'd sat in the bleachers supporting my boyfriend, Hank, the star quarterback. Back then, cheerleaders in short pleated skirts constantly chased after him.

When we married immediately after college, it never occurred to me that short-skirted adult women would continue to chase after my husband decades later. But that was past history. Hank had moved on to greener pastures and so would I. Today my concentration would focus on my son and the grassy green soccer field.

I threw on a turquoise sleeveless shirt, khaki shorts, and a pair of matching turquoise straw mules I'd found at the mall, fifty percent off. The weather should be in the mid-eighties. I could multitask and work on my tan while I watched the game.

The second grade teams play in a park located four miles from our house. With the influx of so many new residents in the area, the league was forced to hold games on Sundays as well as Saturdays, until a new field could be constructed. Thirty minutes later, I stood on the sidelines of an emerald green rectangle, cheering along with the other parents.

My son had inherited my athletic genes, or lack thereof, which was a huge disappointment to his jockstrap father. Ben had spent the summer practicing his soccer skills by dribbling his soccer ball back and forth across the front lawn. All I could do was cross my fingers and hope for his success.

A whisper of a cloud temporarily blocked the sun as the ref blew his whistle for the second half kickoff. One of the forwards on Ben's team kicked the ball backwards and it smacked into my son's foot. He stood in place, stunned, undoubtedly from the shock of gaining possession of the ball.

Ever the supportive Mom, I screamed, "Go Ben."

Whether it was my yelling or the pack of soccer players bearing down on him, Ben finally began dribbling the ball down the field, a sea of blue and gold hot on his rubber-spiked heels. One of the other team's players, a gold number two emblazoned on his royal-blue shirt, towered over my son.

Suddenly number two's foot shot out and kicked Ben above his shin guard. My baby flew over the white-and-black-patchwork ball. When he landed, his body was as still as...

My heart.

CHAPTER THREE

I sprinted across the field as fast as a woman wearing turquoise mules can run. Never having experienced an injury to my child in a soccer game, I assumed it was natural for his mother to run to her baby's rescue. The tiny kitten heel of my left shoe became mired in a rut so I left it behind in my frantic attempt to get to Ben.

By the time I reached my son, his teammates had gathered around his recumbent figure. Ben's coach ambled over and a big guy from the opposite side of the field joined us.

"Honey, are you okay? What hurts?" I clutched his tiny hand as I knelt beside him. Tears shimmered in Ben's eyes but he didn't cry. I looked up at the craggy-faced coach. "Dan, that little boy intentionally kicked Ben."

The coach ignored me. "Ben, can you stand up?"

"I think I can," Ben whimpered, "but can you make my mom go away?"

I stood and stomped my remaining sandal, which sank into the soft grass. "That monster should be disqualified from playing soccer forever. I'd like to talk with his parents."

A hand tapped my shoulder. I looked up, way up into a pair of hot fudge sundae-brown eyes, fringed with outrageous black eyelashes. Only a man would be blessed with natural eyelashes like that.

He scowled. "I'm Kristy's father. You want to talk with me?"

"Kristy? Your son is named Kristy?"

The bear of a man folded muscular arms over a faded brown T-shirt that matched his faded brown ball cap. The brown eyes that glared at me weren't faded at all. "Kristy is my daughter. I can assure you, ma'am," he said, with a pronounced emphasis on the last word, "she would never deliberately kick your son. She's been taught to play soccer fair and square."

He drew his daughter close and she leaned against him. Now that Papa Bear was protecting her, little Goldilocks had resumed her aggressive stance, shooting me a defiant look. Hard to believe the super-size girl was Ben's age. She was almost my size.

"Ms. McKay, can we get on with the game?" Coach Dan asked, his lined face looking weary. "Ben can rest a few minutes and come back in when he's ready."

Ben struggled to his feet. "I'm fine, Mom. Go back to the sidelines and stay there."

I brushed off the dirt that had caked on my knees.

"Yeah, 'Mom.'" A deep baritone parroted my son. "Go to the sidelines where you belong."

The middle finger of my right hand itched to respond but I restrained myself. Kristy's father turned and I watched as his long legs loped to the opposite side of the field.

"Men," I muttered, frustrated with the bunch of them. Small and tall.

With a valiant attempt to look dignified, I limped across the field and retrieved my ruined sandal. As I approached the sidelines, my eyes made contact with a familiar pair of green eyes. Swamp-green eyes, as our daughter affectionately described them.

"When did you get here?" I asked Hank.

"I arrived just in time to see your performance." My ex tipped the visor of his black Giants baseball cap to me and snickered. "Nice job embarrassing our son."

I glared at him. "At least he has one parent who cares." Despite the fact he lives only thirty miles away in Sacramento and was a self-employed contractor, Hank's attendance record at Ben's games was far from perfect.

I turned away and tried to concentrate on the game. Ben appeared to be fine. He could have limped a little and made me feel less like an overprotective hysterical mom.

Hank cleared his throat. "I heard you had a date last night."

"Yup." I didn't see any reason to elaborate. One of the kids must have told him I had a date. I'd better institute a "need to know" policy concerning their father. Basically he didn't need to know about my social life.

"Do you think you'll go out with him again?"

Not in a million years, but Hank didn't need to know that. "I don't think that's any of your business."

His face flushed and he shot me an angry look. "Of course it's my business. What kind of mother are you? Your job is to focus on our children, not your love life."

My mouth opened so wide in protest I almost swallowed a wasp that had been circling. What kind of mother was I? What kind of father was he, leaving his family and moving in with the woman who had hired him to replace some broken tiles on her roof? It took Nadine Wells less than a week to woo him down from her roof and into her bed.

He didn't just replace her tiles. He replaced me.

Cheers from the parents who were not engaged in close verbal contact with their ex-husbands erupted. The game was over and we'd won. I was furious with my ex so I stood off to the side while he and Ben talked. Hank promised Ben he would attend the game the following week. I'd believe it when I saw it. His erratic appearance in our children's lives was one of the reasons I had started the search for a replacement.

The boys clambered into the back of my periwinkle Prius, a tight fit for the seven-year-olds, but my car made me feel like I was contributing to making the world greener, one gallon of gas at a time.

I took the boys out for lunch then dropped them off at Jimmy's house. My next stop was the Love Club, located in Placerville, one of the more infamous gold country towns whose beautiful Victorian houses were portrayed by Thomas Kinkade in his early paintings.

Driving down Main Street, I automatically looked up at the mustached man in frontier clothing hanging from the pole above the former Hangman's Tree Tavern. The man is a dummy, but it's still kind of cool. During the gold rush, the locals used two enormous oak trees to eliminate a couple of troublemakers. After the hanging of "Bloody Dick" it was called Hangtown for a brief period. I thought about my encounter with bloody Garrett and decided those pioneer women would have been proud of me.

The Love Club rented space in the refurbished brick Cary House, best known as the hotel that provided beds for Mark Twain,

Buffalo Bill and Ulysses S. Grant. Too bad Buffalo Bill wasn't around last night. I wouldn't have minded if a few shots of lead had pelted Garrett's posterior.

The Club's young receptionist greeted me as I pushed open the heavy oak door. With her perky nose, violet-blue eyes and blond-streaked mane of hair you could tell she wasn't a member.

I grabbed a few books from the shelves and settled into a chestnut-colored leather club chair. The agency wasn't large, but it claimed to be the most successful matchmaking service in northern California. Hard to argue with a seventy-five percent success rate.

Member profiles were separated by gender and divided alphabetically by first name into individual volumes. Garrett had been the one to select me, so I decided I would choose this time. I skimmed through the *H*, *I* and *J* books. If I found a profile that I liked, I could watch their DVD. Unlike the online dating sites, the agency required that photos and videos be updated annually. No false advertising at the Love Club.

The Harrys, Henrys and Hermans were all too old. On the plus side, they were probably too feeble to attack me. The *I* prospects looked like baby-faced boys, too young for me. I wasn't ready to be a cougar. I moved on to the *J* book.

The Love Club required that all clientele go through a credit check and complete a comprehensive psychological profile, supposedly to weed out any weirdos. They evidently needed a little help with their system. But like Liz said, Garrett was probably an aberration.

New members filled out a six-page questionnaire, which included vital statistics like age, religion, and education, hobbies, pet peeves, ideas for a romantic evening. A more practical approach would be to ask if the men left the toilet seat up, dropped their clothes all over the floor, and were attached to the TV remote.

There were enough potential suitors in the *J* book to keep me occupied for my entire enrollment. I entered one of the screening rooms, sat down and scrutinized the videos of four men. One of the reasons I'd agreed to go out with Garrett was that not only was he attractive, his video had portrayed him as a man of integrity.

Did his attack mean that when it came to judging men, I was clueless? Maybe I wouldn't be able to tell the good eggs from the rotten ones. Or was I such a hot babe Garrett couldn't help himself?

In my dreams.

After reviewing their bios once more, I finally ended up choosing a doctor named Jeremy and an engineer named Jack. Neither of them made my heart hum, but after last night's excitement, dull seemed almost appealing.

Once I turned in my choices, the club would notify the member by both email and voicemail that someone had selected them. If Jack or Jeremy were interested in me, the club would give them my contact information. A simple concept, but it worked. I scribbled my selections on the member request form then walked up to the glossy cherry wood reception counter.

"Hi, Laurel," said the gorgeous blonde, batting her two-inch eyelash extensions at me. "Did you choose anyone today?"

"Hi, Sunny. I thought these two men looked interesting. And safe. You wouldn't believe what happened last night when I went out with this guy named Garrett Lindstrom."

Her face grew paler than the white forms I held in my hand. "You were with Garrett last night?" she squealed.

"Uh, yes. Why? Did he tell you what I did to him?" I was surprised Garrett would have divulged what happened.

"You mean, you're admitting it?" Her voice rose to a crescendo, her eyelashes flickering so fast they created a breeze.

"Of course. I'd do it again if the same thing happened on my next date."

Sunny looked at me like I was crazy. I was beginning to think she was missing a few screws herself.

I leaned forward, resting my elbows on the counter. "What exactly did Garrett say?"

Sunny pointed her crimson-tipped index finger at me. "Garrett didn't say anything. He's dead. You killed him."

CHAPTER FOUR

"You killed him. You killed him." Sunny had backed against the paneled wall, her forefingers crossed in front of her, as if she was trying to ward off a vampire. Or prevent the homicidal woman standing in the reception area from attacking her.

"What are you talking about—Garrett's dead?" The room started to tilt so I collapsed into one of the overstuffed chairs, bent over and breathed deeply. I lifted my head and stared at the receptionist. "Are you sure we're talking about the same person? Garrett Lindstrom?"

Sunny picked up a black cordless phone, staring at me with anxious eyes. Was she going to call the police? Or use it as a weapon against the supposed murderer in the lobby.

"A sheriff's deputy stopped by a few hours ago. A neighbor found Garrett this morning. Sitting in his car. In his driveway." Her arms performed mini calisthenics as she expostulated. "His head was bashed in."

I shuddered and slumped back against the chair. This could not be happening. All I did was hit Garrett on the nose with his phone. You can't kill anyone that way. Although his head smashed into the window and blood spattered everywhere, but I thought that was normal with any head injury.

"You really didn't know he was dead?" Sunny clutched the phone as if she'd been given an extra lifeline, but at least she hadn't dialed the police. Yet.

"No," I whimpered.

16

She hesitated, set the phone down, and inched closer to the reception counter. "You don't look like a killer."

I chose to take her comment as a compliment. "Thanks," I said with a half-hearted smile.

Sunny must have decided my nonthreatening visage meant it was okay to confide in me. "The deputy found one of our invoices on Garrett's desk and guessed he was a member. They asked me to find the women who selected him, and who he picked in the last few months. I found twenty so far, but I didn't come across your name yet."

Twenty women? Who did this guy think he was—Don Juan Lindstrom? Well, with his amorous assault-style maneuvers, it was unlikely he ever went on a second date with anyone.

My head buzzed with unanswered questions, but a line of single females had formed, waving their selections at Sunny. I stared at the women waiting in line. Had any of these women been on a date with Garrett? Perhaps they too fought off an attack by him.

Or...killed him.

The line of restless women distracted Sunny as she immersed herself in paperwork. I slipped out the door and walked through the parking lot, mulling over this startling development. Sunny wasn't the brightest bulb in the chandelier. She could have mixed Garrett up with someone else.

During our dinner, Garrett had mentioned he lived in Villa Dolce, one of the gated subdivisions that comprise the massive Serrano housing development in El Dorado Hills. A brief drive-by couldn't hurt, and might make me feel better.

Fifteen minutes later I was driving up Serrano Parkway. Villa Dolce was located near the top of the Parkway on the south side of the street. By riding the bumper of a blue SUV, I was able to sneak through the gated stone entry. After aimlessly driving up one street and down another, all lined with earth-colored stucco McMansions that blended into the earth-colored hills, the futility of my mission sank in.

Hoping to find an escape out of the maize maze, I turned right then slammed on my brakes. It would be impossible to miss the spacious one-story house with the beige Lincoln Town Car in the driveway. The two sheriff's cars parked in front of the house. Yellow tape stretched...everywhere.

Sunny was right.

My first thought was that Garrett must have been one heck of a CPA in order to afford a house this expensive. Maybe he was involved in something shady. One of his clients might have disagreed with his method of depreciation and accelerated Garrett's death.

As my car crawled down the street, two of the county deputies, clad in pressed khaki shirts and forest-green pants, glanced up. The dark-haired officer with the miniature Hitler moustache frowned at me. Time to move on. My pastel vehicle wasn't designed for undercover detecting.

As I drove to Jimmy's house to collect Ben, I pondered my predicament. Should I contact the police and tell them what happened on our date? I didn't think a *Dating for Dummies Guide* would have any advice on what to do when your date is found dead less than twenty-four hours after you hit him with a cell phone.

The car rolled to a stop in Jimmy's driveway. Before I could open my door, Ben ran out of the house and slid into the backseat. His navy backpack, which reeked of antique bananas, was unzipped as usual. Its messy contents scattered everywhere.

"Mom, I'm so hungry I could eat a Tyrannosaurus Rex." He rubbed his stomach for emphasis.

"Sorry, Ben, no T-Rex burgers tonight. Maybe tomorrow."

"For real, Mom?" he squealed in delight.

Since I had to dash Ben's hopes for a prehistoric burger, I promised to whip up his favorite fudge for dessert. Once he cleaned up the gummy bears, banana peels and G.I. Joes strewn across the back of the car.

The message light was blinking on our phone when I arrived home. "This is your mother, Barbara Bingham. Call me."

Did she think her only daughter forgot her name? Mom would have to wait until I called my best friend. The last thing I needed was maternal advice from the woman who could do no wrong. At least in her own mind.

I didn't want the kids to overhear my conversation. I walked upstairs, plopped on my bed and speed-dialed Liz.

"He's dead," I sputtered into the mouthpiece.

"Laurel? What are you talking about? Who's dead?"

"Garrett. My date. I went to the Love Club this afternoon to complain about him and they told me he was found in his car. Dead."

"Oh, my. That's a bit of a downer."

Talk about British understatement.

"You don't think there's any way I could have–" I gulped "– killed him?"

"Don't be silly. With a cell?" She paused as if contemplating the odds of a mobile phone killing. "There must be a reasonable explanation for his death."

"I hope you're right. What should I do?"

"Let me see if Brian has heard anything."

Brian, her fiancé, is an assistant district attorney for El Dorado County and a terrific guy. I blew out the breath I'd been holding. "Thanks. I appreciate it."

"Don't worry. Everything will be fine. Trust your Auntie Liz."

Humpf. If Auntie Liz hadn't talked me into joining the Love Club I wouldn't be in this situation. I tried to calm myself by cooking dinner, an old family recipe called Pasta a la Ragu. I washed the dishes, made a batch of my special gold nugget fudge, then a batch of brownies. I figured it was better to work off my angst chewing on chocolate than chewing off my nails.

The doorbell rang while I was upstairs in the bathroom. I heard voices then the sound of Jenna's size tens pounded up the stairs.

"There are two men from the sheriff's department downstairs. What's going on?" she whispered. "You're not dating both of them, are you?"

The anxiety in her cornflower-blue eyes mirrored my own. I hadn't expected an official visit this soon. I pulled her close and attempted a reassuring smile. "No, I think they're investigating an accident. Nothing to fret over." There was no point in worrying my daughter about my situation.

"Okay." She smiled suddenly. "Too bad. One of them is a real hunk."

Hunk? Despite her scholarly pursuits, Jenna wasn't totally oblivious to the opposite sex. He must be one of the baby-faced deputies I'd noticed in front of Garrett's house. I told her to tell the men I'd be down in a couple of minutes.

I changed from my sweats to a denim skirt and white blouse. I swiped gloss over my gnawed lower lip and slapped on extra blush.

Murder suspects probably look pale and wan. My rosy cheeks would hopefully proclaim my innocence.

My mind and heart raced as I trod down the stairs. Was it normal for the sheriff's department to appear on your doorstep without any warning? Did they consider me a suspect or was this a routine questioning? And despite hearing the phrase repeatedly on TV, what the heck was a routine questioning?

Lost in thought, I tripped down the two stairs leading into our sunken living room, landing with my legs spread out in a position I hadn't been in since my divorce. The muscular arm that lifted me up made me feel as light as a marshmallow. A familiar pair of Godiva-brown eyes gazed into mine.

"You?" I said to the annoying man from the soccer match today; the dad with the super-size daughter.

His eyes registered recognition and he responded with a tight-lipped smile. "Oh, yeah. The shoeless soccer mom. Small world, isn't it?"

He held out his right hand. "Detective Hunter."

"Hello, Detective Hunk, I mean Detective Hunter." I floundered as his large, capable hand engulfed my much smaller one.

His face remained expressionless so he must have missed my faux pas. My daughter did not. Muffled laughter emanated from the stairs, followed by a growl originating from one of the velour wing chairs in the corner of the living room. I turned and caught a fleeting glimpse of Jenna's shoes disappearing up the steps. I glanced at the mauve chair. Who or what was growling?

The creature in the corner unfurled his gangly legs and introduced himself as Detective Bradford. Tall and bald, with a bulbous nose and bags under his eyes the size of dinner plates. His steel-gray eyes looked sharper than my steak knives.

"Please sit down, Ms. McKay," he said in a gravelly voice, as he lowered his oversized frame back into the chair. I tried not to wince as it creaked in response.

I walked over to my outdated blue flowered sofa and perched on one corner. Detective Hunter looked at the remaining delicate wing chair and wisely decided to join me on the more comfortable couch. He settled into the cushions, uncapped a pen and pulled a small navy note pad from his sport coat pocket. "We have some questions about a friend of yours."

"Of course, oh, before we start, would you like some coffee, brownies, fudge?"

"Not now, perhaps later," Hunter said.

As I settled against the sofa cushions, my skirt slid up my thighs. Hunter's gaze briefly drifted to my bare legs then quickly returned to his notes.

"We understand you dined with Garrett Lindstrom yesterday evening. You're both members of a matchmaking agency called the, uh, Love Club?" A smile briefly flickered across his face but he quickly stifled it behind his hand.

I glared at the younger detective. "Garrett was my first encounter with someone from the Love Club. Our date didn't go that well."

"Would you care to elaborate?" Hunter sat poised with his notebook and pen, probably waiting for some sizzling comments.

I could talk all night but that wasn't the point. Was Sunny not supposed to tell me about the murder? Was the detective trying to trip me up with trick questions?

"Are you are aware Lindstrom was found dead in his car Sunday morning?" he asked.

"Yes, I am." I slumped against the cushions. "One of the Love Club staff told me when I stopped in today. You don't think I had anything to do with it, do you?"

"That's why we're here asking questions. Tell us more about your not-so-great date."

I proceeded to give the detectives all of the gory details. When I mentioned that I Nokia-ed Garrett's nose, Detective Bradford grunted, his only input into the conversation so far.

"That was the extent of our time together. His car was gone when I returned to the parking lot and met the AAA driver. I was home before ten. Garrett couldn't have died from me hitting him with the cell, could he?"

"We haven't seen the full autopsy report yet, but I can tell you the examiner discovered a significant contusion on the back of his head as well as a broken nose. Do you remember anything else about your, um...altercation?" Hunter asked.

All I remembered was rolling around the front seat of Garrett's car while I tried to extract myself from his unwanted embraces. My fingerprints must be plastered all over the seat and the windshield.

21

A strange expression flitted across Hunter's face. I could feel the heat rising up my face then working its way down to another zone.

"How did you find out about our date?"

"His laptop. He used Outlook to manage his appointments. The time and the name of the restaurant. And the initials—L.M. It might have taken us awhile to figure out who he met with, but we received a call from one of the Love Club employees a few hours ago. She confirmed you went out with him last night."

Thanks, Sunny.

"Did Lindstrom mention anything during dinner that could help with our investigation?"

I tried to recall if Garrett had said anything revealing during his monologue on depreciation. All I could remember was blah, blah, blah.

"Anything suspicious inside Leonardo's?" Detective Hunter asked. "Or later when you walked through the parking lot?"

I crinkled my nose at him, puzzled. "Suspicious? Like what?"

"Someone observing the two of you while you were eating. Following you outside." He shot a questioning look at me. "You realize you could have been attacked as well."

My stomach did a backflip cartwheel combination. It had never once crossed my mind that I could have been in danger. "What time was Garrett killed?"

"The medical examiner said it was sometime between ten and midnight."

I didn't like the sound of this at all.

"Can you account for your whereabouts after leaving the restaurant, Ms. McKay?" boomed Tall and Bald.

I jumped. "Whereabouts? Like where I was, uh…about?"

Hunter snorted but maintained his deadpan expression. "Did you stop anywhere on your way home? Can your children confirm what time you arrived?"

"They were in bed by the time I got here. After I drove out of the parking lot, I felt shaken up so I went through the McDonald's drive-through and bought a coffee. I don't know if anyone would remember me."

They exchanged glances, which must have been some type of secret signal. Detective Hunter rose from the sofa and slipped the tiny notepad into his pocket. Detective Bradford unfurled himself from my chair, lumbering out the door without a goodbye.

The younger detective followed. He paused to shake my hand.

"Thank you, Ms. McKay. Perhaps the next time we see each other it will be under more pleasant circumstances—like another soccer game."

I wouldn't describe meeting over Ben's prostrate body as pleasant, but it was preferable to being involved in a murder.

"Please call if you have any more questions. I'm anxious for you to solve this crime. I promise not to injure any more dates."

I thought my comment might get a laugh out of the detective, but his expression remained blank. This guy had absolutely no sense of humor.

I leaned against the door. "Goodbye, Detective Hunter."

He paused on the sidewalk and glanced over his shoulder, a slight smile briefly flitting across his face. His response filled the chilly night air.

"Don't you mean Detective Hunk?"

CHAPTER FIVE

The thump of the heavy oak door slamming shut could not mask the thuds of two children pounding down the stairs. Ben landed first, Jenna close on his heels.

"What happened? Why were those detectives here?"

I curled an arm around each child's waist. It was time for full disclosure.

"Okay, kids. My dinner Saturday night turned into a disaster. I locked my keys and my cell in the Prius. My date offered to let me sit in his car and use his phone to call AAA. He got a little too friendly, so I bopped him in the nose with his cell. It turns out someone murdered him in his car later that night and the police wanted some details from me."

Ben bounced up and down. "Murder. Sweet."

"Mom, that is so gross," Jenna said. "How could you do this to me? What if my friends hear about it?"

"Can I tell Jimmy?" Ben asked.

"No. Let's forget about this incident. I had nothing to do with the murder and we don't need to share this information with any of our friends. Go upstairs and get ready for bed."

The best advice I could give myself was to forget about Garrett. If he could attack me on a first date, imagine what other nasty things he could have been involved in. He probably had a drug habit and his supplier did him in. That theory worked for me.

My thoughts turned to Detective Hunter's parting remark, but the shrill sound of the phone interrupted my reverie. I peeked at Caller ID. Mother.

"Hello, dear, how was your weekend?" I visualized my mother, from the top of her silver-blond flawlessly cut hair to her frosted-pink-pedicured toenails.

"Hectic." Talk about the understatement of the year.

"Honey, you have no idea how hectic life can be unless you're in the real estate business. It's nonstop 24/7. I sold two of my listings this weekend, but of course, I priced them realistically. Something the other agents need to learn."

I sighed with relief. I would receive a short lecture on the foibles of the real estate industry from the thirty-five year veteran on the other end of the line and with luck, escape any maternal nagging.

She paused for a second. Uh oh.

"I heard the strangest rumor tonight. Since the rumor included *your* name and the term *corpse* I thought you might want to share something with me."

Not really, but in a small town like ours who knew what kind of stories were flying around. I updated her on the demise of my date. She was quiet for a few seconds before she let me have it. "I told you signing up for that Love Club would be a huge mistake. It's undoubtedly full of psychopaths and con men."

My mother. The optimist.

"I keep telling you the agency is designed for professionals." I said. "It's too difficult for single working people to meet each other, especially here in the foothills. You wouldn't believe the horror stories my friends have shared about online dating." I grabbed one of the glossy agency brochures and read the verbiage aloud. "The Love Club is a highly intellectual process for discovering your future mate."

"Humph. Well, I think you should forget about that stupid club. I don't think it's safe. There's a new agent in my office you should meet. Peter is about your age, single and highly successful. He recently transferred from the Folsom office. Wouldn't you rather go out with someone I can vouch for?"

Would I rather go out with someone my mother worked with every day? No way. We wrangled over the merits of the dating agency for a few more minutes. I finally told her it was late and time to say goodnight to the kids. I hung up the phone and trudged up the stairs to Ben's room. At his age he didn't need me to tuck him in, but it's part of our nightly regimen and something we both look forward to each evening.

I crossed the threshold into Ben's unique fantasy world. Posters of a prehistoric Triceratops and a Brontosaurus hung between glossy prints of Chewbacca and Batman. He was already in bed, his blue and gray light saber resting on top of his Spider-man bedspread.

"Honey, you know you're not supposed to sleep with your toys." I held out my hand for the plastic sword.

"No. Mom. I need it." He grabbed the saber and hid it under his Batman sheets.

"Now, Ben..."

He sat upright against crumpled pillows. "I need it...to protect you. What if the murderer comes here?" A tear rolled down his cheek and he quickly swiped at it. "I'm the man of the house now."

Tiny droplets welled up in my eyes. What kind of mother was I, subjecting my impressionable young son to murder? When you're raising children, it sometimes feels like you make one bad decision after another. I sure didn't remember Dr. Spock covering a situation like this one.

I climbed in the twin bed and wrapped my arms around my son. I held him close and explained it was a coincidence that I'd gone on a date with Garrett the same evening he died. The murder had nothing to do with me, or the kids. The detectives merely hoped I might possess some information to help with their investigation.

Ben seemed satisfied with my explanation. We nestled together, his shaggy brown mane that was so overdue for a haircut tickling my chin. Once he was out, I slipped from under the covers. Ben could sleep with his sword tonight. Not a battle worth fighting right now.

As I closed his bedroom door, I once again pondered my decision to start dating. Maybe my daughter was right and I should hold off until both kids were out of the house. Of course that meant that by the time I started the search for eligible men, I would also be eligible for early bird dinners.

Considering what happened the previous night that would be fine with me.

CHAPTER SIX

The McKay family is never at its best on Monday morning and today was no exception.

"Mom, there's no bread for my sandwich," Ben whined. He waved the empty plastic bag in front of my face. My son is not a morning person, another gene we shared.

Drat. "You can have cheese and crackers. Won't that be a treat?"

He crossed his arms and frowned. "Jimmy's mother would never run out of bread."

Okay, so I'm not the West Coast's answer to Martha Stewart. "I'll bet Jimmy's mom would never let him have four cookies for lunch." The bribe produced a beaming smile. Sometimes working moms have to compromise to save their sanity.

Jenna had misplaced her homework so we left five minutes late. The kids jumped into the car and I zoomed down our street. I turned right on Wagon Wheel Lane and glimpsed the canary- yellow bus pulling away.

That bus driver and I have a love-hate relationship. I'm positive she waits at the bus stop until she sees my car fly around the corner. Then she shifts gears and hauls you-know-what, forcing me to follow her to the next stop.

I stomped on the gas pedal and all four cylinders responded with a resounding "ping" as we caught up to my nemesis. Ben's pals waved from the back window of the bus. At the next stop Ben flew out of the car and jumped on board the bus. One kid down. One to go.

Our next stop was the high school.

"I'm probably the only kid in the junior class who doesn't have her own car," Jenna complained as I pulled up to the loading and unloading area in front of the high school.

"Great. That means there are 361 kids who can give you a ride." I chuckled, silently patting myself on the back.

"Very funny." She grabbed her green backpack and slogged up the sidewalk towards the ponderosa-pined campus. I watched as two of her friends joined her. Within seconds, they were giggling, heads close together.

I would have loved to provide my daughter with her own transportation. Jenna was a straight-A student and other than her penchant for playing Texas hold 'em, a good kid. But even a junker was too much for our budget. I turned left out of the parking lot and headed to the office. My job might not be a cash cow, but it was the only cash coming in right now.

My employer is Hangtown Bank, established 150 years ago and located only a few doors down from the infamous hanging tree in Placerville. Before Ben was born, I was a manager for one of the bank's local branches. Someone had to bring home the bacon and eggs since my ex kept getting involved in one idiotic get-rich scheme after another.

When the last feathered mammal from his ostrich-farming venture sold, Hank decided to go into construction. The real estate boom combined with a surprising knack for building spec homes provided us with sufficient income so I could quit work and stay home for a couple of years. After Hank and I split up over his extracurricular female activity, the only available position at the bank was mortgage loan underwriter.

I pushed open the glass double doors and smiled at Vivian Vaughn, the bank's receptionist, who also specialized in nosiness. The seven-foot carved wooden bear the president of the bank had purchased to enhance the lobby décor, greeted me with a snarl. I snarled back and walked past the old-fashioned oak teller stations to the area reserved for mortgage staff. I stuffed my purse in my drawer. Seconds later, my cubicle neighbor popped her head over the five-foot wall of gray tweed that divided us.

"How was your date?" Mary Lou, a five-eleven Barbie look-alike, who maximized her assets and minimized nothing, had discovered online dating to be an underwhelming experience. My coworker had gone on twenty-five "meet and greets," as she referred to her first-time meetings with online matches. The men she met through a website called Supermatch.com were frequently three inches shorter, thirty pounds heavier or far more hair-follicle-challenged than their online photos disclosed. She swore some of them posted their high school yearbook pictures.

Vivian had joined a different site, which proved even worse. Three of the four men she met over the Internet turned out to be married. We had warned her about those profiles that said, "Ask me for my photograph." We dubbed her dating site Mismatch.com.

Rosa Martinez, an unmarried processor, and Stan Winters, my underwriting assistant, joined us.

"I want to know everything." Rosa's dark eyes were hopeful. She'd signed up for a third online site that analyzed your personality profile then provided matches with potential partners. So far thirty-nine of their forty suggested matches had rejected the fifty-year-old processor. The reason being "other." At five-foot-one, Rosa didn't know if she was too short, too chunky or too old. She only knew she couldn't take much more online rejection.

All the single women in the office, and Stan, were waiting to see if the Love Club would prove to be as successful as it claimed. Based on my one and only date, none of us would need to hire a wedding planner in the near future.

They all looked so hopeful about the dating agency's prospects that I decided to withhold a few facts. Such as my date's current residence–the morgue. I relayed the few dismal details of my dinner with Garrett ending with our minor altercation. Mary Lou spit out her coffee when I admitted I'd discovered a new use for a cell phone.

"Hey, Laurel, I wouldn't mind taking your rejects," snickered Stan. "As long as they're not battered and bruised."

"Ahem." Our boss stood in the doorway, glaring at the assemblage. Within seconds, my co-workers vanished to their respective cubicles. I wondered if he'd noticed none of his direct reports had been doing anything remotely related to work in the past ten minutes.

Earl Fisher leaned forward, his double cheeseburger stuffed stomach resting on my desk. "How was your weekend?"

My weekend sucked and I didn't think it was any of his business, although I couldn't be rude to the head of the mortgage division. "Why?"

"Always interested in the welfare of my staff." Earl winked and walked away.

Weird.

I grabbed a loan file and soon became absorbed reading the borrowers' letter of explanation for multiple credit card delinquencies. They claimed their mail carrier had deliberately not delivered their credit card statements because their basset hound bit the carrier's ankle. They scored a nine for originality. Zero for integrity.

Reject.

I grabbed another file but my mind drifted to the events of the past weekend. It was difficult concentrating on loans when there was a high probability I could be involved in a murder investigation. I finally confided in Stan and Mary Lou.

"Your date was killed? As in dead?" The furrow in Mary Lou's brow deepened. "And I thought my date was a disaster. Does this mean you're a suspect?"

"I don't think so," I said.

"Are you kidding? Of course you're a suspect. You need to hire an attorney," advised Stan, our resident crime show aficionado. "Otherwise they'll try to trap you into saying something you'll regret."

"But I don't know anything. How can they trap me?"

Stan rolled his eyes and graced me with a pitying look. "Trust me. If the detectives think you're the killer, they sure aren't going to waste time looking for anyone else. The next thing you know you'll be wearing matching metal bracelets."

"And an orange jump suit," Mary Lou chimed in.

As far as I was concerned, the words orange and jumpsuit should never be combined. Particularly in a sentence referring to me.

It was only Monday, but already I could tell it was going to be a long week.

CHAPTER SEVEN

Whether the detectives were busy hunting bad guys or not, there were no further calls or visits from the sheriff's department in the next couple of days. Wednesday evening I received a call from Jeremy Slater, the physician I'd selected during my last trip to the Love Club. I had totally forgotten about the two agency choices I'd turned in the previous weekend. Right before Sunny shared the news about Garrett.

The last thing I wanted to do was go on another date, but after conversing for an hour, I decided Jeremy might be a pleasant diversion. We exchanged the usual information hapless singles share, number of kids–zero for him, number of divorces–another zero for him, where we worked, what we liked to do, etc. Jeremy suggested we meet for lunch on Friday. A lunch date seemed safe. I wouldn't have to worry about any front-seat acrobatics during daylight hours.

Friday morning turned into another wardrobe time waster. I didn't want to reprise my Bimbo Banker look, so I finally selected a tailored white blouse, my good black suit and heels.

Since Fridays are dress down days at the bank, my appearance created a buzz.

Vivian was the first to grill me as I entered the bank lobby. "Do you have another date today? You are so lucky."

Considering how my last date ended, I didn't think *lucky* was the most appropriate word to define my dating success so far. But I was proactive.

Stan was next to comment. Seconds after I settled in my cubicle, he plopped his slight frame in my tweed visitor chair, pushed his wire-rimmed glasses up his pointed nose, and whistled.

"Do I sense a love bug circling today?" he asked.

"Stan, some days you are a royal pain in the patootie."

My smart-ass responses needed a little work.

"Sweetie, you're looking good. We all want you to meet the man of your dreams. I'm sure the other Love Club members won't be like that first jerk."

"Thanks. I hope you meet the man of your dreams too." Stan had recently broken up with his partner of ten years. It wasn't easy meeting gay men in the foothills, but Stan grew up here and he preferred living in a small town to the big city social scene.

Since the practice Jeremy shared with his partner, Dr. Radovich, closed at noon, we agreed to meet at a restaurant in downtown Placerville. I entered the Main Street Bistro a socially correct five minutes late. Jeremy was easily recognizable from his video. An inch or two over six feet, with a full head of curly gray hair, a big Roman nose and a disarming smile. Not even remotely drop-dead gorgeous, which was fine with me. I didn't need any more drop-dead dates in my life.

"Laurel, it's a pleasure to meet you." He proffered his hand from a safe distance. We were shown directly to a green marble-topped table overlooking a tiny fern garden. The soothing sound of a waterfall helped diffuse the noise of the other diners.

Jeremy quickly peeked at the glossy menu then laid it on the table. I checked out their salad selections, pleased with the variety.

"What are you going to order?" I asked.

"Oh, I'm kind of a boring diner. I usually order turkey on whole wheat, with a small salad on the side. Fiber, fiber, fiber, I always say."

Yeah. Me too. Between Kit Kat bars. His fiber mantra seemed a little weird but doctors need to be serious about nutrition.

"Have you tried any of the new diets, like South Beach or the Zone?" he asked.

That was quite personal. Was Jeremy intimating I needed to lose weight?

"I tried the South Beach diet last spring," I said with a wry smile. "It lasted for all of six hours. I'm afraid the only diet that works for me is the 'See no chocolate, eat no chocolate' diet.'"

"It's certainly not unusual for women to crave chocolate. Of course, the more refined carbohydrates you eat, the more you'll want. But you can overcome those cravings if you change your lifestyle." He gazed at me with intensity. "Soon you'll discover you desire something else."

Oh no. Not another man with an overactive libido.

Fortunately, our server arrived to take our orders. A turkey sandwich for Jeremy and a healthy Cobb salad for me—with plenty of fiber, just like the doctor ordered. I reached for a piece of garlic bread and Jeremy grabbed my hand.

"Laurel, that's exactly what I'm talking about. If you avoid bad carbohydrates, eventually you won't crave them anymore. You'll crave the healthy foods your body needs."

"Oh...right." I released my hand from his and shook my head at my unsavory thoughts. He was concerned about my health. That was sweet. Nevertheless, I kept my hands under the table until our food arrived.

We continued to talk throughout lunch. Other than his fetish for fiber, Jeremy was personable and the time flew by. I wasn't sure what to do when the bill arrived. Did the man pay on the first date? Was lunch considered a date? Somebody needed to write a rulebook on this subject.

Our middle-aged waitress must have her own set of rules because she plopped the bill next to Jeremy's plate. He picked it up and reached for his wallet.

"Can I split that with you?" I asked.

"Thanks for the offer, but it's my treat. I do have a question for you, though."

I hoped he didn't want to know my daily carbohydrate count.

"I'm in the middle of applying for a loan and I've experienced some problems. I'd love to pick your brain about the mortgage application process. Not to mention I enjoyed your company today. Would you like to go to dinner next Saturday? I haven't been to the River Inn for awhile, and they have an excellent and healthy menu."

Decisions, decisions. I fiddled with the cloth napkin as I tried to decide whether to accept his invitation. Jeremy seemed nice, although a trifle obsessed about nutrition. One of the articles I'd read in a women's magazine said you should go on a minimum of six dates with someone before you decide they aren't right for you.

I couldn't imagine six dates with someone I wasn't interested in, but one dinner with a financially secure doctor wouldn't be such a hardship. He could assault me with loan questions as long as he didn't attack me in his car.

Or deprive me of dessert. "Sure. Saturday will be fine," I replied.

"Great. Shall I pick you up at your house?"

Darn, more trick questions. I gnawed at my lower lip debating whether to let him come to my house. But he was a doctor. I could always check out his references before he knocked at my front door.

We shook hands goodbye and I strolled down the sidewalk, peering into the shop windows. They were far more intriguing than the loan files I had to look forward to when I returned.

A sunny fall afternoon is not conducive to reviewing loans. Usually I'm very conscientious about my loan files. It didn't take more than a few loans going into foreclosure to put a small lender out of business. Even big banks aren't immune to a foreclosure crisis. One CEO of a failed mega bank bragged about how they funded the most loans in the country. What is it with men? Why do they always think bigger is better?

The phone rang and I grabbed it, thrilled for the interruption. "Hi luv, can you lunch tomorrow?" Liz said.

"Sure. Where do you want to meet—the usual?"

"There's no place better than Sweetie Pie's as far as I'm concerned."

We settled on a one o'clock meet. Now all I had to do was find a babysitter for Ben. Jenna had made plans to go to the mall with a friend who had just received her driver's license. I still couldn't decide what was worse: letting Jenna ride with a friend, letting her drive my car, or chauffeuring her back and forth.

Young mothers with toddlers think their lives are stressful, but nothing can prepare a parent for the daily fear they experience the minute that laminated driver's license is in the possession of their offspring.

I hated to ask Jenna to cancel her plans so I called several of Ben's friends Saturday morning. No one was home, which left me with only one possible babysitter. My mother. She was at the real estate office—AKA her second home. Heaven forbid she miss out on a potential walk-in customer looking for a real estate bargain.

In my best suck-up-to-Mom tone, I asked, "Do you have any showings this afternoon?"

"No, dear. Only paperwork to catch up on. What do you want?"

That's my Mom. She doesn't waste a second.

"Liz and I want to get together for lunch today. Jenna is going to the mall so she can't watch Ben. Would you be able to babysit him for a few hours?"

Her sigh resonated over the line. My mother loves her grandchildren, but she prefers that familial visits be booked weeks in advance. "There is a potential listing I want to preview in your area. I'll pick him up at your house then take him to McDonald's and get him one of those happy plastic meals."

McDonald's might not be pleased with her description of their kids' meal, but Ben would be thrilled to add a new toy to his collection of colorful plastic items. None of which will ever be played with again.

I donned a sleeveless white top and my denim skirt and was pleasantly surprised to see the waistband was loose. Did dating stress burn off calories? Or the stress of knowing there was a murderer out there.

Jenna agreed to stay with Ben until her grandmother arrived. I slid into my compact car, shoved in a Shania Twain CD, and popped open the sunroof. My hair flew in all four directions as Shania belted out "I Feel Like a Woman." I relaxed for the first time all week as my car zipped past hundred-year-old farms and newer stucco ranches on five-acre parcels. Horses cantered alongside the road as I careened down the twisty ten-minute drive into Placerville.

Tourists clogged the sidewalks in front of the brick and pastel clapboard buildings lining Main Street, most likely on their way to Apple Hill, home to over forty apple and pumpkin farms, as well as wineries famed for their medal-winning Syrah and Zinfandel.

I squeezed my pint-sized car into a parking space between two massive SUVs. Clusters of hungry people mingled on the sidewalk outside the mauve Victorian house built in 1865 that housed Sweetie Pie's Restaurant. I politely pushed my way inside, hoping Liz was already seated.

Like a moth to a flame, the cinnamon-scented air drew me to a glass bakery case piled high with their world famous cinnamon rolls drenched in a gooey caramel glaze. My stomach gurgled in response to the mouth-watering display.

I needed to find my friend before I succumbed to eating a two-thousand-calorie cinnamon appetizer. I waved at Patty, the owner, who was scurrying around the high-ceilinged room with its flower-sprigged wallpaper, attending to her customers. I found Liz seated at a corner table, her hazel eyes glued to the menu, gold corkscrew curls askew.

Liz and I became acquainted our sophomore year of college. She had just arrived from Kent, England, as a participant in an exchange program with the University of California at Davis. We met at a fraternity party during which both of our dates decided to drink themselves into stupidity. After hiking the three miles back to campus, we formed a friendship that has lasted twenty years. She's the Yin to my Yang, or maybe I'm the Abbott to her Costello.

While I married immediately after college, embarked on a sensible banking career, and bore two children, Liz traveled to exotic locales, seduced by the glamour of foreign countries. Not to mention foreign men, of all shapes, sizes and nationalities. After acquiring health and beauty tips from spas all over the world she eventually returned to El Dorado County and opened a state-of-the-art luxury salon in El Dorado Hills. Once her Golden Hills Spa became a success, she moved on to the next goal on her "to do" list: getting a man. Enter the Love Club and Brian.

I slid into the chair across from my pal, losing one of my red slides in the process.

"Are you ready to order?" Her bracelet-laden wrists jangled as she waved her arms at a server.

"Well, hi to you too." My buddy is always hungry and subsequently always dieting.

"Sorry, luv. I arrived early and I'm starving."

"Give me a second. I think I'll try something on the healthy side for a change." I scrutinized the menu as I tried to wiggle my shoe back on my foot.

"I'll have the pastrami with extra cheese," Liz told our server, snapping her menu shut.

I stared at her. Didn't she have a wedding coming up?

"So I'll spend an extra hour on the Stairmaster." Her dimples appeared as she grinned at me. "It's worth it."

I ordered a chicken Caesar salad, dressing on the side. The server promised to bring our iced teas right away.

"Do you have any more dates on your calendar? I was afraid you'd give up after what happened with that first guy." She patted my hand, her gold bracelets clanking against the varnished wood table.

"You know if I hadn't already selected a couple of guys from the Love Club before I found out about Garrett, I probably would have dropped out. But I had lunch with a doctor yesterday and we're going out again next week."

"Ah. A doctor. Now we're talking." She lifted her left eyebrow and leered. Liz needed to stop watching soaps. That one eyebrow lift was almost professional.

I shrugged. "I didn't hear any bells ringing."

"Don't expect to hear bells right away." She shook her charm bracelet and it tinkled in response. "It takes time, persistence and patience to find the right guy. Dating isn't a game—it's a full time occupation. Remember how many losers I went out with?"

How could I forget? Before she met her fiancé, Liz had dated and dumped so many men that I'd lost count. She'd demonstrated classic signs of becoming a serial dumper when Brian popped into her life.

Strangely enough, I could have sworn I heard a faint tinkling when Detective Hunter said good-bye the other night. Must have been the brass wind chimes on my porch.

"So tell me what happened with the detectives. Any guys I might know?"

"Some old grump named Bradford and a big burly guy called Hunter."

"Oh...I've heard about that Detective Hunter," Liz said, her eyes dancing. "The dispatcher at the sheriff's department said as far as eye candy goes, he's a Godiva God."

A vision of the detective's chocolate-brown eyes popped through my head.

"I heard he has a cute bum. What did you think?" She winked at me as she reached for a roll.

"I didn't notice."

Liz opened her mouth, aghast at this lack of anatomical perception on my part. Our server arrived with our lunch and I escaped a lecture. I eyed Liz as she inhaled her sandwich. "Your lunch looks delicious, but is there any chance you can eat and discuss the murder at the same time?" I asked.

"Laurel, luv, you need to slow down and enjoy lunch with your best friend," she admonished me. "Remember, *carpe diem*—seize the day."

Carpe diem? Today I was more concerned with *corpus delicti*.

I speared an oversized piece of romaine lettuce. "Brian must have shared something about the Lindstrom case. I'm not really a suspect, am I?"

Liz put her fork down and dug through the emerald-green Marc Jacobs tote that perfectly matched her silk blouse. I admired the fine workmanship and tried not to slobber on the buttery leather. The only chance I had of owning a designer purse was to get lucky at a garage sale.

"I was afraid I'd forget what he told me so I took notes." Liz rummaged through the capacious bag and finally yanked out a sheet of lined pink paper.

"Let's see. Okay, this isn't good. The sheriff's department doesn't have any suspects other than you."

"Oh, c'mon. There must be someone else who didn't like the guy—clients, family members, probably every woman he went out with."

"Yes, but your fingerprints were the only ones found in his car." She lifted her perfectly arched eyebrow. "Some of them in highly unusual spots."

My fork fell out of my hand, clanging against the delicate china plate. I shuddered, remembering Garrett's attack and our front seat gymnastics.

"The coroner said Lindstrom was hit with some kind of blunt object. Brian implied that Garrett's head smacking the window probably wouldn't have created that type of injury." She peered at me over her notes. "You didn't whack him with anything other than his cell, did you?"

"Of course not. What do you think I am?"

She cocked her head. "Correct me if I'm wrong, but you did hit Hank in the forehead with that dinner plate. The night he announced he was leaving you for Nadine."

"That was an accident. It was supposed to fly over his head, like a Frisbee. It's not like I wanted to break a hundred-dollar piece of china over his lame-brained head."

She nodded in sympathy. "Men may come and men may go, but Royal Doulton lasts forever."

We finished our lunches, paid our bill and cruised down Main Street. Placerville is an antique road show mecca for buyers with the energy, time and knowledge to wade through piles of crap.

I mean valuable antiques.

We stopped in Placerville Hardware, the oldest operating hardware store west of the Mississippi. The scuffed wooden floors creaked as we squeezed our way down the narrow aisles. The bulging floor-to-ceiling shelves always looked like they were a sneeze away from toppling over. A few gold pans were stuck next to some shovels so I decided to buy one for Ben. I'd been promising to take him to Sutter's mill in Coloma where the first nugget of gold was discovered.

Liz purchased a china teapot in a cream and violet pansy pattern. As the cashier wrapped the teapot in bubble wrap, Liz turned to me. "He's single, you know."

I must have looked confused because she punched me in the forearm. "Detective Hunter. The Godiva God. He's a widower."

"What a shame." I remembered the detective's protective stance at the soccer game. Having lost my father at a young age, I could empathize with his motherless daughter.

"Keep it in mind, in case your date with the doctor doesn't work out."

I rolled my eyes. "Liz what are the odds that a widowed detective, who's investigating a soccer mom for murder, would want to go out with said soccer mom suspect?"

She grabbed her bag and smiled. "Good point. Have fun with the doctor."

After supplying me with enough seaweed and cucumber moisturizer samples to keep my face glowing for the next year, we parted. I sped down the hill towards the Centurion Cameron Park office as fast as my little hybrid could move without drawing the attention of the CHP. I couldn't decide which was worse, getting a ticket, being a suspect in a murder case, or arriving late and risking the wrath of my mother.

I pulled into the parking lot, jumped out of the car, flung open one of the Centurion Realty glass double doors, and found myself chest to stomach with a tall man wearing a dark suit. He dropped a few manila folders, which scattered across the slate-tiled lobby.

"Let me help you." I bent over to pick up the files.

"No. That's okay." He knelt down and quickly scooped them up.

"I'm sorry. I'm in a hurry to pick up my son. My mother is Barbara Bingham and she's been watching Ben all afternoon and I'm late as usual," I rambled on.

A broad smile creased his face and a lock of blond hair fell over his forehead as he nodded sympathetically. "Ah, the formidable Barbara Bingham. I can understand why you wouldn't want to be late." He held out his right hand. "I'm Peter Tyler."

"Laurel McKay." His handshake was firm, but not crushing.

"I'm new in this office, but Barbara has mentioned your name several times," he said.

How embarrassing. I tried to imagine what she could have told him. The chatter of voices and footsteps interrupted us.

"Hi, Mom," Ben said. "Grandmother bought me a happy meal and it came with a Spider-man. Isn't that cool?" Ben thrust the tiny blue-and-red plastic figure in my face. I admired the miniature toy and thought how uncomplicated life is at that age. Maybe if I stuck to small plastic figures my life would be simpler too.

"Peter, you've met my daughter?" My mother looked only slightly frazzled from the three hours spent with her hyperactive grandson.

"Yes. She is every bit as delightful as you said."

Delightful? I thought it far more likely she would refer to me as difficult.

I grabbed Ben's hand and turned to Peter. "It was nice meeting you."

"My pleasure," he said, opening the door for us.

"Mother, thanks for taking care of Ben," I said. She frowned at our hasty departure. I anticipated a lengthy lecture in my future.

By the time Ben and I arrived home, Jenna was already there, having survived the ride to and from the mall. She assured me everything she bought had been reduced at least eighty percent and showed me the marked down price tags to prove it.

The three of us spent the evening nestled under an afghan on the sofa, munching on a bowl of buttered popcorn and watching a classic Julia Roberts film, *Runaway Bride*. The movie depicted the way Julia's character redefined her personality every time a new man entered into her life. If the right man came along, would I turn into a different person?

I thought about the men who had recently appeared in my life. The doctor. The real estate agent. The detective. My ex.

The dead guy.

The metamorphosis was beginning. Whether I liked it or not.

CHAPTER EIGHT

An arctic frost icing my cheeks woke me early the next morning. The temperature had dropped more than thirty degrees. With the heat turned off, it was only fifty-five degrees in the house. Dark gray clouds glared balefully at me and I glared back.

After a long dry summer, most Californians welcome the first rain of the season. Rain and soccer, however, are not a great combination from a mother's perspective.

I peered through the showers pouring off the rim of my turquoise umbrella. If Liz were here, she'd say it was peeing rain. Blue and gold merged with muck brown as arms and legs tangled on the sloppy field. I was so engrossed in the action on the field I didn't notice the man standing next to me. It wasn't until his size twelve Nike bumped against the toe of my running shoe that I looked up to see Detective Hunter, his oversized black umbrella almost a foot above mine.

"You take soccer quite seriously, Ms. McKay. I've been standing here for over five minutes and you haven't blinked once."

I couldn't blink. The rain had welded my waterproof mascara to my eyelids. I opened my mouth to respond when a roar from the parents turned my attention back to the field. Just in time to see my son kick a ball through the legs of the other team's goalie, a perfect shot.

"Yay, Ben," I screamed, totally forgetting the man standing next to me.

"That was a well-placed kick. Your son is a smart player. He must take after his mother."

My eyes narrowed as I looked up at him. Are detectives allowed to give compliments to murder suspects?

"I'll take credit for Ben's intellect, but I'm afraid the only time I received an A in P.E. was in square dancing," I said. "I was the do-si-do diva."

"I have no doubt you're a hit on the dance floor." He smoothly segued into another question. "Do you have any more Love Club dates on the horizon?"

Odd. Was the detective investigating me or flirting with me?

I shrugged my shoulders nonchalantly. "Well, you know the life of a single woman, one pressing social engagement after another."

His eyes twinkled and a brief smile hovered over his lips. Didn't he believe me?

"For your information, I have a date next weekend with someone else from the Love Club. A doctor. We're having dinner at the River Inn."

"Good to know. I might have dinner there myself." The look he shot at me penetrated through my windbreaker. "Just to make sure nothing happens. To your date."

He checked the gold watch on his left wrist. "I need to get over to Kristy's game. She'll be wondering what's keeping me. My daughter thinks she's going to kick up a storm, so to speak. Congratulations again on your son's goal."

With that remark, he strode down the sidelines toward one of the other playing fields. Remembering Kristy's tenacity in her last game, she undoubtedly would be kicking major butt, so to speak.

I gazed down the field and contemplated her father's broad shoulders and fine posterior as he walked away. Liz would be so proud of me.

But what did he mean by that last comment? Did he think Dr. Slater could be at risk by going out with me? Was that supposed to be a warning? As I watched his burly form disappear down the side of the field, I felt the nudge of an umbrella. Swamp eyes.

"How's the game going?" Hank asked. Wisps of dark blond hair escaped from beneath his cap and brushed the collar of his beige windbreaker. For a second, it looked like he was going to kiss me, but I checked his advance with my own umbrella.

"Ben made a goal."

"He did? You're kidding?"

43

I drilled him with a look. How about supporting your son instead of knocking him? Ben would never be the athlete his father was. Thank goodness. The last thing the world needed was another high school quarterback who couldn't stop reliving his victories from two decades ago.

A few seconds passed before Hank broke the silence. "Do you have any more dates coming up?"

I lifted my head from under the umbrella, a strategic error that resulted in a deluge of rain down my face and chest. Good thing I didn't need to make an impression on Hank. This man had seen me at my worst, during my twenty-hour labors with each child.

"Why?"

"I'm worried about you, honey. What if something happens when you're out with one of these bozos? Are you checking these guys out? Think about our kids." The gaze he fixed on me surprised me with its intensity. "And us."

Wow. Hank was displaying more passion this afternoon than in our twenty years together. What brought this on? Maybe he finally realized what he'd given up when he broke up our marriage. The impact his leaving had on his young children, not to mention his wife. I was about to question Hank further when I noticed our son slipping and sliding towards us with the apparent intent of giving me a hug.

"Did you see my goal, Mom? Wasn't it awesome?" Ben's grin reached literally from one side of his mud-speckled face to the other. Then he noticed his other water-soaked parent.

"Dad. You made it," he squealed. "Did you see my goal?"

"I'm real proud of you, big guy. You're a chip off the old block."

I snorted. Chip off the old blockhead was more like it. Hank performed some kind of complicated male bonding fist thing with Ben then attempted another kiss on my cheek. I outmaneuvered him but he grabbed my hand and held it tight.

"Be careful, Laurel. Don't take any chances." He hugged Ben and walked away leaving me in an unusual state. Stunned silence.

The rest of Sunday passed uneventfully. Ben called all of his pals to swap stories about their soccer games and make sure they heard about his goal as well. I did four loads of laundry and pondered my future.

My eagerness for my pending dinner with health-conscious Jeremy Slater had waned. Since the kids would be with their dad the following weekend, maybe I should embark on Liz's shotgun approach to getting a guy. My friend used to schedule four to five dates a week. But her goal was to find a husband and the father of her future children before her estrogen clock stopped ticking.

My goal was…what was my goal? Did I want a friend, an escort, a lover, or a husband? Was my decision to join the Love Club merely loneliness and the desire for intimacy with someone? Or was I trying to replicate the happy home Hank and I had for most of our marriage? Was I truly ready to spend the rest of my life with that special someone, the man who would not only keep my feet warm, but also my heart?

Very heavy thoughts, which should be contemplated when I wasn't so tired. After soccer and a full day of laundry, all I really wanted was to hit my sheets. The phone rang as I brushed and flossed. One of the kids picked it up and a few minutes later Jenna called out, "Hey, Mom, Grandmother Bingham for you."

My mother refused to go by Grandma or Granny.

I grabbed the phone and plunked into my overstuffed plaid wing chair. "Hello, Mother, how are you?"

"Laurel, your name popped up on my 'to do' list and I realized you never told me what happened with that murder investigation."

I could visualize it now. Item twenty—check on status of daughter to determine if necessary to raise bail on Monday.

"No need for the bail bondsman yet," I replied.

"Good." A few seconds elapsed. I think she really did check me off her list.

"I wondered if you would accompany me to a dinner they're having next Saturday at the country club, to honor the top producers in our company. Remember we went together last year."

I did remember. My mother, the queen of Centurion Realty, had been in her element. I felt like her ugly duckling daughter. She forgot to tell me it was a formal affair so I wore one of my old suits. Thank goodness I didn't have to face that designer-dressed group again.

"Sorry. I have a date Saturday night. At the River Inn."

"Not another of those Love Club people," she groaned. "I thought you were finished with that foolishness."

"I've only been on one date. Just because it was a disaster, it doesn't mean I shouldn't try again. He's a doctor."

"Why would a physician resort to joining a club like that? Certainly he can find dates without assistance."

I sighed. There was no pleasing my mother.

"What are you going to wear? The River Inn is quite elegant. I think men are supposed to wear coats and ties," she said.

Coats and ties. That was unusual for a California restaurant. Now I'd have to find time to buy a new dress. Too bad my mother and I aren't built the same. How my five-foot-seven, slender mother produced a short, curvy daughter was beyond me. Guess I had my dearly departed fireplug of a father to blame. I would love to go shopping in her walk-in closet, which was almost the size of my bedroom. Plus all of her designer suits and dresses were organized by color. Talk about anal with a capital *A*.

"I haven't decided yet. I'll fill you in at church next weekend."

"I'm sure Pastor Brown will be delighted to see you again."

Did I detect a hint of sarcasm? I opened my mouth to respond but she cut me off. "Try not to spoil your next date."

That was a low blow, but the dial tone came on before I could give a pithy reply. I hung up the phone, set my alarm clock and crawled into bed.

The clatter of squirrels rearranging the slate tiles on my roof woke me early the next morning. I love living in the country, but I wished my furry neighbors would find a hobby that wasn't so noisy or expensive to repair. Even so, the joy of living in the foothills is worth it. Starry, smog-free skies, snow-capped mountain vistas, herds of deer grazing peacefully on my front lawn. Eating all the petunias in my window boxes.

Okay, it's not pastoral perfection all the time. But I live only ten minutes from the office. If I lived in Sacramento, a forty-mile commute on clogged highways, I'd have to get up an hour earlier. Or get rid of my children.

Monday morning I arrived early at the bank. I exchanged growls with the wooden bear and with Vivian who seemed even surlier than usual. She didn't even quiz me about Friday's lunch date. After storing my purse, I sauntered down to the breakroom. Mary Lou entertained several of our co-workers with a description of her

Saturday night date. I nodded sympathetically when she confided he was a lousy kisser.

At least her date was alive and kissing.

I grabbed my mug, scurried past the rows of gray cubicles and reached my own miniscule six-by-six cube. The pile of loan applications formed a barricade around my desk. I was glad I worked for a conservative bank that stayed true to its mission statement—making sensible loans to qualified borrowers.

"Hey, gorgeous." I recognized Stan's deep baritone and looked up. "What's up?" I asked. "Do anything exciting this weekend?"

Stan draped himself over the tweed chair. His pressed lilac shirt and matching satin tie were perfectly coordinated as usual. "The highlight of my weekend was helping my sister pick out a dress to wear to a wedding if that gives you any idea of my hot social life."

"Hey, I need to buy a new dress. Can you think of someplace suitable for me—as well as my budget?" I added. Given Stan's excellent and expensive taste, further clarification was necessary.

Stan stroked his chin, gray eyes thoughtful behind his wire-rims. Not that he had much of a chin to stroke. "Honestly, I think we visited every boutique in Sacramento. Jeannie is such a perfectionist it took *forever* to find something, and she never lets a price tag stand in her way."

"Great." I rubbed my hands together in anticipation of a shopping expedition. "Do you have any evenings free this week?"

"Between my baseball league, knitting class and the church choir, I think I can squeeze you in." We settled on Thursday since most of the stores would be open late.

Wednesday evening I called Coach Dan and he agreed to bring Ben home from practice the next day. I could ramp up my Visa to my heart's content and my bankcard's limits.

Stan and I left the office promptly at five. He offered to drive us in his new Beemer. I wasn't about to refuse the offer and entertained myself on the drive to the city by trying out all twelve of the different seating combinations.

"This is such a terrific car," I said. "Do you think I'll ever own one like it?"

"If you don't mind being indentured to a finance company for the rest of your life, you too could own a BMW. If we find the right dress tonight, you may end up marrying the doctor. Doesn't the Hippocratic oath state they have to drive a BMW or a Mercedes?"

I chuckled, but his comment made me pause. Could our shopping excursion eventually result in marriage to the respectable Dr. Slater? Was marriage my ultimate goal? The sensible thing would have been to spend the next three hours evaluating what I wanted in a man. Instead, we spent the evening trying to decide what I wanted in a dress.

Stan suggested we start at the Pavilions. Since the Plaza is more than forty miles from my house, I hadn't shopped there in years. As we strolled up the brick-lined sidewalks, I ogled the mannequins in the windows. A soft black chiffon number caught my attention. It looked like it would be perfect for my less than perfect figure.

A rhapsody of tinkling bells greeted us as we entered. A willowy sales woman dressed in a sage green silk suit, her left hand enhanced with a diamond the size of a snow globe, greeted us. "Hello. Can I help you find anything in particular?"

"How much is that black dress in the window, the floaty one?" I asked.

"The uh, floaty one? I believe it's either twenty-two ninety-five or twenty-three ninety-five. What size are you?" Her aquamarine eyes sized me up, down and sideways.

"I'm a ten or twelve. I can't believe that dress is less than twenty-five dollars. This is better than Ross."

The sales woman and Stan gawked at me and managed to synchronize the rolling of their eyes. She turned the price tag over and read aloud, enunciating every patronizing syllable. "This Roberto Cavalli is twenty-three hundred ninety-five dollars. Let me see if I have your size available." She stared down her perfectly shaped nose at me. "If you still wish to try it on."

My cheeks blushed hot pink. What was Stan thinking? I was on a Payless budget, not a Prada budget.

"Of course. I'm sure it will be the perfect dress for me," I muttered.

The minute she walked into the back room, I grabbed Stan's sleeve and dragged him to the front door.

"Are you nuts?" I said. "That dress is the equivalent of three months of house payments. Or eight hundred mochas."

"You said you needed the perfect dress," he said with a sheepish look. "Sometimes my champagne taste collides with my common sense. But it may be exquisite on you."

Luckily, the exquisite overpriced dress was unavailable in my size. We browsed through several other stores but couldn't find anything in my price range that made either of us rave.

"Don't get discouraged," Stan said, as I slumped in the leather seat of the Beemer. "We still have lots of boutiques to check out in mid-town and East Sac."

We found a parking space on H Street in front of a store called Serendipity. Twinkling white miniature lights lent a festive look to the fall fashions in their window. Stuffed pumpkins strewn throughout the display reminded me it was less than a week to Halloween. Ben and I hadn't even discussed his costume yet. This mother had her priorities all screwed up.

"I'm getting some good vibes here." Stan's head swiveled as his eyes scanned the room. "You take the racks on the left and I'll head over to the ones on the right."

I'd forgotten how tiring shopping could be since I rarely indulged in my favorite pre-divorce hobby. I was ready to call it a night when Stan cried out, "Hoochy Mama."

Huh?

Hoochy Mama was a sapphire-blue dress with sheer sleeves, ending in beaded cuffs at the wrist. The empire waist dress with its low rounded neckline would flatter my curves. I snagged the dress from Stan's clutches, entered the dressing room and closed the louvered door. I held my breath when the zipper stuck, but a little jiggle and it made it to the top. I slipped on my heels and peeked in the mirror.

A young sales woman tapped on the door. "We have a three-way mirror out front. I'm sure your boyfriend wants to see how you look."

I snickered as she pushed open the curtain. "Stan's not my boyfriend. He's just the best personal shopper a girl could have. We'll let him make the final decision."

I model walked through the store ending my performance in front of Stan's chair.

"Babe," he said. "You've been hiding yourself under those Betsy Banker clothes. You look good enough to make a gay man go straight."

"Ok.a.a.y...I'll take that as a compliment. Guess I'm buying the dress."

I changed into my slacks and sweater, hung the dress on its hangar, and walked back into the store straight into—her. Nadine Wells. The golden goddess who for some strange reason clung to the arm of—another man? Not my ex?

"Nadine, um...hello." I turned to Stan. My expression must have screamed help because my buddy jumped in to rescue me.

"Hello. I'm Stan. Laurel and I were just leaving. In fact we were just getting into my new Beemer, the silver 660 parked over there..."

I recovered in time to save Stan from receiving the "gay dork" award of the week. "Where's Hank?"

Nadine tittered as she tottered on four-inch gold stilettos. Every time I encountered the woman I expected her to topple over, her super-sized man-made breasts at odds with her size double-zero body. At least I had a decent size frame to haul around my excess soft tissue.

"Honey, I kicked him out a few weeks ago. This is Dr. Hugo Black. Plastic surgeon extraordinaire, aren't you sweetie?" Her breasts tilted up in homage to the man who must have been responsible for their design and construction.

A plastic surgeon far surpassed Hank financially. My ex could barely keep up with my child support payments since the bottom fell out of the construction industry. Had Nadine grown tired of supporting him?

The plastic couple sauntered to the back of the store as I paid for my dress. Stan and I were both quiet as we drove up Highway 50 toward Placerville. Nadine's revelation stunned me. Were Hank's recent overtures due to a realization that our children had suffered when he'd moved out of the house? Or were financial considerations involved?

Stan dropped me off at the bank parking lot. I thanked him for his help, climbed in my car and headed home to a house ablaze with lights. I couldn't wait for the day when my kids received their first utility bill.

I parked in the garage and removed my dress from the back seat. Despite the high wattage emanating from every room, neither of the children was downstairs. I walked into the kitchen, the dress in its navy bag, draped over my arm.

A note lay on the table. Jenna had scrawled the words a mother never wants to read.

CHAPTER NINE

I read the note a second time. DON'T FORGET—SNACK FOR SCHOOL.

The two most dreaded words in a mother's vocabulary. Snack Mom.

Ben's teacher had decided that every Friday one student should bring a treat for the entire class. It would give the kids something to look forward to at the end of the week. An excellent concept, assuming the mother of the designated student remembered her snack-mom detail.

I'd totally spaced out and forgotten it was Ben's week. I would quickly check on the kids then head to the supermarket. I climbed up the stairs and entered Ben's room. He was asleep, a contented smile on his face. Probably dreaming of a soccer goal. I tucked in his covers then crossed the hall to Jenna's room. I knocked on her door and she gave me permission to enter.

She glanced at my garment bag. "Did you find what you were looking for?"

"Uh-huh. I bought this amazing dress. I was going to try it on for you but then I saw Ben's note. I have to drive to the store and buy a snack for his class."

"Nah, you're good. We made brownies and stacked them in the Tupperware carrier. I wrote the note so he wouldn't forget to take them in the morning. We figured you had enough on your mind and didn't want you to screw up this date, too."

In my opinion, I *wasn't* the one who screwed up my last date, but I was thrilled by Jenna's helpful attitude. I plunked down on her apricot embroidered bedspread. "Guess who I ran into tonight?"

She gave me the look that only a sixteen-year-old daughter can give. Okay, maybe she is too old for guessing games. "Nadine. According to her, she and your Dad split up."

Jenna's eyes lit up and her smile was the widest I'd seen since our divorce. "Now you and Dad can get together again." She jumped up from the desk chair and twirled around the room. Her mattress whooshed as she landed in a happy sprawl on the bed.

My heart plummeted. Why hadn't I realized what her reaction would be? With Nadine out of the picture, Jenna assumed Hank and I would reconcile. My garment bag fell onto the floor as I embraced my daughter.

"Honey, your dad and I aren't getting back together. It just means he's no longer living with Nadine." I frowned when I realized her father had neglected to inform me he was residing elsewhere. "Did you know he moved?"

She gave me a sheepish look reminiscent of the man in question. "He told me he and Nadine were having problems so he moved in with his friend Bill. I thought...I thought maybe we could all be a family again..." Her voice trailed off as she slumped against me.

All the anger I felt when Hank left two years ago erupted in full force. How dare he let Jenna get her hopes up that we would reconcile. It was a good thing he wasn't standing in front of me because I definitely had murder on my mind.

I kissed the top of her tangled auburn hair. "We'll discuss it tomorrow." The shopping expedition had worn me out and I didn't have the emotional stamina to think about my ex-husband's deceit right now.

Friday morning Hank left a voicemail informing me he would pick up the kids from school. I would have to wait until he brought them home on Sunday before I could chastise him. While our divorce decree granted joint custody, lately it seemed more like an eighty/twenty split. I hoped their lack of quality time with their father wouldn't make them any more dysfunctional than most children.

Considering the amount of time they spent with me, that was probably a given.

Despite Jeremy's courteous demeanor during our previous meeting, I was somewhat apprehensive about having him come to my house. He probably wasn't used to tripping over the G.I. Joes and Matchbox cars that normally decorate our family room.

After a restless night, I awoke early, determined my house would be clean enough to invite Martha Stewart to dinner. I swept, vacuumed, scrubbed and polished. Once the house was immaculate, it was my turn to become scrubbed and polished. I skipped lunch and by six o'clock, I was ready. Thanks to Liz, my face was aglow with sunny sheen foundation, an organic product that guaranteed I'd look ten years younger. Too bad it couldn't make me look ten pounds lighter.

With extra time on my hands, I paced through the house. I was looking forward to the date but also dreading it. My pacing eventually led me to the kitchen. I decided a little wine might relax me. I uncorked a bottle of chardonnay just as the doorbell rang. I took a sip of liquid fortification the size of a Big Gulp, set the glass on the counter and walked to the front door to greet my suitor.

Jeremy stepped into the entry, tall and slim in a gray suit, blue shirt and darker blue tie. He smiled as his eyes appraised me. "Laurel, you look terrific. Are you ready to go?"

"Yes. Do we have time for some wine before we leave? There's a bottle of chardonnay open."

"Sure. Sounds good." He followed me into the kitchen and perched on one of the oak barstools.

I poured a glass for Jeremy and topped off my own. Our glasses clinked as he toasted, "to a beautiful woman and a beautiful evening."

Aww. What a lovely sentiment. Both his words and the wine made me feel all warm and toasty inside. Jeremy was definitely a step or an entire staircase up from my last date. I beamed at him. He smiled, sipped his wine then grimaced. The doctor must not be a connoisseur of the McKay house brand, the infamous Two Buck Chuck. He set the glass on the counter then swiveled around, surveying my kitschy yellow kitchen.

"Nice house. Very cozy."

"Thanks. My ex built it. Lots of flaws just like him."

Jeremy looked taken aback. I forgot that complaining about your ex is a no-no. Love Club rules.

"I guess all men are flawed to some extent. No matter how hard we try, perfection eludes us." He shrugged. "Are you ready to go?"

Strange remark. Jeremy looked troubled but since he didn't elaborate, I didn't want to push. Maybe once we reached the restaurant he'd feel comfortable confiding in me. I eyed my glass of wine. I hated to waste good chardonnay.

I also hated to waste cheap chardonnay. I took another sip then put the glass down by the sink.

I locked my front door and we walked out to Jeremy's navy Mercedes. He politely helped me in without making any anatomical detours. I settled into the passenger seat admiring the gleaming burled walnut paneling and array of controls on the dashboard. "Nice car."

"Your cars are the clothing you drive in." He shot me a sideways glance. If that were true, I was currently riding in a tux. But what did my pastel hybrid say about me?

It was a short drive to the restaurant. Jeremy handed the keys to the valet and we strolled down the slate pathway to the entrance of the River Inn. Between the vaulted ceilings, pine-paneled walls and enormous green plants interspersed throughout the restaurant, it was like entering a primeval forest. We followed the hostess to a romantic corner booth overlooking the American River.

Jeremy perused the wine list while I admired the tumultuous river crashing over the rocks below. When the waiter appeared, my date lifted his gray curls from the menu. "We'll have a bottle of the 1976 Dom Perignon."

The waiter looked impressed, nodding his head in approval. "Excellent choice, sir. I'll be back shortly."

I was also impressed and displayed my approval by emitting a tiny burp. Uh, oh. Maybe I shouldn't have drunk that chardonnay on an empty stomach. Our waiter arrived with a silver ice bucket, two crystal flutes and the two-hundred-dollar bottle of champagne. A muffled pop and—voila, I was holding a fifty-dollar glass of booze.

The bus boy delivered a basket loaded with some garlicky smelling focaccia bread. Jeremy was still engrossed in the wine list so I withdrew two pieces and slathered on some butter. I sipped the champagne and munched on the excellent refined carbs.

My date finally looked up from the two-inch-thick gold embossed wine list. "Laurel, do you have any preferences?"

My only preference was that the wine didn't taste like grape juice. How could I convince him I was a connoisseur as well? "I prefer a full-bodied red." I had no idea what that phrase meant, but I figured it should narrow it down to a couple hundred choices.

Jeremy finally selected a local 2010 Petite Sirah from the Lava Cap Winery. The award-winning wine was undoubtedly a better choice than the $1.99 bottle I'd served earlier. The waiter stood, pen in hand, primed for our orders.

I held the menu at arm's length then brought it closer, but it was still out of focus. Why was it the fancier the restaurant, the smaller the font. "I'll have the Caesar salad to start and the prime rib, petite cut."

Jeremy was ready with his order. "Spinach salad with nonfat Italian dressing on the side, and the sautéed sea bass, no sauce." He handed his menu to the waiter.

"You have such control over your diet," I said in admiration.

"Everything in moderation." He traced his index finger around the rim of his crystal champagne flute. "It's an easy motto to follow. But there are those who just can't help their addictive personalities."

I looked at the crumbs littering my bread plate. Time to turn the conversation in a different direction before another nutrition lecture was forthcoming. "What do you like to do for fun?"

His smile lit up his face and his shoulders relaxed. "I really enjoy going to Lake Tahoe. Last summer I hiked most of the Tahoe Rim Trail. In fact, I'm thinking of buying a vacation home on the south shore."

My mother would so love to get her hands on Jeremy. A doctor and a multiple homeowner.

"Your practice must be doing well."

His pensive look returned as he drank his champagne. "It is. I've been very fortunate. But something odd came up when I made the offer on the property. Laurel, since you're in the mortgage business, I thought you could explain how...."

A buzzing noise interrupted us. I jumped and banged the crystal flute into the table. Champagne droplets landed on the beads of my new dress. Jeremy grabbed his cell from his belt and silenced it.

"I didn't realize you were on call tonight." I bent and dabbed the spots with the black linen napkin. Smart restaurant. No white lint speckling our dark clothing. Too bad they couldn't guarantee my dress remain in a spill-free zone.

Jeremy seemed perplexed as he stared at the number. "It's not an emergency, but I need to make a call. I'll go outside so I don't disturb anyone. Enjoy the champagne."

Being the obliging person that I am, I sipped the bubbly that hadn't landed on my dress. I don't normally drink champagne but this Dom stuff tasted pretty good. I wondered if Jeremy treated all of his dates to such fine wine and cuisine.

My eyes glanced wistfully at the empty breadbasket as I poured more champagne into my flute. The servers must be waiting until Jeremy returned before they brought our salads. My bladder suddenly announced it needed to make an expedition. I pushed my chair back. The waiter quickly materialized and slid it out for me. My hands gripped the back of the chair as the room did a 360 rotation.

"Are you all right?" asked the solicitous server.

I nodded. I was fine except for being a lightweight when it comes to alcohol. I negotiated my way through the restaurant, bumping into two chairs. At least I avoided landing in anyone's chef's special.

The ladies' room was located in the back of the cocktail lounge. There was no sign of Jeremy in the restaurant or the bar so he must have gone outside to make his call. It wouldn't hurt to take a quick peek. The fresh air might dispel some of the champagne bubbles fogging my head. I grinned at the valet and sauntered around the side of the building.

I squinted in the direction of the river. Two men stood in the shadows along the riverbank, a hundred feet or so from the restaurant. The moonlight shining on the back of one man's head indicated he might be bald. The man facing him had a full head of hair and was about Jeremy's height, but I couldn't be certain at that distance. The only thing I was sure of was that it was too cold to stand outside wondering.

I went inside, weaved my way around the black leather bar stools, and entered the ladies' room. After using the facilities, I tried to decide what to do next. Should I go back to the table or wait in the lounge? The beige microfiber chair in the corner of the lounge beckoned me. I plopped my feet on the matching ottoman.

The door burst open and I woke with a start as two chattering women headed for the stalls. I peeked at my watch.

Good grief. Almost fifteen minutes had elapsed since I'd left the table. I stood and smoothed my dress over my hips. Either Jeremy would be back at the table or Mr. Dom Perignon and I would become bosom buds. Although after the purchase of my new dress, there wasn't enough credit left on my Visa to pay for dinner, much less the Dom.

I stepped into the bar, which was deserted. In the dining room, most of the patrons stood in front of the large arched windows overlooking the river. I joined them and addressed the armpit of a navy pinstriped suit. "What's going on?"

The tall man glanced at me. "A woman seated by the window thought she saw someone in the river. Several of the staff ran outside to check."

Even in my somewhat befuddled state, I knew this was a treacherous part of the river with craggy rocks and boulders strewn everywhere. With temperatures in the fifties, surely no one would intentionally be swimming.

The woman who spotted the person in the river might have imagined it. Perhaps she'd downed most of a bottle of champagne herself. At the rate I'd been drinking, I'd probably see pink elephants taking a dip.

Several people gasped. The man next to me said, "It looks like the river rescue team has arrived. I hope they can save the poor sucker."

So did I. Unfortunately there wasn't anything I could do in the way of river rescue, so I wandered back to my romantic booth and gulped down a glass of water, hoping it would dilute some of the champagne. I spotted our server and waved. Maybe he would take pity on me and bring out my salad.

"Sorry, I don't wish to ignore you. You heard what happened?"

"Yes. My date has disappeared and I wondered if he's helping? He's a doc..." I burped. "tor."

The server shook his head. "I don't recall seeing him, but a lot of the guests ran outside. Do you want to check out there? I'll bring your salad as soon as you return."

Sure. Jeremy had to be around here somewhere. I walked through the nearly deserted restaurant and stepped out on the patio. The cold air felt invigorating.

Much as I hated admitting I'd lost my date, I needed to find out what had happened to him. An El Dorado County deputy was deep in conversation with an emergency technician. I tapped the husky officer on his khaki-clad shoulder.

"Excuse me. Is one of the guests at the River Inn helping your rescue team?"

"Sorry, ma'am. I can't say for sure. We've received several offers of assistance from the diners at the restaurant."

"Is the person in the river okay?"

The young deputy shook his head, his red-rimmed eyes weary. "No, unfortunately. The EMTs tried to resuscitate him but they weren't successful."

"How awful. Was he dining here?"

"We assume he was. He was wearing a light gray suit." The deputy's expression was bewildered. "But no one has reported anyone missing."

My Dom Perignon addled brain produced a giggling frenzy as I visualized Jeremy jumping into the river to escape my boring conversation. The two men appeared startled by my inappropriate outburst.

"Sorry, I've had way too much champagne. You see, my date left the table a while ago and hasn't returned."

They exchanged glances. The deputy spoke first. "We may be able to help." He pulled out a notebook and pen. "His name?"

"Jeremy Slater." My stomach growled. "Sorry. I'm in desperate need of some food."

"I'll see what I can do," he assured me. "In the meantime, why don't you go back to your table?"

The restaurant was devoid of customers with the exception of a silver-haired couple seated at a table in the bar. They glanced my way then resumed their quiet conversation. I plopped down in our booth in the empty dining room. I hoped the deputy had some pull. All I wanted was Jeremy and my salad, and at this point, I wasn't sure in which order.

After a few minutes of waiting, my patience was maxed out. I slid out of the booth then realized my purse was resting under the table. My chiffon skirt shimmied up my thighs as I grabbed the leather strap. I backed up and bumped into something solid. Jeremy had finally returned.

I turned around to chastise my date and was startled to see Detective Hunter. I said the first thing that popped into my mind. "What are you doing here?"

He frowned. "I had a dinner reservation but just as we arrived, someone noticed the person in the river." The detective seemed uneasy as he shifted from one leg to the other. "One of the deputies told me you were dining with a Jeremy Slater."

"Yeah, I spoke to someone a few minutes ago. Jeremy left to make a call right after we arrived and never returned. He's a physician so I thought he might be helping but no one seems to have seen him." I wrinkled my nose and frowned. "I won't be going out with *him* again."

The detective's gaze softened as his eyes met mine. "No. I'm afraid you won't."

CHAPTER TEN

The room spun in a kaleidoscope of colors and I pitched forward. The quick-thinking detective caught me before I connected with the floor. His arms wrapped around me and I curled into his chest as my brain absorbed the fact that Jeremy Slater was dead.

Hunter gently disengaged my limp frame from his and assisted me back to my seat. He slid across from me, not an easy task given his size and the confines of the booth.

"I know this is a huge shock," he said, "but I have to ask a few questions." He took a familiar looking pad and pen out of his shirt pocket. "You mentioned to one of the deputies that Dr. Slater was missing for quite some time. Was this typical behavior for him?"

"I don't know." Tears streamed down my cheeks. I grabbed a napkin and attempted to staunch the flow of hot teardrops mixed with inky rivulets of mascara. "This was only our second date. Oh no," I moaned.

"What's the matter?"

"He didn't get to try the Dom."

"The Don?" He looked puzzled.

"Dom Perignon. Right after we placed our dinner orders he received a page and disappeared to make a phone call. He never got to sample the champagne." I hiccupped. "It was very tasty."

"Evidently." A hint of a smile crossed his face before it disappeared. "Ms. McKay, you realize in the last two weeks, both men you've dated have died. Two men. Two dates. Two deaths."

I couldn't respond. I could only stare at him with tear-blurred eyes.

"I can't decide if you have an unerring ability for ending up in disastrous situations, or if I'm sitting next to a killer."

"Killer?" My flowing tears froze in shock. "Jeremy was murdered?"

He shrugged. "I don't know yet. It could have been an accidental fall. Until we discover exactly what occurred this is a crime scene.

He paused and fiddled with his tie. "We identified Dr. Slater from his wallet, but we can make it official if you confirm it's him. Do you think you're up to it?"

My eyes widened in alarm as I contemplated viewing the drowned body of my dead date.

He shook his head. "Never mind, that was a bad idea. I don't think you could handle it."

Hey, mister. I may be a woman, but I'm a mother. We do what we have to do. I stood, placed my hands on my hips, and glared at the detective. "I'll do it for Jeremy."

Weak female, indeed.

He slid out of the booth. His gaze wandered down the length of my dress, slowing as he contemplated my bare legs. "Do you have a coat? It's chilly out and your dress doesn't look like it provides much warmth."

"No, I didn't bring one with me." I shivered. "I'll manage."

He took off his sport coat and draped it slowly, almost sensually around me. I noticed his broad shoulders—the kind you wanted to lean on after your date dropped dead.

I squared my own shoulders as he escorted me towards the entrance, his hand resting lightly on my back. As we passed the lounge, he halted. "Would you mind waiting here? I need to speak to that couple."

He walked over to the elderly pair I'd noticed earlier. Could they be witnesses? He must have spoken to them previously because they jumped right into conversation. It was fine with me if we waited before I viewed Jeremy one last time.

As I sniffed in the woodsy scent of Detective Hunter's brown tweed jacket, I briefly wondered what it would feel like to have his arms around me. Oh, dear. Not an appropriate reaction considering

61

my date was gone. Forever. Must be the residual effects of the champagne.

The detective returned. "Sorry about the wait. I needed to check with them about something."

My mind raced with possibilities. "Suspects?"

His laugh rang through the room. "Hardly. They're my parents. I can personally vouch for them."

Hmm. So he was with his parents. Not a hot date.

Fewer people lingered outside than on my previous visit. The patio was cordoned off with that increasingly familiar yellow ribbon. I was running into crime scene tape far more frequently than a soccer mom should.

One of the deputies stood next to what resembled a gigantic black baggie. My heart plummeted two feet when I realized it was a body bag. The deputy nodded to us. "Evening, Tom. Is this the woman who was with the victim?"

"Yes, Sam. She's agreed to identify the body. Ms. McKay, are you sure you're ready?" Detective Hunter's palm rested on my back as he gazed sympathetically at me. Was this the same man who interrogated me less than two weeks ago? He appeared to have at least one compassionate vein running through his body.

I swallowed and braced myself for the unveiling. "As ready as I'll ever be."

Sam slowly unzipped the bag then looked at me for confirmation.

His eyes were closed, but the pale face and damp curly silver hair were undeniably recognizable.

Omigod. I gasped and frantically looked around as the butterflies in my stomach morphed into an assault team of flying pterodactyls. Hunter took one look at my face and astutely led me to some shrubbery alongside the patio. A hundred dollars' worth of champagne eliminated within seconds. The detective grabbed a clean paper napkin off one of the tables and handed it to me. I wiped my mouth and face and collapsed into one of the patio chairs. I barely knew Jeremy but to see him like that was devastating.

"I take it that was Dr. Slater?" Hunter asked.

"Yes." I pressed my hands against my heaving stomach and tried to erase the picture of Jeremy's pallid face from my memory. "I don't know how you detectives get used to it."

"Your first body is never easy."

I sat straight up. "I'm not planning on making a practice of viewing dead bodies."

"Glad to hear it. I'm not sure our sheriff's department is large enough to handle your social life."

I lasered an angry look at the detective.

"Sorry," Hunter apologized and placed his hand on my forearm. "That was uncalled for. Look, we have to complete an in-depth interview with you, but we're shorthanded and I need to spend time with the crime techs. I hope I'm not going to regret this but I'm sending you home. I assume the two of you drove here together."

"Yes, the valet parked his car. It's some type of large Mercedes."

"We'll need to examine his vehicle as well. One of the deputies will have to drive you to your house."

I was about to respond when the elderly man Tom had spoken to earlier approached us. "Hello, I'm Bill Hunter, Tom's father." He extended his hand to me.

I checked to see if there was any icky champagne residue left on my palm before I shook his hand in response. There was a considerable resemblance between the two men. Bill Hunter's eyes were a soft faded brown, and he had the same high cheekbones. I detected some Native American influence in their bloodline somewhere. The senior Hunter possessed a very engaging smile. I vaguely recalled Detective Hunter having an equally appealing smile but it wasn't something he displayed with any frequency.

"Your mother is getting tired. Can we leave now or will you need a lift home?"

"Why don't you and Mom take off? I need to arrange transportation for Ms. McKay."

"Where do you live?" Bill Hunter asked me politely. Detective Hunter rattled off my address.

The older Hunter looked mystified. "You know each other? Is there something you've been keeping from me, son?" he teased.

The detective flushed. "No, Dad. I interviewed Ms. McKay a few weeks ago when her date was found..." his voice faltered.

This was the first time since I'd met Detective Hunter that he'd lost his composure. He was human after all.

Maybe.

"Both of our children play soccer in the same league, on different teams," I explained.

"Oh, so you've met our adorable granddaughter," Bill said with pride in his voice. "Isn't Kristy a sweetheart?"

"Um, yeah. A real sweetheart." Except for those occasions when she was attacking players on the soccer field. It sounded like Kristy had her grandpa wrapped tight around her pinky finger.

"You don't live very far from us. We could drive you home. Are you having car problems?"

"Not exactly," I said, grateful for his offer. I rose from the chair and glanced at Detective Hunter. His face had reddened to a dark aubergine.

"Dad, I think, it would be best if she, uh…was driven home by a deputy."

A deputy? What did that mean? Were they taking me into custody?

Bill Hunter winked at me. "I understand why you want to make sure this lovely woman gets home safe. It was nice meeting you, Laurel."

The senior Hunter walked to the back of the restaurant where he joined his wife. They waved as they exited. The detective and I stared at each other. Was this what novels describe as a palpable silence?

I was the first to break it. "Am I under arrest?"

He shook his head. "No, but it's not appropriate for my parents to drive you home. Plus I want an officer to check your house and make sure it's safe. Until I find out more about Dr. Slater's death, I still don't know if I should treat you as a suspect—or a potential victim."

Great. I didn't know whether I should be more afraid of a murderer running amok, or being arrested for a murder I didn't commit. He gently removed his tweed jacket from my shoulders. "I'll get you a blanket from the EMTs. Let me see if Sam is free to take you home."

I nodded my assent then waited in the lounge for my official chauffeur. A guy hefting a huge video camera lumbered in and glanced around. The TV crews had arrived. I hoped I'd be out of there before someone mentioned the dead man wasn't dining alone. It was horrible enough that Jeremy was dead. My children didn't need to see their mother's tear-streaked face plastered all over the eleven o'clock news.

Sam, the deputy I'd met previously, was assigned to transport me home. He handed me a navy blue fleece blanket, which I promptly turned into an oversized pashmina shawl. He escorted me to his patrol car, which was parked a short distance from the restaurant.

I wanted to interrogate my official chauffeur, but he spent most of the drive on the phone. Once we entered the house, Sam checked all the rooms. He ensured that each window was locked and waited until all bolts were bolted before he took off.

I stared at my watch in disbelief. It felt like three in the morning but it was barely after eleven. I was halfway up the stairs when I realized I still hadn't eaten dinner. I didn't feel tipsy so my purge behind the bushes must have eliminated the champagne I'd consumed.

Comfort food was required and any form of chocolate was the obvious choice. Unfortunately, I'd prioritized house cleaning over grocery shopping. The pantry was barren when it came to my favorite food group. A rummage through the refrigerator scored one bruised apple. A little fiber—in Jeremy's honor.

My eyes misted as my gaze drifted to the wine glasses sitting on the counter. A tragic event certainly made a person more appreciative of the simple things in life. To have your life cut short in an instant of time was heartbreaking. I reflected on the difficulties of my life. Trying to make financial ends meet. Struggling between my career and the needs of my children.

The death of my marriage.

All of those problems were mere hiccups. I was blessed with two terrific and caring children, a mother who loved me in her own peculiar fashion and an array of wonderful and loyal friends. Who would be mourning Jeremy's tragic death tonight?

I plodded up the stairs and put on a pair of flannel jammies, perfect for providing the solace I needed. Soft red ones covered with cavorting puppy dogs that my mother had given me the previous Christmas. She didn't think I needed anything sexier and she was probably right. I lay there in my flannel splendor pondering the tragedy of Jeremy's death. What were his last moments like? Was it an accident? Or murder?

Could I be in jeopardy? Or my children?

Sometime in the wee hours of the morning, I finally fell into a troubled sleep. I dreamt I hung by my fingertips from a bridge over the American River. A tall man with a bald spot on the back of his head stomped on my hands. Finger by finger, I was losing my grip as the turbulent river crashed against the rocks below. A siren wailed in the distance, the piercing sound increasing in volume until the siren was next to my ear.

CHAPTER ELEVEN

The shrill ringing of the phone on my nightstand announced an unwelcome wake-up call. "Hello," I croaked, cradling the receiver against my left ear.

"Is that you, dear?" Mother asked.

Good question. I wasn't so sure of the answer myself. It felt like the entire percussion section of a drum and bugle corps was marching through my head.

"Hello, Mother, how are things?"

"How are things?" Her voice crescendoed to a high pitch.

Oh, that was unpleasant.

"Things are not good, Laurel. Not good at all. I'm sitting in my car in the church parking lot. You were supposed to meet me for the ten-thirty service. It's ten-twenty. Are you running late?"

Not exactly. I wasn't running at all. I'd completely forgotten I was supposed to meet my parent for the late service at church, followed by brunch in Apple Hill.

"Sorry. I got home late and forgot to set my alarm. Why don't you go to church and we can get together for brunch afterwards. Do you still want to meet at the Cozy Apple Cafe?"

"You've become very inconsiderate lately, Laurel. Your social life should not interfere with your obligations to your church. I can't imagine what Pastor Martin will think. You've missed services several weekends in a row."

Missing church was the least of my worries. I just hoped our minister didn't find out I was a double murder suspect.

"I'll be at the café by noon."

"All right. Don't be late."

Our family has attended the same church under the leadership of Pastor Martin for the last thirty years. He's a kindly man as I'm sure all men of the cloth are. He is also a very forgiving minister. I was certain he wouldn't hold my lack of attendance against me. Although with the rate the bodies were piling up, I might need someone with God's ear on my side.

I dragged myself down the stairs into the kitchen. Rays of sun shimmered off my bright yellow walls, which did nothing to alleviate the throbbing in my head. I eyeballed the rooster clock. Time for at least one high-octane cup of caffeine.

I swallowed four aspirin while the coffee perked. Even my automatic drip seemed noisier than usual. Despite the hangover mist hovering in my brain, I couldn't forget the events of the previous evening.

How did Jeremy end up in the river? Was it an accident? And what about those two men I saw talking on the riverbank? If Jeremy was the gray-haired man I'd seen, the other man might have left the restaurant before anything happened. He could be totally unaware of the incident. This topic needed to be discussed with Detective Hunter.

I gazed at the clock. Not enough time. I would contact the detective later. It was almost eleven-thirty and I still hadn't made it into the shower. That meant arriving at the restaurant with no makeup and bed hair. I flew up the stairs into my bedroom, slipped on a pair of khaki slacks and a coral blouse that bore two tiny spots on the front, both of which my mother would undoubtedly notice.

My hair resembled Ben's, but with an additional twenty cowlicks. The silver hairs threading their way through my copper mop seemed to be cloning one another. I reached into my closet and smashed an ivory straw hat on my head. My flat hat hair couldn't be helped.

If our pastor was his usual loquacious self the service would run over. My mother normally would stay afterwards to glean any new gossip such as job transfers, which could mean a potential listing. With a little luck, I would get to the Cozy Apple Cafe before she did.

I managed to hit every red light on the drive to the Apple Hill area east of Placerville. My mother's white Chrysler Le Baron, a testament to her fastidiousness, gleamed in the parking lot. I pulled into the slot next to her car.

I jogged across the asphalt parking lot and entered the restaurant. Mother sat in a cracked red vinyl booth not far from the cash register, dressed in a rose knit suit that complemented her platinum coloring. I smiled fondly as she pored over every inch of the large glossy menu, her matching rose-colored reading glasses balanced on her straight nose. She was undeniably the most annoying woman on earth but...she was my mother.

I air kissed her cheek and slid into the opposite side of the booth. "Church must have gotten out early."

She looked up from the menu and frowned. "What's the matter with your hair?"

I chose to ignore her comment. A bad hair day was the least of my concerns.

"How was the service? Did you hear any good gossip?" That should occupy her until I decided what to order from the extensive menu. Almost twenty-four hours had passed since anything substantial entered and remained in my stomach.

Should I continue to watch my diet or just say screw it? The café specialized in six different versions of eggs Benedict, and my favorite was a poached egg sitting on a slice of tomato, perched on a crab cake then drenched with creamy Hollandaise sauce. Breakfast didn't come much more fattening than that, unless I added bacon and fried potatoes on the side.

Engrossed in the bounty of Benedicts, I missed her next question.

"Did you hear me?" she asked, her glare magnified fourfold by the reading glasses.

"Sorry." I slapped the menu shut. "What did you say?"

"All the talk at church was about an accident at the River Inn. They said a man fell in the river but he'd drowned by the time the rescue workers pulled him out. The Parkers were dining there and saw the whole thing. Hugh Parker said the police roped off the patio with crime scene tape. Did you hear or see anything while you were there?"

She looked at me with anticipation, probably hoping I would have first-hand knowledge she could share with her cronies. Once she heard my "up close and personal" information, I doubted she would want to share it with anyone. Our conversation was interrupted by the arrival of the waitress, holding a full pot of coffee. I needed more caffeine before I dealt with my mother's questions.

"Didn't you notice anything at all?" she asked. "And you haven't even mentioned how your date went."

I gazed at the six-tier dessert showcase displayed next to the cashier. The revolving tiers of fruit-filled cobblers and whipped-cream-topped lemon and chocolate pies spun around and around, exactly how the carousel of my life felt right now.

"Let's place our order then I'll fill you in."

Our server materialized the minute our menus were set down. Her cheeks were as rosy as the apples dotting her crisp white apron. "Ladies, what will you have this bright sunny day?" she asked way too cheerfully.

Bet none of her dates drowned last night.

"I'll have two eggs lightly basted," Mother said, "and three slices of bacon, not undercooked but not burnt, and an English muffin, lightly buttered with butter, no margarine."

The server scribbled quickly to make sure she didn't miss any of my mother's precise order. You have to admire a woman who knows exactly what she wants. When the waitress glanced at me I decided to go whole hog. "I'll have the crab Benedict. Lightly sauced," I added, with a grin.

"Yeah, right." She winked. "I'll be back with a coffee refill."

Mother folded her arms against her chest. "No more delays. Tell me about last night."

I commenced with Jeremy's arrival at my front door. I had just mentioned the high-end champagne when our server arrived with a huge tray loaded with our breakfast orders. It looked like the eggs, bacon and muffins were all cooked to my mother's specific directions. No wonder she kept coming back.

"This Dr. Slater seems like quite a catch." Mother delicately bit into her toast. "Perhaps I was too hasty in judging the Love Club. I can't believe he ordered Dom Perignon. Did you enjoy it?"

Did I ever. I nodded, my mouth dripping with savory Hollandaise sauce.

"Did he ask you out again?" She poured some cream into her coffee and slowly stirred it while she waited for my response. I shoveled the crab Benedict into my mouth, hoping she wouldn't expect an answer if my mouth was full.

"Slow down, dear. You're eating much too fast. Did Dr. Slater ask you to go out with him again?"

I swallowed a bite of crab. Time to bite the bullet as well. "No, Jeremy isn't going to be available."

"Why not? Is he going out of town?" With the skill of a surgeon, she cut a piece of bacon and placed it in her mouth.

"No, Jeremy is uh, uh..." I couldn't think of anything more circumspect to say so I finished with, "dead."

Mother's eyes bugged out and she started choking. Ever the dutiful daughter, I grabbed her water glass and handed it to her. She swallowed a few sips, eyes contemplating me as she set the glass down. "Dead?"

I winced and nodded. She picked up her fork. The utensil hovered over her plate like a helicopter, finally landing on a bite of egg. I marveled at her calm, waiting for the barrage of questions to begin.

"Am I to assume Jeremy is the man who drowned in the river?"

I nodded and shared the details without a single interruption. She was either marvelously in control or totally in shock.

"I'm at a loss for words," she admitted. In thirty-nine years, this was the first time I could recall my mother acknowledging such an event.

"Do you see any reason why it wouldn't have been an accident?" she asked.

"I can't imagine anyone intentionally pushing Jeremy in the river. It's a good thing I was in the bathroom when this occurred or I'd be a suspect."

She pursed her thin lips in disapproval. "I hope you finally realize how foolish this Love Club idea is. Obviously, they haven't screened their members. It's much too dangerous for you to go out with these strangers."

"Mother, you're making some rash assumptions. We don't know how or why Garrett was killed. And we still don't know if Jeremy drowned accidentally or not." My lips twisted as I smiled wryly. "The only danger appears to be when someone goes out with *me*."

Our waitress brought more coffee and inquired whether we were finished. We both seemed to have lost our appetites so I grabbed the bill and paid at the cashier station. As far as I was concerned, this was enough mother and daughter bonding for today. As we exited the restaurant, my mother halted in the middle of the pavement. Tears welled in her eyes.

"Mom, what's the matter?"

She foraged in her purse and pulled out a pre-packaged tissue. She gently wiped her eyes and blew her nose before continuing. "You know how worried I am about you going out with these strange men. I don't know what I would do if anything happened to you."

I was touched. It was so seldom my mother showed any emotion, especially in public.

"Honest, right now I have zero desire to go on another date."

"Well, don't totally give up on men. You just need to go out with someone you can trust."

We hugged and headed toward our respective vehicles. We were almost to our cars when she asked, "What kind of costume is Ben wearing for Halloween?"

Oops. Time I focused on my children instead of my primal urges. "We're going to work on his costume tonight, as soon as the kids come home from their weekend with Hank."

We parted company, she in her pristine sedan and me in my dusty hybrid. Since the kids wouldn't be home until six I decided some quiet time was in order. I drove to my favorite orchard and sat at a picnic table surrounded by apple-laden trees overlooking the farm's trout- filled pond. The sun caressed me with its warmth while I gnawed on a caramel apple. Between the sunshine and the high dosage of sugar, the tension eventually eased out of my shoulders.

Driving home, I decided it wouldn't hurt to emulate my mother. I scrubbed my car from one sparkling periwinkle end to the other then whipped up some chocolate chip cookies for the kids. And possibly their father. When we were married, I used to hide cookies in my lingerie drawer to keep Hank from devouring the entire batch.

Hard to believe a man would stray from a wife who smelled like chocolate.

My arms were elbow deep in suds when the timer beeped. I wiped my hands on a dish towel, grabbed a potholder and opened the oven door. The front door blew open and the kids serenaded me with their theme song, "Hey Mom, where are you?"

Perfect timing. I turned to greet them, baking sheet in hand, when a furry animal scurried over my bare foot. I screamed and the metal pan flew into the air. Hot cookies rained melted chocolate on the floor.

"Kids, there's a rat in the kitchen." I opened the pantry door and looked for a weapon. A can of Pringles would have to suffice.

"Mom," wailed Ben, "that's not a rat. It's our new kitten. You've probably scared her to death." Ben picked up the furry creature cowering next to the stove. He cuddled her in one arm, while he chomped on one of the few cookies that escaped landing on the floor.

Jenna bent over and began picking up the cookies splattered everywhere.

"Mom, you need to get glasses. Can't you tell it's a kitten? Isn't she adorable?"

I took a closer look at the "adorable" kitten. She was a strange blend of orange and black hair with enormous pointed ears. The homeliest cat I'd ever encountered.

"We got her at the mall and named her Pumpkin cause she's orange and black and it's almost Halloween. We can keep her, can't we? Dad said you wouldn't mind." Ben looked over my shoulder and I turned to glower at a sheepish Hank.

"Sure, honey, I mean, Laurel. I know you had a tough weekend, so we went to the mall to pick up a costume for Ben. He said you'd been too busy to work on one."

My ex. Master of the guilt trip.

"Dad bought me a terrific Spider-man costume." Ben transferred the kitten to Jenna's willing arms then proceeded to climb the cabinets in Spider-man style, leaving chocolate imprints all over my oak-paneled doors.

"We picked up cat food and a litter box. We promise to clean it every day. Honest." Jenna's eyes pleaded with me as she stroked the tiny critter. The odds were fifty to one that my children would remember to empty the litter box every day. But I was grateful the costume issue was resolved, so I grudgingly nodded. How much trouble could a tiny kitten be?

Hank looked relieved at my acquiescence. The four of us, plus their furry friend, trooped outside to bring in the kids' suitcases and the kitten paraphernalia. We were outside less than twenty seconds when Pumpkin leaped out of Ben's arms and decided to investigate our garden.

What I didn't anticipate was Pumpkin discovering a butterfly and chasing it. She had probably never been outside before and here was her opportunity to explore the wonders of nature. Ben discovered a nine-week-old kitten moves faster than a seven-year-old boy. Pumpkin streaked across the lawn, Ben and Jenna racing after her. I was right behind them.

We couldn't let little Pumpkin turn into pumpkin pie!

The kitten miraculously avoided the street. She climbed up the back tire of the Prius, jumped on the trunk, clambered up the rear window onto the roof of the car, leaving a trail of tiny paw prints for us to admire. She paused and calmly began washing her paws.

"See, Mom." Ben scooped up the kitten. "Pumpkin is smart enough to stay away from the street." Too bad she wasn't smart enough to stay off my car. There went my plan to emulate my mother's immaculate habits. With two children and a new kitten, I should concentrate on things within my control—as soon as I could think of any.

The kids hauled their stuff, including their new pet, upstairs. I offered Hank some cookies. I neglected to mention the treats had adorned the floor a few minutes earlier. He inhaled them in seconds. "You still make a great chocolate chip cookie."

I narrowed my eyes. I knew when my ex was buttering me up.

He cleared his throat. "I need to tell you something."

"Like you and Nadine split up?"

He stopped mid-chomp. "How did you find out?"

"I have my sources." I grabbed a cookie and nibbled on it. I needed chocolate—but strictly for medicinal purposes. "So what happened between the two of you?"

"I broke it off. I've missed being with you, Laurel."

I snorted. Not a wise move with my mouth full of cookie crumbs. I grabbed a tumbler from the cabinet and filled it with tap water. Once I stopped choking, I continued. "This concerns me, how?"

"Well, I..."

I thought Hank was reaching for another cookie, but he grabbed my right hand instead and pulled me close, my five-foot-four inches nestled against his six-foot frame. For a brief moment, I relaxed against his familiar chest. My eyes closed as he gently massaged my back in that way that had soothed me on so many nights. It felt good to be held by someone who wanted me, cared about me, desired... Hey?

I felt a movement that brought back familiar memories. I jumped back and swatted his hand. "What do you think you're doing?"

He smirked. "See, hon, you still turn me on. When Jenna told me you joined the Love Club it made me realize how much I miss you. We had twenty great years together. Don't turn your back on me. Doesn't everyone deserve a second chance?"

Evidently our definitions of twenty great years differed dramatically. I wanted to kick his sorry butt through the back door but I merely shoved him in that direction. "Get out."

He snatched two more cookies and exited the kitchen with one last parting shot.

"Just remember. I love you and I want you back."

CHAPTER TWELVE

I dreamed I was kissing a mustached stranger. I woke to discover a furry paw glued to my moisturized chin. Blech. I pushed the kitten off my face and attempted to remove strands of her hair from my mouth. She howled and ran across the bed, knocking my fake Tiffany lamp to the floor. Then she raced down the stairs.

I finally cornered Pumpkin in the kitchen where she was amenable to a bribe of roasted turkey. After shutting her in our oversized laundry room, I crawled back into bed. 2:15 a.m. Less than four hours until my alarm went off. Hank was probably sleeping just fine tonight. Perhaps the kids should get him a kitten for Christmas so their dad could also experience the joy of owning a pet.

Seconds before I drifted back to sleep I remembered Hank's comment about my tough weekend. Was he referring to my tragic date? Or brunch with Mother?

Getting the kids ready for school with the distraction of our new pet made me late to work. As I walked into the lobby, decorated with pumpkins and hay bales, Vivian pointed at the clock hanging over the double doors. I hustled down the corridor past two rows of cubicles, turned the corner and bumped into Stan. He waited, holding a newspaper in hand, undoubtedly hoping to interrogate me. He watched in silence as I hung my jacket on the coat rack and stored my purse in the bottom drawer. Then he laid the front page of the paper on my desk.

The headlines of our local newspaper, *The Mountain Democrat*, screeched at me.

DISTINGUISHED DOCTOR DIES DURING
DEADLY DINNER

That got my attention. The newspaper must be giving brownie points for excessive alliteration. I tried to read but couldn't concentrate with Stan staring at me. I pictured imaginary question marks dotting his broad forehead.

"Dare I ask about your weekend?"

"Shush." I pressed my index finger to my lips. "We'll have the whole office asking questions if they find out I was involved."

I lowered my voice and leaned across my desk. "Have you heard anything about the accident from anyone else?"

He nodded. "Mary Lou mentioned it this morning when we were getting coffee. She said her entire family had been going to Dr. Slater for almost ten years since he initially opened up his practice. She raved about what a wonderful doctor he was, very caring and friendly. Not the kind of doctor who gives you a ninety-second exam, then moves on to the next patient."

Stan stood and plucked at the pleats in his perfectly pressed khaki pants. "I'll give you time to read the article. Buzz me when you want to talk."

I read the article word for word. It contained numerous glowing references to Dr. Slater, his career and contributions to local charities. His closest relative was a younger brother who also resided in El Dorado Hills. The reporter didn't mention any specifics other than a statement that the authorities were looking into all possibilities and nothing was ruled out at this time.

My stomach knotted as I continued reading. The last paragraph concluded: *The El Dorado County Sheriff's Department has indicated that Dr. Jeremy Slater was dining with a female companion on the evening of his death. Her identity is being withheld pending further investigation. The waiter at the River Inn described the woman as a short, middle-aged redhead.*

Middle-Aged? The nerve of that waiter. He was probably upset he didn't get a tip.

Well here was a tip for him. Don't expect to get tips from women you describe as middle-aged.

I was grateful the newspaper hadn't mentioned my name. My employer is a conservative bank that caters to an equally conservative clientele. Management would not be happy if I became implicated in a criminal inquiry. But what did the sheriff's department mean when they referred to further investigation of Jeremy's dinner companion?

If only Liz were in town, so we could discuss my latest Love Club debacle. She and Brian had gone to Monterey to scout for wedding sites. My phone's shrill ring disturbed my reverie. I answered, hoping it was Liz returning one of the many messages I'd left on her home phone.

"Laurel McKay," I said.

"Ms. McKay, good morning."

I recognized the caller immediately, but the formality in his voice did not bode well. Was this what they meant by further investigation?

I could be equally formal. "Good morning, Detective Hunter."

"Detective Bradford and I would like to ask you some questions. Could you set aside a few minutes this afternoon for us to come to the bank?"

"Not here," I said, evidently too loudly. Mary Lou's blond waves popped over our adjoining cubicle wall. I really was going to have to get a promotion so I could get my own office. These cubes were not designed to conduct a personal conversation in private although that's probably why they were constructed that way to begin with. "I doubt my boss would appreciate having officers interview me in the bank. You would be a bit of a distraction."

I wasn't sure what would create the greater distraction—the uniforms or Detective Hunter's imposing presence.

"There's a Starbuck's right around the corner. Would it be possible to meet there?" I asked.

I heard him confer with someone else. "That's fine. What time?" We agreed on two-thirty for our meeting. The minute I disconnected, Stan ambled over to my desk. He must have grown tired of waiting for me to buzz him.

"C'mon, the least you can do is share feedback with your personal shopper." He eased into the chair in front of my desk. "Was the doctor so dazzled by your beauty he fell into the river?"

I frowned at Stan's warped sense of humor but realized I would never get any work done until I explained. Stan listened intently and only interrupted once.

"He ordered Dom Perignon for your first date? What a great catch he would have been. You need to be less careless and stop losing your dates."

"Okay, that's it. Go annoy someone else." I swiveled my chair around and watched the icons on my computer screen blur together as tears of frustration clouded my contact lenses.

The springs on the chair squeaked as Stan abruptly stood. I immediately regretted my small outburst. "Sorry, Stan. I'm shook up and your comment was the last straw."

He walked around the desk and squeezed the back of my neck. "You're right. I was totally out of line." His gaze veered to the left. "Uh-oh. You better get back to work. I spy Earl heading this way." Stan quickly disappeared down the aisle to his own cube.

Having learned from previous experience never to be empty-handed when Earl appeared, I rummaged through my file drawer pretending to be searching for something. I felt a brief touch of a beefy palm on my shoulder and spun around, narrowly missing colliding with my boss.

"Laurel, I haven't had an opportunity to say good morning to you yet. Did you have a nice weekend?"

"Huh? Oh, yeah, fine," I mumbled and continued my drawer ravaging. Earl eased his hefty frame into the chair Stan had vacated.

"Anything new and exciting in your life?" he asked, as a chorus of squeaks protested his visit.

Nope. Nothing I planned to share with my far-too-curious boss.

Earl clasped his hands behind his neck and leaned back. "I wanted you to know how pleased the bank is with your performance. The delinquency ratio on the loans you've underwritten is the lowest in the department. I know you're handling more volume than any of the other underwriters."

Whew, that was a relief. My life had been so chaotic recently I worried about screwing up some of my loans. My shoulders relaxed and I blasted a broad smile at my boss. "Thanks, I appreciate the feedback."

"Just thought you should know we recognize your hard work. I was afraid you might apply for that branch manager position." He winked at me. "I wouldn't want to lose such a valuable and attractive employee."

Branch manager? How did I miss that? Maybe if I paid more attention to my career than my sex life I might have noticed. As soon as Earl stepped away, I would check the job postings in the break room.

But what was this about a valuable *and attractive* employee?

"Anything else I can do for you," he asked, "with the exception of a raise, ha ha?"

Ha ha. "No, everything is fine. Bye." Hopefully he would get the hint that I had work to do. Like finding out what the bank is paying branch managers these days. I could use a pay increase, especially now that we had an extra mouth to feed, albeit a tiny mouth. At the rate Pumpkin was streaking through our house, our breakage costs could well exceed any salary increase.

Earl reluctantly left my cube, giving me another one of those gentle pats on my shoulder.

I spent the next four hours trying to cram in a full day's work. I wasn't sure how long the meeting with the detectives would take and that branch manager posting needed to be checked out when I returned.

On my way out, I stopped in the ladies' room to refresh my lipstick and peel off some stray orange and black hairs from my teal blouse. I zipped through the lobby, walked outside and shivered. Although the sky was as bright as the sky-blue crayon in Ben's Crayola box, it was chilly—probably only in the mid-fifties. My jacket, unfortunately, was still hanging in my cubicle. I increased my pace to a slow jog, flung open the door and barreled straight into one massive detective.

"Whoa, little lady," he said, in a fair imitation of Gary Cooper.

Little lady. How cute. Way better than the newspaper description of a short, middle-aged woman.

My nipples hardened and I drew back. The brisk wind outside must have produced that effect. It couldn't possibly be the proximity of my chest to his. My face flushed as I apologized. "Sorry to crash into you. It's cold outside."

"Any time," he replied with that sexy half-smile of his.

Any time?

"I saved that table for us." He pointed to the rear of the restaurant. "A hot drink should warm you up. What can I get you?"

"I'll have a grande nonfat mocha with one Equal and two squirts of cinnamon syrup, but hold the whipped cream."

He rolled his eyes. "Women. Even their drinks are complicated." He whipped out his pen and his dog-eared notebook from the inside pocket of his leather jacket. The dark brown leather looked soft and touchable.

I wanted to reach out and caress him.

I meant the jacket. I wanted to caress the soft leather jacket.

"Okay, repeat that one more time." His pen hovered over his pad. "Are you sure you didn't forget anything?"

I described my concept of the perfect mocha again. It was a good thing Detective Hunter had that notepad handy to write down my order. Or did my coffee order now permanently reside next to his notes on the investigation?

I meandered back to the table he'd saved. The scent of freshly roasted coffee, chocolate and cinnamon permeated the room. This store provided an ample number of wooden tables and chairs, plus some seating areas with deep green upholstered chairs. The only other occupants were two fortyish women at one table surrounded by shopping bags and a single man carrying on a conversation with himself. Or maybe not. A Bluetooth stuck out of his ear.

A few minutes later, Detective Hunter strode toward our table with my mocha grande and a plain cup of coffee for him. Typical policeman. It was too bad Starbucks didn't sell jelly doughnuts. That might have softened him up.

The two women eyed him as he carefully wove his way down the aisle trying not to spill the drinks. They simultaneously reached into their purses, grabbed their respective compacts and applied fresh lipstick.

Interesting effect he had on women. Present company excluded, of course. Hunter placed the drinks on the table then hung his jacket over the chair. I couldn't help but notice how his soft tan turtleneck molded to his muscled chest. The sound of his voice interrupted my pectoral musings.

"One nonfat grande mocha with one Equal, two squirts of cinnamon, no whipped cream, and good old French roast for me. How did I do?"

"Excellent," I replied. "If you ever decide to make a career change, you can always get a job here."

"Well, if I don't start making progress on these two murders, the sheriff may give me the option of being recruited by Starbucks."

"Two murders?" I parroted.

"Two murder investigations with one common thread." His dark eyes, the color of my mocha, pierced right through me as he sipped his coffee.

I gulped my mocha. Ouch. Hot. Very hot.

He lifted the notepad from his pocket and picked up his pen again.

"Taking another order?" A little levity couldn't hurt.

His brow furrowed as he contemplated his notebook, then me. Okay, maybe it could. "Ms. McKay..."

"Please call me Laurel," I interrupted. "After all, our kids play soccer together. You don't think a soccer mom could possibly be a murderer, do you?"

"Are you kidding? I've seen soccer moms on the sidelines. They're scary." He softened his words with a slight smile. "Ms. McKay..." He hesitated then continued, "Laurel, the waiter at the River Inn told us you disappeared from the table several minutes after Jeremy left the dining room. He said you were gone quite a while, sufficient time to venture outside the restaurant and confront Jeremy. Where did you go and why?"

I gnawed at my thumbnail, a precursor to heavy cerebellum activity for me, and reflected back on that evening. "Well, the waiter kept pouring champagne in my glass so I kept drinking it, waiting for Jeremy to return. Eventually I needed to use the restroom. Wait a minute. Did the waiter say anything about those two men by the river?"

"What men?"

I was about to chastise him when it dawned on me we had never discussed the mysterious strangers.

"When you were grilling me," I paused as he frowned. "Okay. Poor word choice. "When you and I discussed the incident Saturday night, I was kind of in an alcoholic haze. Yesterday I remembered the two men. I meant to give you a call today but you beat me to it."

He picked up his coffee cup and drained it. "Tell me more."

"I wish there was more to tell. I stepped outside looking for Jeremy and noticed two men standing along the riverbank. One man's back was to me. He was on the tall side and it looked like he was balding, but I'm not positive because it was dark out, although the moon was shining, kind of...."

He looked confused, and I didn't blame him. I backed up and tried again.

"Anyway, there were two men talking but I couldn't see them clearly, and one of them was about Jeremy's height. It was chilly out so I went inside and then into the ladies' room. I relaxed in their comfy lounge chair and fell asleep for about fifteen minutes."

He cocked his eyebrow at me.

"Honest." I held up my right hand. "That's the whole truth and nothing but the truth."

He slammed the notebook shut and threw it on the table. "Laurel, this is no joking matter. Do you have any idea how serious this is?"

I slumped in my chair. "I just can't believe I'm a suspect in both of these deaths. Who needs an alibi when she falls asleep in the ladies' room?" My face lit up as I remembered something pertinent to the investigation. "What about the fact that Garrett was killed by a blunt instrument and not from me smacking him with his cell? Doesn't that exonerate me from his murder?"

His smile evaporated in less than a second. "You know this how?"

Darn. When was I going to start engaging my brain before my lips? I needed to divert his attention from the fact that someone in the District Attorney's office might have shared some official inside information with his fiancée, who might have shared it with her best friend.

"Where's Detective Bradford?"

"He'll join us shortly. He was called away to look into another incident. Would you feel more comfortable if we went down to headquarters and you made a formal statement there?"

Headquarters? Nope. Not really.

"Detective, you can't seriously think I'm some type of a Black Widow knocking off eligible bachelors? Trust me, there are not enough decent single men in this town as it is. Why would I want to eliminate some great candidates? Garrett wasn't much of a prospect, but Jeremy was charming and generous. I think we could have developed a wonderful relationship."

He leaned back in his chair and crossed one blue-jeaned knee over the other. "Really?" The intensity in his voice was surprising.

I nodded vigorously in response. "Absolutely."

Despite the clatter of cups banging against the espresso machine, the silence between us was deafening. And getting on my nerves.

"So, what is Kristy wearing for Halloween?" Better to engage in useless drivel than sit in morbid silence.

Hunter's shoulders shook and the next thing I knew he was laughing. Aw, he did have a nice smile. Too bad he didn't use those facial muscles more often. "Honestly, if you are a murderer, you are the coolest, smoothest killer I've ever encountered. What is Kristy wearing for Halloween? I wish I knew what to do with you," he said, still chuckling.

"Well, for starters, "I gazed at him with what I hoped was a look of pure innocence. "You could share your little notebook with me."

"My notebook?" His face wore a blank look. "Did you want to review your drink order?"

"No. I want to know what you've found out. Don't you have notes on the murders in there?"

"Possibly," said my infuriating companion. He flipped the pages of his notebook back and forth.

I forced myself to take a few calming breaths before I barreled on. Lamaze breathing often comes in handy. Except for the two occasions when I was in labor. "Let me rephrase my question. Isn't it possible that I, the common thread, as you referred to me a few minutes ago, could assist you in this investigation? I seem to be the only link between the two murders."

"Yes indeed. You are the only link," boomed a voice from behind my back.

Startled, I shot up and knocked my chair over backwards which resulted in Booming Voice spilling hot coffee all over his baggy brown suit. His uncensored remarks sent the barista scurrying to the back of the store.

Detective Hunter stifled a smile by holding his napkin to his lips. His partner yanked a chair from the table opposite ours. He deposited himself and his nearly empty cup of coffee at our table.

Bradford was even scarier than I remembered. Still tall. Still bald. And definitely still crabby. Hunter retrieved my chair and indicated I should sit.

"So, Ms. McKay," growled the hulk. "You've managed to get yourself in even more hot water. Are you ready to book her, Tom?"

Book her? Wait a minute. There were loans to review, children to pick up from soccer, and Halloween cookies to bake, um... purchase. I wasn't certain what booking meant, but it didn't sound like something I wanted on my agenda.

"Ms. McKay has been very cooperative," said the younger detective.

I looked at him suspiciously. Was this one of those good cop–bad cop routines?

Bradford crushed his empty cardboard cup and hurled it at the garbage can. It bounced on the metal rim then smacked the barista right on her pierced nose. She screamed and disappeared into the back room again. It was a good thing there were only two people waiting in line instead of the usual ten. They both shot Bradford an evil look.

"Detective, why do you refuse to believe I'm innocent?"

The broken capillaries around Bradford's nose turned an unattractive shade of magenta as he scowled. "Lady, you had the opportunity and the motive. We just haven't determined the means. But we will."

Huh?

He ticked them off, one meaty digit at a time.

"You had dinner with both men. And no alibi for the time either of them was killed."

Okay, but so what? That didn't prove anything.

"You have a reputation for assaulting men."

"What?" It was my turn to shout.

Hunter nodded as Bradford explained. "One of the people we interviewed said you attacked your ex-husband. You obviously have a problem with your relationships with men."

"I don't have a problem with men," I said, grinding my teeth together. "I have a problem with idiots. That is not a proper motive."

"All we're missing is the murder weapon," Bradford said. "Trust me, we will find it."

I stared at both of them. Bradford, the belligerent bulldog looked as pleased as if I had delivered a full confession. Hunter, the brawny bear looked...puzzled. Or could that be concern on his face.

I was frustrated and I was scared, and there wasn't enough chocolate in the Starbucks to calm me down. "Detective Hunter, are we done here?"

He exchanged a look with Tall and Bald.

"Sure. We know where to find you." Bradford's smile was chillier than the temperature outside. "But don't leave town."

I grabbed my purse, slung it over my shoulder and strode out the door. I might as well get back to work and pursue my career options. At least until they arrested me.

CHAPTER THIRTEEN

The temperature had dropped even more so I race-walked back to the office. I hadn't seriously thought the detectives considered me a suspect, but Bradford made me feel like I was the number one most wanted criminal in town. Certainly, there had to be another suspect or two, or three.

As soon as I reached the office, I stopped in the break room to check out the branch manager posting. Hundreds of rainbow-colored flyers were thumbtacked to the bulletin board. I finally located the job posting dated over a week ago. Applications would be accepted through the next day. I still had time, but was it worth the effort if I was about to be arrested?

I mentally slapped myself. With two children to support, there was no way I would let those overbearing detectives haul me off to jail without doing something about it first.

After work, I stopped at the supermarket and bought a rotisserie chicken, fruit salad and cold broccoli salad. Then I dashed over to the soccer field. Ben was cold, dirty and sniffling. One of Jenna's friends had given her a ride home so by the time we arrived, she sat curled in a recliner with Pumpkin perched on her shoulder, gnawing at her auburn strands. I didn't see any signs of recent cat-astrophic activity.

I left two more messages for Liz. By nine, Ben and Pumpkin were tucked into their respective beds. I was tucked into my own bed, boning up on detecting techniques in a new book by my favorite mystery author. The phone rang and I shrieked, the book tumbling to the floor. That's what happens when you get too engrossed in murder.

"Hello?" I whispered into the phone.

"Laurel, what's going on?" asked my best friend. "You left five messages on my home phone. Why didn't you call my cell?"

"I didn't want to bother you and Brian on your romantic getaway. I'm so glad you're back."

"We came home early. The District Attorney called Brian about a new case they've opened up. A doctor who drowned under suspicious circumstances."

Dead silence on each end of the phone.

"Please tell me this wasn't the doctor you were meeting," she said.

"Okay, I won't tell you. But I met with the detectives again today. And according to Bradford, I'm their number one suspect in both murders!"

"Wow. That is a sticky wicket."

Sticky wicket? I'd say being accused of murder was more like being sentenced to the Tower of London, waiting for the axe to fall.

"So what are we going to do?" I asked.

"We? As in the royal *we*?"

"If the *royal we* means you and I, then yes. I need help and you've got the inside track."

"Of course I'll help. But I'm not sure how much info I can wangle out of Brian."

"Visit Victoria's Secret and pick out something irresistible. Like some black-feathered handcuffs."

"That would certainly get Brian's attention. But maybe you should visit Victoria's Secret. Do you think Detective Hunter fancies you at all?"

"Fancies me as a suspect," I muttered.

"Well, that's the kind of input I may be able to get out of Brian, even without killer lingerie," she said.

"Back to the topic of killers, what are we going to do about finding this murderer ourselves?"

Her phone clattered to the floor. "Bloody hell. Are you off your rocker? This is not one of those mysteries you love to read. Neither you nor I are equipped to investigate a murder."

88

"But the Sheriff's Department considers me the only suspect. How much time and energy do you think they'll expend to find the actual murderer? Or murderers. They could arrest me any day now."

"Oh, sweetie, I wish there was something I could do to help."

I thumped my pillow in frustration. "This is so unbelievable. What are the odds the only two Love Club men I met were both murdered?"

Bingo. "The Love Club!" we shouted in unison.

"Now that's something we could look into without getting into trouble," Liz said. "You're still an active member. You could talk to the staff about both men. There must be a connection between them."

"Wouldn't the police have determined if the two men knew one another?"

"They might not waste the time if they think they already know who the killer is. It's not like they have that big of a detective force up here. You could nose around, discover something they missed."

"I suppose I could try."

Liz must have discerned some hesitation in my voice. "It sounds like you're getting cold feet."

"I'm imagining Sunny's expression when I stop by their office. It was bad enough when she thought I killed Garrett. If she finds out I was with Jeremy the night he drowned, she'll probably pass out. For all I know, they've evicted me from the club by now."

"Hey, just because you're a murderer doesn't mean you aren't entitled to meet the man of your dreams."

Liz always knew how to cheer me up.

On that note, we agreed I would visit the Love Club as soon as possible.

The following morning I woke before dawn. I'd been so tired the night before, I'd forgotten to complete the job application. I tiptoed down the stairs to avoid waking the kids. The sound of mewling cries emanated from behind the laundry room door. I opened the door, thinking Pumpkin deserved a break from her jail.

No sign of the kitten anywhere. A ball of fluff suddenly flew from the top of a cabinet, landed on all fours and skidded across the floor. I jumped back, knocked over my ironing board, which narrowly missed flattening the bundle of fur cowering at my feet.

As if I didn't have enough aggravation. I picked her up, carefully watching out for her small but deadly claws. We went into the kitchen and I sat down at the table. Pumpkin settled on my lap while I completed the online application.

As soon as I arrived at the office, I wandered into the break room for a cup of coffee. Three creams, two sugars, one squirt of Hershey's chocolate syrup, and my budget mocha was ready. I felt a tap on my shoulder and turned.

"Did you read this morning's newspaper?" Stan asked.

"No, was there anything important in there?"

He dramatically flourished said paper. "An article on the second page says the doctor's death was probably not accidental. The sheriff's department is currently investigating persons of interest. The reporter asked about the mystery woman but the officer said he couldn't reveal anything."

"Good. I don't need that kind of notoriety right now. I'd never get that job if the bank knew I was involved in a murder investigation."

"What job?" Stan's very broad brow wrinkled in confusion.

"Sorry, I forgot to tell you. I'm applying for the branch manager opening in Cameron Park, the position I held before Ben was born."

"You mean you'd give up all of your wonderful friends at corporate for a measly increase in pay?"

"In a heartbeat," I replied. "I'm tired of making life and death underwriting decisions. I want to work with the public again. You can visit the branch and annoy me any time you want. Assuming I get it. I'm sure they have a lot of eligible candidates."

"Well, my vote's with you, sweetie. Hopefully these murders will be solved before the bank hears about them."

"Murders?"

I whirled around to find myself confronted by the bank's receptionist. Vivian's pale moon face with its two double chins hovered inches from my face. Although we get along fine, I'm always careful when I talk with her. Vivian could transmit office gossip faster than a Twitter feed.

I moved a few feet away from the pale orb of her inquisitive face. "Stan and I are discussing a murder mystery we're both reading."

"Oh, I love a good mystery," she said. "What's the name of it?"

Stan and I looked at each other in dismay.

"Murder on the Orient Express," I said while Stan said at the same time, "The Drowned Man."

Vivian looked confused. "What did you say the title was?"

I jumped in before we could make that mistake again. "Uh, the title is Murder of the Drowned Man on the Orient Express. It's a s-sequel to the original m-mystery," I stammered.

Stan grabbed his coffee cup and said a quick goodbye, leaving me alone to deal with Vivian. I made a mental note to get him later.

Vivian reached into the cabinet for a mug. "Since you're so interested in murder mysteries, did you hear about the guy who drowned in the American River last weekend? Dr. Slater was my doctor. The paper said the sheriff doesn't think it was an accident."

I was anxious to move the conversation away from the homicide aspect of Vivian's family physician. "Did you like him?"

Always anxious to share, Vivian didn't disappoint. "He was terrific. I'd gained so much weight this past year and couldn't seem to lose it. Dr. Slater devised a diet and exercise plan to help me. He was very sympathetic about my condition."

I nodded in agreement. "He was so slim you probably just needed to follow his personal diet."

She moved closer and thrust both chins in my face. "How did you know Dr. Slater was slender?"

Note to self. Never have a conversation with Vivian before my first caffeine infusion.

"Someone in the office mentioned it yesterday." Who did Stan say was also a patient of Jeremy's? "Mary Lou."

"What about her?" Vivian's eyes narrowed into a squint. Someday I would have to tell her it was not an attractive look.

"She mentioned Dr. Slater was her family physician as well. So, what was his helpful advice?" I said, hoping to distract her.

Vivian filled her cup with black coffee then elaborated her diet plan for me. "He prepared a chart of food groups to follow, told me to keep track of my carbohydrate and fiber grams and recommended that I try a mild strength-building exercise program. Dr. Slater was so kind to me. Said men are often attracted to large women. In fact, he told me he had a date coming up with a woman he described as pretty, but pleasingly plump."

Pleasingly Plump? I hoped he was describing his date for Friday night. If Jeremy had said that to my face, I probably *would* have pushed him in the river.

We needed to shift from the fat-fighting conversation to something more constructive—like who done it.

"Can you think of a reason why anyone would want to harm him? Do you know anything about his family or friends?"

She averted her eyes and stared at the fingerprint-grimy break room cabinets. "No. He was a terrific guy. I kind of hoped that once I lost some weight he would become interested in me."

She sighed and I tried to cheer her up. "I'm sure you'll find another terrific doctor. Did you ever see his partner, Dr. Radovich?"

She frowned. "Just one time when Jeremy was unavailable. Dr. Radovich was really brusque. No bedside manner at all."

Hmmm. Someone to investigate. "I've been looking for a new doctor," I said. "Maybe I should try this Dr. Radovich." It couldn't hurt to talk to Jeremy's partner.

Vivian looked at me like I'd lost even more of my marbles.

"I like doctors that are abrupt. They're much more efficient with their time, and mine."

"If you say so." She dumped her coffee in the sink and scurried out of the room.

Our conversation had lasted so long my own coffee was now lukewarm. I placed my mug in the microwave and set the timer for thirty seconds, mulling over our recent conversation. The bell rang and I eased the cup out carefully. No point in scalding myself with overly hot coffee.

I'd already promised Liz I would visit the Love Club. My conversation with Vivian pointed me in another direction—Jeremy's medical practice. I might not be one of their patients, but that could be rectified easily enough.

I didn't have a clue what kind of clues I would encounter at either location, but anything would be better than nothing. Especially something that would tie Garrett and Jeremy together. Something besides me.

So far, all I'd netted from my investigation was that Jeremy thought I was fat.

I returned to my desk and received a call from Anne in the HR department. We arranged for an interview on Thursday. She seemed pleased with my previous branch experience.

My second interruption was from my mother.

I rested the receiver on my shoulder so I could underwrite while she chattered.

"Hello, dear, I wanted to see how you were feeling after your dreadful weekend. Thank goodness, those newspaper articles about Dr. Slater's death didn't mention your name. Can you imagine what would happen to my real estate business if people found out you were his date that night?"

I personally didn't see how having a daughter as a murder suspect had any bearing on her ability to sell real estate, but what did I know.

"Have the police contacted you regarding that evening?" she asked.

I pondered the advisability of telling my mother that a detective by the name of Bradford had informed me I was his chief suspect. "Nothing to worry about."

"Well, that's good news. Are you bringing Ben here on Halloween?"

A few years ago, I'd taken Ben trick-or-treating in my mother's neighborhood so she could see how cute he looked in the costume she'd made for him. My mother can write up a real estate contract, cook a five-course dinner and sew a child's Halloween costume simultaneously. I still question whether I'm adopted.

"Sorry. Patti is taking Ben and Jimmy through her neighborhood then she'll drop them at my house."

Wait a minute. If his grandmother was dying to see her grandson, maybe she could pick him up from soccer practice today. Then I could run over to the Love Club and begin my investigation this evening.

"Mother, it would help if I could work late and catch up on my underwriting. Could you pick Ben up from practice?"

"I guess so. Some clients are coming in to write a contract tonight. Can you get him before seven?"

I eagerly assented and we said goodbye.

The majority of my workload was completed by four so I devoted the next half hour to perfecting my detecting. Having been an avid murder mystery fan since my first Nancy Drew novel at age eight, I must have developed some innate investigating skills from all the mysteries I'd read in the past thirty years.

Every amateur detective seems to make a list so I wrote down potential questions for my visit to the Love Club.

1. Were Garrett and Jeremy acquaintances? Did they share something in common that could be determined from their biographies?

2. Was someone from the Love Club out to get male clients?

3. Was someone out to get my dates?

4. Was someone out to get me?

5. Were my children in any danger?

Those last two questions tied my stomach in multiple knots, but it only made me more determined to find the answer.

I arrived at the Love Club office shortly after five-thirty. Another young, perky blonde stood behind the front desk. We exchanged smiles as I walked past and into the room with the alphabetized member books.

An attractive woman clad in a smart charcoal pinstriped suit, and a silver-haired, silver-goateed man sat at separate tables, books and DVDs piled high in front of each of them. They were so intent on reading the profiles that neither of them looked up as I entered.

First I would re-examine Garrett's and Jeremy's biographies. The book labeled *G* was available, but I couldn't find the *J* book anywhere, even misfiled among the other alphabetized books. Several black notebooks were stacked in front of the woman so one of them might have the *J* entries.

I flipped through the pages until I found Garrett's biography. By now, they should have removed his bio. Instead, I found a large red inactive banner stapled over his picture. When a member became involved with someone—regardless if they met through the Love Club or not—they were to notify the club, which would place the inactive banner over the member's photo to discourage anyone from choosing them.

I agreed that death automatically made someone inactive, but it didn't seem like the most appropriate category. Although they could hardly place a banner shouting "murdered" on their member's photos. Maybe the police asked them to keep the profiles in the books so they might retrieve some additional leads. Nothing startling jumped out in Garrett's biography but I wrote down his ID number—3377. Now I needed to get my hands on the book with Jeremy's data.

I drifted over to the other woman's table to see if she had the *J* volume. She added a name to her selection list. The club advised members to limit their picks to a maximum of eight at a time. Even though less than fifty percent of your selections would normally respond, arranging meetings with four new members of the opposite sex could be quite time consuming.

I discreetly glanced down at her choices. I saw a James, Jared and, uh-oh, a Jeremy #4155 on the list. I couldn't remember Jeremy Slater's ID number, but for her sake, I hoped there was another current member in the book named Jeremy.

I tapped her on her shoulder. She looked at me quizzically, her shiny chestnut hair swinging forward then falling back in place. She shouldn't have a problem meeting the man of her dreams. As long as she didn't pick any of the men I'd chosen.

"Sorry to bother you. Would you mind if I borrowed the *J* book for a few minutes? I need to look up one of the members I selected a few weeks ago."

"Sure. I already have five candidates. That's probably enough for tonight. I usually have a one hundred percent positive response so I don't want to get too booked up."

One hundred percent? Some women have all the luck. On second thought, it was a good thing I'd received only two positive responses. I couldn't handle any more dead bodies.

I skimmed through the pages and quickly located Jeremy. No inactive banner so he was still eligible from a Love Club perspective. I checked out his ID number—Jeremy, 4155.

Ms. Pinstriped suit would not get a perfect response rate this time.

I compared both men's bios carefully. Other than the fact that they were both forty and childless, there were no other similarities I could discern. Garrett was divorced and Jeremy had never married. Of course, the biographies weren't that detailed. And not particularly original—over eighty percent of the male members said their idea of a romantic evening was to take a moonlight walk on the beach.

My idea of a romantic evening was dinner with someone who was still *alive* the next day.

Since Jeremy's number had been issued later, Garrett could have been the one to recommend him to the Love Club. I sauntered over to the front desk. The receptionist's nametag read Sorrento. Maybe she was conceived while her parents honeymooned in Italy.

"Sorrento, I wondered if you could help me. I know the club pays a fee for any referrals that end up joining. Is there a way to check your records that would show whether my friend recommended me?"

"Yeah, sure. The referrals are like listed by number." She chomped on a piece of gum with the vigor of a cow masticating her cud. "What's your number? I can see if her name is mentioned."

I rattled off Jeremy's number with the ease of an experienced liar. My ability to tell white lies has never been my strong suit, but if I kept up this investigation, I could become an expert.

"Nope, no referrals listed. Wait...that number belongs to Jeremy Slater." She crinkled her pert little nose and looked baffled. "Are you sure that's the right one?"

"Sorry. My ID number is 5498."

She looked confused. "I thought you said 4155. It doesn't sound much like your number."

"I get my ID here confused with my bank PIN. It's so hard to keep track of all of these PINS these days," I said.

"Boy, that's for sure. I like have to write my PINS on stickies everywhere or I can't remember them at all. Okay, under that number it shows Liz Somerville was the referral. Do you want me to see if a check went out?"

"No. Thanks for looking it up."

Okay. That took care of question number one. Garrett didn't refer Jeremy to the Love Club, and Jeremy couldn't have referred Garrett, since Garrett joined first. As far as question number two, unless someone was systematically removing all the forty-year-old males who enjoy moonlight walks along the beach, there was no way I could tie their murders to the Love Club.

CHAPTER FOURTEEN

I zoomed out of the club managing to arrive at the Centurion office at exactly 6:59 p.m. Punctuality is not my strong suit and my mother is not very forgiving if you screw up her carefully structured schedule.

My mother stood in the reception area conversing with a middle-aged couple. Ben sat cross-legged on the floor, racing bright metal Matchbox cars across the parquet until they crashed into an unlikely obstacle. A large tasseled black cordovan loafer. I shot a glance at Ben's oversized buddy who was also seated on the floor. A thick swatch of blond hair fell over one eye. He looked up at me and winced as a cherry-red miniature fire truck rammed his knee.

"Okay, Ben," he said. "Your mother is here to pick you up." He unfurled his long legs easily. He must hit the gym more than I do. But then who doesn't.

"Hi there, um... " I couldn't remember his name.

"Peter Tyler. We met last week."

My mother excused herself from her clients. "Laurel, you remember Peter, don't you?"

"Yes, thanks for keeping Ben occupied."

"My pleasure." A shadow crossed his face as if he remembered something from the past. "My wife and I tried to start a family, but it turned out she couldn't have kids and then we divorced and..."

He shrugged off his somber thoughts and smiled shyly at me. "I enjoyed spending time with Ben. He's a great kid."

My great kid, who seemed to have added a few fruit juice stains to the front of his previously clean sweatshirt, was busy picking up his toys from the carpet.

"Ben, please thank Peter for playing with you," I said.

My son smiled his gap-toothed grin. "Thanks."

My mother chose that moment to demonstrate her matchmaking skills. "Laurel, maybe you can thank Peter by taking him out for a cup of coffee some time."

My face flushed. That was so not subtle.

Peter grinned graciously. "Sounds good to me."

I was too embarrassed to do anything but nod and grab Ben's hand. We hustled out of the office as fast as Ben's short legs could move.

"Are you going out with Peter?" Ben asked as he struggled with his seat belt.

"I don't know, honey." I waited to make sure he was securely fastened before I backed the car out of the parking space.

"Why don't you go out with Kristy's dad?"

My foot stomped on the brake pedal, causing Ben's head to whip back and forth. Thank goodness for seat belts. I waited until I had eased out of the parking lot before I continued our conversation. "How do you know Kristy's father?"

"He came to our school last week and gave a talk about staying away from strangers. He's nice and real smart and he gets to wear that cool uniform. And he has a badge. I'm gonna be a detective when I grow up."

Ben's revelation shook me so much I missed the Greenstone Road turnoff.

"You should go out with him, Mom. He'd keep all the bad guys away."

"I don't think Kristy's dad has time to go out with me. He's busy investigating both murders right now," I said, without giving any thought to my comment.

"Two murders?" squealed Ben.

Darn. When would I learn to censor my remarks in front of my impressionable young son?

"Give it up, Mom. I want to know about the other murder."

"I don't know any of the details." Except for the tiny detail that I was a suspect in *all* of the murders currently under investigation in our county.

"Bummer. I'm gonna ask Kristy tomorrow."

Now I was totally confused. "There's no soccer tomorrow. It's a school day."

"Guess I didn't tell you. Kristy is in my class now. She's not so bad, for a girl. And she can sure kick a soccer ball."

Talk about out of the mouths of babes. Not only would I be running into Detective Hunter at the soccer field, we'd see each other on Open House nights. Picturing the six-foot-three detective attempting to squeeze into the miniature second-grade desks made me smile. Remembering our last meeting at Starbucks quickly erased the grin from my face.

Once we arrived home, Ben disappeared into the pantry. I could hear him counting out loud. "Mom, I don't think we have enough Halloween candy."

"I bought twelve bags. That's enough for this neighborhood."

He walked out of the pantry, arms laden with plastic bags filled with an assortment of miniature candy bars. He scowled at me. "We don't want to run out like we did last year."

That had been a tad embarrassing. I meant to buy extra candy but forgot. We ended up handing out plastic bags filled with carrots and broccoli stalks. It was months before the neighbors let me live that down. Sometimes the benefit of living somewhere long enough that you know all of your neighbors is offset by the fact they know all of your little foibles. I had to put up with them calling me Mrs. Broccoli for the rest of the year.

Shortly before ten, the phone rang.

"I hope I'm not calling too late," Mother said. "I just finished with those clients. They went back and forth trying to decide what to offer, but we finally came to an agreement on a fair price."

And why are you calling me with this fascinating piece of information at this time of night? I scanned my closet trying to decide if I should wear Halloween attire to work the next day.

"So, dear, what do you think of Peter?"

Ah ha. I should have known there would be a grilling once I left the office. "He seems very nice."

"He's quite a catch, you know. He's been divorced about a year now so I know he's available. He developed that Bella Lago subdivision off Salmon Falls Road. Isn't that a romantic name?"

Her voice rose to a higher pitch when I didn't respond. "Laurel, I asked you a question."

Oops, I hadn't been listening. "Salmon, yes, that would be great for dinner."

The sound of teeth gritting echoed through the receiver. "I don't know why I even attempt to introduce you to suitable men."

Okay, maybe we weren't talking about salmon for dinner.

"Mother, I don't think I should go on any more dates until these murders are solved. Peter could be putting himself in danger by going out with me."

"Nonsense. Obviously you didn't have anything to do with the deaths of those men. Just promise me you won't go out with anyone else from the Love Club."

"You'll be pleased to know we are in total agreement there."

Wednesday dawned cold but sunny, perfect weather for Halloween ghosts and goblins. I decided to forego wearing a costume to work, but I brought a batch of my gold nugget fudge to the office, always a surefire hit. Anything remotely edible was welcomed with open arms and mouths. Just the mention of "free food" and seconds later a line would stretch throughout the building.

Patti agreed to take the boys around her neighborhood until I arrived at her house. I pulled into the driveway and the two superheroes hopped in my car. Once we arrived home, I walked through the kitchen door and bumped into a gruesome figure. Ben and Jimmy followed me in, engrossed in counting the candy in their bags.

"Hello, my pretties," Jenna cackled, her olive green skin and rubber putty nose repulsive in the fluorescent lighting of my kitchen.

Jimmy jumped two feet into the air. Ben barely glanced at his sister. "Lo, Jenna. Cool makeup."

The doorbell rang and all three kids raced to the front door to meet, greet and scare the newcomers. I ran upstairs to transform myself into a clown. The neighborhood kids expected it. I slathered white paste on my face, drew huge eyelashes above and below both eyes, painted two red circles on my cheeks, and outlined my mouth with bright red lipstick. A black bowler hat topped a curly red wig.

My costume included a red polka-dot blouse with puffy sleeves my mother bought me twenty years ago. It must have been after a three-martini lunch. Red suspenders attached to a pair of baggy red shorts, knee socks covered with red polka dots, and gigantic red plastic shoes completed the outfit. My full complement of clown paraphernalia included a loud horn, buzzer, and the *pièce de rèsistance*, a yellow plastic flower pin that squirted water.

As I attempted to maneuver down the stairs in my clown shoes, the doorbell pealed. Ben opened the door but there was a noticeable absence of noise. My son stood paralyzed in the doorway so I waddled over to see what was wrong. Walking in these shoes was like being ten months pregnant.

No wonder Ben was speechless. I gazed into the mirror image of my child—although a larger version. I wasn't surprised to see another Spider-man costume, but Ben wasn't prepared for it. I looked to see if I recognized the parent.

The boy's father was dressed in black pants, a white tuxedo-style shirt and a cape. A white mask covered half his face. Brilliant amateur detective that I am, I recognized the Phantom of the Opera standing on my doorstep. If this guy could sing "All I ask of You," he would receive all of our candy without hesitation.

"Hello, Spider-man. Mr. Phantom, how are things at the opera house these days?"

The phantom smiled, his one brown eye twinkling at me. That twinkling eye looked vaguely familiar.

The annoyed voice of the Spider-man at our door interrupted my thoughts. "Trick or treat, trick or treat. Are you gonna give me any candy or what?"

The phantom finally spoke. "Kristy, that's not polite. Please apologize to Ms. McKay and Ben. I'm sure they're surprised to see us on their doorstep."

Kristy? The soccer terror was Spider-man? What happened to little girls who dressed up like Cinderella or Snow White?

Ben finally broke the silence. "You can't be Spider-man, Kristy. You're a girl."

"Hey, it's a free world. I can be Spider-man if I want. Let's go, Dad, we'll never get any candy here." She turned and trudged down the sidewalk, her bag dragging on the ground.

"Kristy, come back," I shouted at her retreating form. "I think you make a fine Spider-man." Okay, it was kind of a weird costume, but the poor child didn't have a mother to help her out. The Phantom detective joined his daughter. They held a brief conversation then walked back to the door holding hands.

"Do you really like my costume?" Kristy's voice quavered as her eyes questioned mine. I could tell my opinion was important to the motherless child.

"I think it's wonderful. We girls have special powers, too."

She beamed a smile so angelic St. Peter would have been proud.

I grabbed the plastic candy-filled pumpkin from Ben. Kristy's smile spread from one freckled cheekbone to the other as I dumped eight different bars in her bag. "Thank you for the candy, Ms. McKay. I'm sorry if I was rude before," she said, without any prompting from her father.

Nice apology. Maybe she wasn't such a hellion, after all.

"You're very welcome. But what brings you to our neighborhood tonight?"

The phantom cleared his throat. Was the detective about to burst into song?

"Kristy still doesn't know many of the kids in our subdivision. They seem kind of standoffish. She mentioned Ben has treated her like a pal at school and she thought maybe he would trick-or-treat with her. Of course, I should have realized Ben would be going out with other friends...."

His voice trailed off as he gazed lovingly at his daughter, her small hand enfolded in his.

This was not the angry soccer dad I'd met across a muddy field. Nor was it the suspicious interrogator I'd encountered at Starbucks. For the first time the detective was cast in a vulnerable role. How terrible to be widowed, raising a young daughter alone. Particularly given his career choice.

I looked up into his eyes—or rather his eye. The other one was still covered by the mask.

Fortunately, my sixteen-year-old daughter who appeared to be maturing by the minute chose that moment to step in. "Detective Hunter, we'd be glad to take Kristy along with us. Mom's staying behind to hand out candy so you can help her. It gets really busy with hordes of kids coming at once."

Jenna shot me a grin and I mouthed a silent thank-you. I doubted hordes of children would congregate on my doorstep this evening, but I was thrilled at the proactive manner in which she'd come to Kristy's rescue. Jenna grabbed the young girl's hand and they walked out the door. Kristy skipped down the sidewalk trying to keep up with my daughter's brisk pace. Jenna paused to look back at the boys.

"Are you guys coming? If you don't hurry the neighbors will run out of candy."

That remark took care of Jimmy and Ben's temporary paralysis. They grabbed their bags and ran after the girls, practically knocking them over in their hurry. I closed the front door and turned around. My giant red clodhoppers stomped all over the detective's shiny black shoes.

"Sorry," I apologized. "I'm not sure I'll ever get used to wearing two-foot long shoes, Can I get you something to drink?"

"No, I'm good." He glanced down and contemplated his shoes for a few seconds. "You have no idea how much I appreciate this. It's only the second Halloween since my wife passed away. She used to make all of Kristy's costumes, Snow White, Cinderella, typical little girl clothes. I think Kristy chooses these outlandish outfits so she won't be reminded of her mother's creations."

I nodded in sympathy. "My dad died in a car accident when I was ten. For a long time I was mad at everyone. It seemed so unfair for him to die so young. Why was I the only kid who didn't have a dad? But eventually I learned to cope. To concentrate on remembering the good times we had and appreciate what a wonderful father he was for the short time he was with us."

"It's been tough. Kristy's been so rebellious it's difficult knowing what to do. What battles to fight or when to give in? That's one of the reasons I moved to Placerville. I hoped being closer to her grandparents would help her cope. She has a hard time making friends. Even in soccer. The boys respect her for her abilities, but they won't play with her because she's a girl. Ben's one of the few kids who's been kind to her."

"That's my Ben." I chuckled. "Of course he's used to being bossed around by three generations of women so one more female in his life is no big deal."

Hunter smiled a twisted smile at me. Extremely twisted, since he was still wearing his mask. Poor guy. Having to contend with his wife's death and his daughter's emotional issues, plus solving the county's proliferating murders couldn't be easy. The unapproachable grizzly bear of a man was demonstrating some teddy bear tendencies. The detective removed his mask, leaving his thick chestnut hair in total disarray. His hair looked like it was aching to be ruffled. Or maybe I was aching to ruffle it. My heart beat louder than a bongo drum.

Was I the only person feeling a frenzy of pheromones?

He stepped close just as the doorbell rang. Never had trick-or-treaters been so unwelcome. I plopped a candy bar in each of the children's bags then felt something brush against my ankle. An orange, black and white blur streaked out the small opening.

"No!" I dumped the candy on the floor and attempted to run after Pumpkin. I managed three steps before my right shoe caught on a sprinkler head along the edge of the sidewalk. I flew over a large azalea bush and landed a perfect face plant in the middle of my crabgrass-filled lawn.

Detective Hunter knelt by my side. "Laurel, are you okay? Did you break any bones? Try moving your foot. Just a little, not too much. Lie still. Don't sit up too fast."

The nonstop litany of medical commands confused me so I chose to ignore all of them. I sat up slowly then leaned over to examine my shoeless right foot. My left foot was still encumbered by its floppy mate. My foot didn't hurt too badly although my brain felt foggy.

Why was I running?

"Pumpkin!" I grabbed the detective's arm as I attempted to stand up.

"You want a pumpkin?" A worried frown creased his forehead. "I think you might have a concussion. You better stay still."

"Pumpkin's our kitten. That's the blur of fur I was chasing." Something sticky caressing my right hand drew my attention. The phantom wasn't drooling on my digits so I glanced down to find the kitten licking my fingers.

The detective stared at Pumpkin with a confused look. "There's a peculiar creature attached to your hand."

"The kids surprised me with her last weekend. She's been a bundle of entertainment ever since."

"She's the most unusual cat I've ever seen," he tactfully replied.

Since I wasn't in the mood to discuss Pumpkin's redeeming qualities, or lack thereof, I grabbed her and attempted to get up.

My right knee buckled and I collapsed back on the lawn. Hunter crouched beside me. "Is it your knee? Your ankle? Hamstring?"

It looked like the detective's interrogation skills also extended into the medical arena. I held up my palm. "Slow down. Let me try to walk and we'll see what happens."

Hunter held on to Pumpkin with one hand, keeping his other arm wrapped around my waist as I limped up the sidewalk. Once inside the house, he locked the door and the kitten scurried off. I hobbled halfway across the living room where I stumbled on a piece of candy that must have fallen out of one of the boy's bags.

Once again, I found myself clinging to my rescuer. I was about to thank him when I noticed his eyes had a peculiar look in them. It almost looked like, like—lust? My heart pumped faster as he leaned toward me. I moved closer as well. My head swam with desire and I could feel my chest getting wetter and wetter.

Huh?

CHAPTER FIFTEEN

Advice to single clowns everywhere. Never wear a water-squirting flower if there is a chance a hunky detective may try to kiss you. And never attempt a kiss on Halloween, I thought, as the doorbell clamored yet again.

The detective strode into the foyer and yanked the door open.

Kristy's voice rang out. "What happened to your shirt, Dad?" Her question was followed by a familiar refrain. "Hey, Mom, where are you?"

Two of the sugar-infused miniature super heroes blasted into the room. "How come you're only wearing one shoe?" asked my pint-size Spider-man.

"I fell down and hurt my knee chasing your kitten." I looked accusingly at the probable offender. "Someone forgot to close the door to the laundry room."

"Is Pumpkin okay? Did you find her?" Tears formed in Ben's eyes. Such a sensitive child. Maybe someday, he would feel the same compassion for his poor mother.

"Hey, Mrs. McKay, your shirt's all wet. Did you guys have a water fight?"

When did Jimmy become so observant?

"I was demonstrating my plastic flower on Detective Hunter and we both got wet." I quickly changed to a drier subject. "Are you having fun, Kristy?"

"Yeah, it's been awesome. You guys ready to go back out?"

The three younger children ran out of the house while Jenna lingered behind.

"Thanks for taking care of the kids, honey." I put my arm around her shoulder as I leaned against one of the chairs. "Are you sure Kristy is having a good time?"

Jenna smirked. "She's having a great time, although maybe not as good as the two of you." She pointed her finger in the direction of my sopping wet shirt then sauntered out after the others.

Tom closed the front door then turned to me. "We need to talk," he said abruptly. "Let's sit on the sofa."

Although the thought of sitting together on the sofa hinted at romance, the serious tone of his voice did not. He offered his arm and I limped to the sofa. The detective grabbed a fringed throw pillow and propped my leg on the coffee table before he settled on the opposite side of the sofa.

"I better get rid of this stupid plastic flower before I douse you again." Was that subtle enough?

"Good idea. Although by the time I'm done with my explanation you may want to do something worse than soak me."

I settled into the cushions. It didn't sound like canoodling was on his agenda. Tom was quiet for a few seconds, his index finger tracing one of the blue flowers decorating the arm of the sofa.

"Laurel, I haven't been in a relationship since my wife passed away. My entire existence revolves around my daughter, my parents and my career. Right now, I don't have room for anyone else in my life. But the first time I saw you running to your son's rescue, racing across that soccer field in those silly blue shoes...."

"My turquoise mules aren't silly," I interrupted, "they're..."

He reached across the sofa and placed a finger on my lips. "Let me finish. Despite our hostile introduction on the soccer field, I haven't been able to stop thinking about you. And not just as a murder suspect."

He took my palm in his and absentmindedly stroked his thumb along my wrist. I could feel a throbbing in my body. And it wasn't in my knee.

"You're the first woman I've been attracted to since my wife died. You're also the primary suspect in two murder inquiries. Do you realize what an enormous conflict of interest this is for me?"

The touch of his thumb was short-circuiting all the fuses in my body including my brain, but I still grasped what he was saying.

Tom grimaced. "I've talked to folks who've known you for a long time: Ben's second grade teacher, your pastor, neighbors. I told the sheriff that everyone I've interviewed says you're a great mother and all around wonderful person. I keep hoping the favorable things I've discovered will persuade him you're innocent of either murder."

Tom had been interviewing people like my pastor? And my neighbors? I tried to digest his words but they were giving me a serious case of indigestion.

"You've been talking to my friends...about me? Without telling me first?" I yanked my hand from his grip and tried to rise. Unfortunately, I had to bend my knee in order to remove it from the top of the coffee table.

"Ouch," I whimpered as I slipped back into the cushions. Tom slid across the sofa and tried to help me.

Forget it, buddy. I pushed him away as I struggled to get up. Detectives must be prepared to deal with criminals who resist arrest, but I doubt Tom's normal method of subduing them is to kiss them. I didn't know if that was his original intent, but I responded like a woman who hadn't been in a lip lock in over three years. The kiss was hot. It was so.... hot. My body had never tingled this way from just a kiss.

Or was it a hot flash?

I pulled back and glanced at him. His face mirrored the surprised look on mine.

My senses reeled. But Tom's disclosure that he was investigating me behind my back ticked me off. I shoved him away and he slid back to the other end of the sofa.

"I'm sorry," he said, "that never should have happened."

"You're darn right." My face was flushed and my body felt like a volcano about to explode.

Tom chuckled suddenly and I glared at him. "You might want to wipe the lipstick smudges off your face before your children come home." His lips curved in a smile. A smile rimmed with red lipstick. I dug into the pocket of my baggy shorts and pulled out a gigantic hankie. Clowns are always prepared. The incriminating lipstick disappeared seconds before the kids burst through the door, their bags overflowing with candy.

Tom stood and checked out each of the kids' booty. I remained seated, still stewing over his disclosure. He squatted next to me, resting his hand on my injured knee. "You should see a doctor tomorrow. You may need to be on crutches."

I folded my arms over my chest. "I don't need a..." my voice trailed off as my brain leaped a few steps ahead. Hmmm. There was a doctor I wanted to visit and now I had the perfect excuse.

Since I continued to glower at him, Tom astutely determined he'd overstayed his welcome. He told Kristy to gather up her stuff. She grabbed her loot, thanked Jenna and me, and waved goodbye to the boys. Her father followed her out the door with a brief troubled glance at the gimpy murder suspect sulking on her sofa.

The boys probably would have stayed up all night exchanging goodies but Ben's crabby, injured mother was ready for bed. After removing my smeared makeup, I put on my red puppy dog pajamas. I briefly wondered what Tom Hunter would think of my attire. If he could kiss me in clown makeup, imagine how turned on he would be by my flannel jammies.

The numbers gleaming on my alarm clock announced it was a little after ten. A little late, but Liz has always been a night owl. I dialed her number and listened to it ring eight times before the answering machine kicked in. She picked up just as I started to leave a message.

"Laurel, do you know what time it is?" She didn't sound thrilled to hear from her best friend. Had I interrupted some X-rated activity?

"Sorry to call so late, but I need your help. I injured my leg tonight and I wondered if you could drive me to the doctor tomorrow?"

"What happened?" she gasped.

"It's a long story. I'll give you the details tomorrow."

"Call me at the office after you've made an appointment with Dr. Templeton."

Dr. Templeton is a terrific family doctor who practices in Placerville. With years of klutziness behind me, I've visited his office so many times I could have earned frequent patient points. But I had other plans.

"I'm going to call Dr. Slater's office and see if his partner can take a look at it. Then we can chat about Jeremy."

"Do you think that's a good idea?"

"It can't hurt to try a new doctor, someone younger than Dr. Templeton, in case my injury is a complicated one. Please don't say anything to Brian."

"I'm too tired to argue with you right now. Ring me when you want to be picked up." I winced as the phone slammed in my ear. Liz was beginning to sound a lot like my mother.

Another sleepless night followed, either due to the stimulus of the detective, the pain shooting out from my left knee every time I rolled over, or the extra caffeine from all of the candy bars I scarfed down for dinner.

The throbbing ache eased by morning, but this was too good of an opportunity to meet Jeremy's partner. I dropped both kids at the bus stop and at nine on the dot called Dr. Radovich's office. I explained to the receptionist that I was a friend of Dr. Slater's and wished to switch doctors since my own family physician would be retiring shortly. This was an emergency since I could barely walk. She kept putting me on hold but finally agreed to squeeze me in at noon, probably just to get me off the phone.

That gave me the morning to skim through the last two days' newspapers. The *Mountain Democrat* was focusing on the upcoming election so there was only a tiny article about Jeremy's demise stuck on the back page. Politics trumped murder.

Liz picked me up promptly at eleven-thirty. I wiggled into her impractical but cute red Miata. At least my small car was roomy enough for a *pleasingly plump* woman.

Yes, Jeremy's quote still rankled.

We shot down the hill to Jeremy's medical practice in El Dorado Hills. I could tell by her demeanor that Liz wasn't thrilled about spending her lunch hour sitting in a doctor's waiting room. I promised to treat her to the fast food restaurant of her choice. As we drove to the office, I briefed her on her part of the investigation. Her initial response was somewhat less enthusiastic than I'd hoped.

"Are you out of your bloody mind? Brian will kill me or worse— he might break off our engagement if he finds out I'm mixed up in a case he could end up prosecuting. Did you suffer brain damage from your fall?"

"Hey, calm down." I noticed the speedometer venturing into ticket territory. "There's no need for Brian to find out. I just want you to chat up the front desk staff while I'm with the doctor. You're such a great schmoozer. All we need to find out is if they know of anyone who would have a reason to kill Jeremy. How hard is that?"

"I suppose I can handle it," she grumbled, "but you're going to owe me more than a lousy cheeseburger."

By the time we arrived at the doctor's office, we had our game plan in hand. Liz was truly concerned about my knee. She carefully assisted me into the reception area. It seemed wise not to disclose it was barely hurting. With any luck, I'd trip over something and writhe with pain by the time the doctor examined me.

Two women sat behind the reception counter. An older caramel-skinned female in a lilac-flowered smock and white pants worked at her computer. Her fingers flew over her keyboard like a skilled pianist. The other significantly younger woman, dressed in a tightly fitted version of the same uniform, filed her nails with an emery board while she held a cell phone against her short platinum spiked hair. She gave me the universal "I'll be with you when I feel like it" wave.

I waited for a few minutes then stood and walked to the desk, announcing that I was a new patient. When Spike didn't respond to my "new patient status," I raised my voice and asked whether there were any forms for me to complete. The older woman shot me a rueful look and reminded Tara, the young receptionist, that all new patients had to fill out a four-page questionnaire.

I smiled in sympathy with the older woman whose nametag read Carol. She could be a valuable ally. I filled in my medical history on the lengthy form while Liz sifted through the magazines on the coffee table. The office didn't maintain a subscription to any beauty or bridal publications, the only reading material that interested her these days.

I looked up from my questionnaire thinking how nicely furnished the office was. Old Doc Templeton still owned the original orange molded plastic chairs he'd bought forty years before. Dr. Slater and Dr. Radovich must consider the comfort of their patients a priority. Or maybe they charged more than Dr. Templeton.

Whatever the reason, the soft cushioned burgundy and navy chairs along the perimeter of the office were comfortable. Large photos of different scenes from the snow-capped Sierras and Lake Tahoe lent a serene ambiance to the room.

After a wait of ten minutes, Carol called my name. I nudged Liz. She was engrossed in a *Newsweek* article on aging. I prodded her with the tip of my Adidas but missed, my foot connecting with her ankle.

"What's the matter with you?" She flashed me a dirty look as she reached down to rub her bruised ankle.

Some accomplice she was. I whispered to her left ear. "I'm going to try to keep this nurse occupied. You need to question the young one while I'm gone."

Carol cleared her throat impatiently. I walked briskly across the room then remembered why I was in the office. I adjusted my pace and limped down a hallway lined with examination rooms. We walked into a room with light blue walls adorned with more photos depicting beautiful views of the Sierras. I complimented the nurse on the décor.

"What a lovely room. Did you help decorate the office?" My flattery seemed to have a thawing effect. Carol produced a tentative smile as she grabbed the blood pressure thingie from a table.

"No, we had a professional decorator. Dr. Radovich didn't care what we did to the office. He wanted to paint everything that bilious green color you find in government buildings because the paint is so cheap, but Dr. Slater insisted we have a nice ambiance for our patients." She sighed softly. "I certainly miss Dr. Slater."

"He was very special to me, too." My sigh was so forceful it blew my patient questionnaire right off her clipboard.

Carol bent over and picked up the form. "Oh, I forgot you said you were a friend of the doctor. Did you know him well?"

"We'd been dating awhile." I guess a lunch date and an abbreviated dinner date could constitute awhile. "I was very fond of Jeremy."

I sighed again but toned it down a few notches.

"Were you with him the night he died?" she asked.

Trick question. One of these days, I need to buy a *Dummies Guide to Detecting*.

I decided I would probably get more information out of Carol if she didn't know I was with him the night he was murdered. "Jeremy said he was having dinner with a business associate and would see me later. I never saw him again."

Thinking about Jeremy's bruised and battered body made me tearful, and really nauseous. It was a good thing Liz and I hadn't devoured any greasy cheeseburgers before this appointment. "He never told me who he was meeting that evening. Do you think it was Dr. Radovich?" I asked.

She shook her head. "No, it couldn't have been. Dr. Radovich told the police he was at a Boys and Girls Club fundraiser that evening. Don't you think it's strange the police would question the staff if his death was an accident?"

"That does seem peculiar. Perhaps they suspect foul play." Foul play? Now I sounded like a character straight out of an Agatha Christie novel.

Carol wrapped the blood pressure cuff around my right arm and pumped like she was pumping for oil. "I thought it was kinda odd myself."

She hesitated then leaned closer. "Plus those articles in the paper. Do you think he coulda been..." She pumped so hard I thought my arm would explode. "Murdered?"

"Uh, Carol." I winced and pointed at my arm.

"Sorry. Guess I got a tad distracted." She let the air out of the gauge, and seemed satisfied with the results as she marked them down on my chart.

"I'd better tell Dr. Radovich you're ready." She picked up my file and walked to the door.

I hated to let her go now that she had finally begun opening up. "Carol, I'm sure it was murder."

Her dark eyes widened until they were double in size. "What makes you think that?" she asked, her hand resting on the polished doorknob.

"I got that impression from the detective who interviewed me. He questioned me about someone that Jeremy knew, an accountant named Garrett Lindstrom. Is that the name of the accountant for this office?"

"I wouldn't know about any of that financial stuff. Dr. Radovich handles all the bookkeeping. I sure don't remember a patient by that name."

The door burst open and a middle-aged man, dressed in a white coat entered. Astute amateur detective that I am, I took a wild guess this was Dr. Radovich.

"Carol, is there a problem? This is my last patient before I can leave for lunch." He grabbed my chart from her outstretched hand.

"Sorry, Doctor, I was just coming to get you." She ducked her head and bustled out of the room.

The doctor paused to look at my medical history before he turned to me. "So Ms. McKay, what seems to be the problem with your leg? You indicated it's difficult to put any weight on it. How did you injure it?"

If I told him the entire story, he definitely would not have time for lunch. An abbreviated version might benefit both of us. "I tripped over my cat and now my right knee buckles when I stand. Last night there was some swelling although it seems to have gone down today."

I rolled my black sweat pant up over my knee to give him a better view of said injury. He sniffed then squeezed my knee. Hard.

"There doesn't seem to be anything seriously wrong with it. You have a little swelling but it's likely that it's merely strained. I don't think you've torn an ACL or the meniscus."

That was a good thing because I had absolutely no idea what an ABC or a missus was. A sprain or a strain I could deal with.

"Ice it every few hours, keep your physical activity to a minimum for the next couple of weeks, and you'll be up skiing in no time."

He had obviously never seen me ski—during ski season, I spend more time lying spread-eagled in the snow than schussing on my skis.

He shook my hand, indicating the exam was over, then walked to the door.

"Dr. Radovich, I have another question," I blurted out before he could make his exit. He turned back with an irritated look on his face. His dedication to the sick must not extend into his lunch hour.

"When you brought up skiing it reminded me of Dr. Slater. The last time I saw Jeremy, he mentioned he was buying a vacation home in Lake Tahoe. He seemed concerned about the financing. Do you have any idea what he was talking about?"

A mottled red flush formed at Dr. Radovich's neck and worked its way up to his matching shaggy red brows. "I hardly think Dr. Slater's real estate activities are any business of yours."

Considering I was the only suspect in Dr. Slater's death, I chose to differ with him. I decided to attack from another direction. "I understand you were at a Boys and Girls fundraiser the night Dr. Slater died. Where did they hold it?"

The angry vein pulsing in his temple looked ready to explode. I shrank back as his menacing form approached the table. "I think you'd better leave now." He snatched my file and strode out of the office without a backwards look.

I caught a glimpse of the back of his head. A bald spot. And he was about the same height as the man I saw along the river the night Jeremy was murdered. If this were an episode of *Law and Order*, I'd say that was a very peculiar response to some innocent questions.

I liked him as a suspect. Now all I needed was a motive.

CHAPTER SIXTEEN

I waited a full minute before jumping off the examining table. Purse in hand, I stepped into the corridor and cautiously approached the reception area. Both nurses seemed enraptured by a magazine Liz had spread open on the front counter. By the time we left the office, my pal would undoubtedly have arranged a spa day for at least one of them.

Since both women appeared occupied, it seemed like a perfect opportunity to examine Jeremy's office. I scooted past the doorway to the reception area and race-limped to the end of the hallway. One door was closed. Probably Radovich's office. He seemed the secretive type.

An open door led to an office furnished with a large polished mahogany desk and a navy blue leather executive chair. My head swiveled back toward the reception area. The coast was still clear.

Bookshelves lined with leather tomes covered two walls. Diplomas and licenses hung on the third wall. I remembered that Jeremy had mentioned receiving his BS at the University of California at Davis, one of many things we had in common. I'd graduated from UCD a couple of years after him with a useless degree in history. His diploma from medical school hung on the wall. Stanford. Impressive. But not helpful.

Photos in matching silver frames rested on the shelves. One picture was of an attractive man, his arms around a pretty blond woman and a very young girl. The man bore a slight resemblance to Jeremy. I picked up a photo of some young men dressed in caps and gowns. I tried to locate Jeremy. There he was. The skinny kid at the end of the last row. A few of his curls had managed to escape from the tight-fitting mortarboard cap.

I turned back to the scrupulously neat desk. Nothing that shouted out "clue." I left Jeremy's office and tiptoed down the corridor. The muted sound of voices indicated that Liz and the nurses were still chatting.

I opened the closed door of the other office. Diplomas hung lopsided on the walls. Files were stacked in haphazard piles on the floor and papers were scattered all over the desk. How did a man this sloppy end up practicing medicine? I certainly wasn't coming back to him for my annual pap. Who knows what tortuous metal instruments he might leave behind?

My arm brushed against a stack of documents and a paper from the top of the pile floated to the floor. The sound of approaching footsteps warned of an impending visitor. I snatched the paper and quickly glanced at it. The first page of a real estate contract for a property on Ski Run Boulevard in Lake Tahoe. The purchaser. Jeremy Slater.

Carol entered the office just as I placed the document back on top the messy pile. "Ms. McKay, what are you doing in here?" She gave me another one of those suspicious looks. At least I think it was a suspicious look. I had a feeling Carol used that look a lot.

"Uh, I just wanted one last memory of Jeremy. I thought there might be some photos of him in here. Is this his office?"

She pointed in the opposite direction. "No, over there."

I followed her across the hall and entered Jeremy's office once again. Carol walked around the desk and stopped in front of the framed photos. I pointed to the family picture I'd noticed in my previous foray. "Is that his brother and his family?"

"Yes, that's his younger brother Mark, and Mark's family. Since Jeremy didn't have any children of his own, he was real fond of his niece, Sammie." She leaned against the credenza, her face pensive.

I lifted the group graduation photo from the bookcase. "Did Jeremy keep in contact with many of his friends from Davis?"

She shrugged. "He went to some type of reunion last summer, but I can't remember if it was for high school or college." She took the frame out of my hands and returned it to the shelf.

"Tara and I are going to lunch. I assume you've seen enough to satisfy you?"

Not really. I wondered why the contract for the Tahoe property Jeremy was purchasing was sitting on Dr. Radovich's desk. But I also knew if I asked Carol, I would definitely get one of those "suspicious" looks.

"Thanks for being so understanding." We walked down the hallway back into the reception area where Liz chatted with Spike. I thanked both women as I pushed my friend out the door. She complained as we walked toward her car. "What's your hurry? I almost signed Tara up for my monthly microdermabrasion special. It's great for getting rid of acne."

Liz stopped abruptly in the middle of the asphalt parking lot. "How come you're not limping anymore?"

I decelerated, slowing my pace as we approached her Miata. "Dr. Radovich is a miracle worker. So did you discover anything useful?"

She shook her head as she beeped the doors open. "I don't think I'm cut out to be your Dr. Watson. Tara has only worked in the office a couple of months. She doesn't know anything personal about either doctor. Carol knew Dr. Slater wanted to buy a condo in Tahoe but she thought the deal had been canceled for some reason."

"This detecting isn't as easy as I thought." I mulled over everything we'd discovered, which wasn't a heck of a lot. Jeremy might or might not have been purchasing a house in Tahoe.

Dr. Radovich is a pig.

A pig who possessed a copy of Jeremy's real estate contract.

"At least I may have picked up some new clients. Feel free to take me along on your next sleuthing expedition." Liz beamed a satisfied smile at me as she shifted into reverse. "By the way, you're looking a little pale. Have you been using that Pumpkin enzyme masque I gave you?"

I shook my head. The only pumpkin in my life lately was the kitten that had instigated this visit.

We ate a quick lunch then Liz dropped me at my house a little after two. The answering machine indicated three messages. The first was from Tom thanking me for letting Kristy go out with the kids and hoping my knee felt better. It was a good thing he didn't know about my detecting foray. The second was a hang-up, and the last message was from Stan informing me I'd missed my eleven o'clock interview for the branch manager position.

Darn. I'd totally forgotten the interview. These murders were a tremendous distraction. I used to be so organized.

Well, maybe not all that organized, but I still couldn't believe I'd totally blown off a job interview in my misguided attempt to solve the murders. I left a voicemail for Anne Lewis in the HR department telling her about my injury and subsequent doctor's appointment. I asked if we could reschedule for the next day. Maybe if I hobbled into the office on crutches I'd elicit some sympathy from Anne.

Without the kids, the house was as quiet as...as a house without kids. I grabbed a diet soda from the refrigerator and sat down at the kitchen table. I thought about my appointment this morning. It was curious how irate Dr. Radovich became when I mentioned Jeremy's real estate deal. He obviously knew about it. What was that phrase? Follow the money.

It was also odd how upset he became when I mentioned the fundraiser he supposedly attended the night Jeremy drowned. Could the doctor have slipped out for a few minutes and killed Jeremy?

I debated whether I should attend Jeremy's memorial service. My mother would know if any of the mourners were in the real estate industry. Maybe she could glean some tidbits about his Tahoe transaction.

Mr. Rooster clock cheeped four o'clock. Both kids would soon arrive home via the school bus so I'd better start thinking about dinner. I rummaged through the cupboards and when I opened the lower cabinet door next to the refrigerator, I discovered Pumpkin asleep on the bottom shelf.

No wonder she hadn't been terrorizing me. The kitten stretched the full length of her tiny multicolored body. When I attempted to grab her, she evaded me and scurried out of the kitchen. Eventually something would break and I'd track her down.

I opened the freezer to see if there was anything recognizable that could be thawed in two hours. The phone rang. Another blocked call. Why I bother with Caller ID is beyond me.

"Hello," I said, distracted by the array of fuzzy frozen foods. How many years can you store ground beef in the freezer?

"Is this Laurel McKay?" asked a raspy male voice.

"Yes…" Is this a trick telemarketing question?

"My name is Neil Schwartz. I'm a reporter from the *Mountain Democrat.* I'd like to ask you some questions about Jeremy Slater. The police report stated that you identified the body the night of his death."

Police report?

"I understand you and the doctor were dating. Would you care to tell me about your relationship? I'm sure you'd like to share your side of the story with our readers."

Relationship? Readers?

A resounding crash erupted from the living room. The kitten had made her whereabouts known.

"Goodbye." I slammed the phone down and tore into the living room to assess the destruction. My brass floor lamp rested on the carpet, the light bulb smashed into a gazillion glass shards. At first, I couldn't locate Pumpkin, then I lifted the lampshade and found her cowering beneath. I was relieved she wasn't hurt, and even more relieved my lamp was intact.

"Pumpkin, thanks for the excuse to get off the phone, but let's make a smaller mess next time." The four-footed pipsqueak scampered off again.

I expected the reporter to call back, but it wasn't until several hours later when the kids and I were eating dinner that the phone interrupted our conversation. Probably the reporter again. Or someone claiming to be conducting a survey. The machine could answer for me.

The voice on the machine got my attention. I dropped my fork and ran to grab the receiver before Detective Hunter could hang up.

"Hello, Tom?" I panted like I'd walked six miles—not six feet. My breathlessness must be due to the sound of his voice. It couldn't be due to lack of exercise.

"Laurel, I was calling to see if your knee felt better. I phoned your office but they said you stayed home from work. Did you get to see your doctor?"

Trick question. Was Dr. Radovich my doctor now?

I carefully crafted my response. "The doctor said it was probably a strain. It feels fine except when I climb the stairs."

"That's good. I was worried you might be on crutches for a while. Is he taking new patients? I need to find a doctor nearby."

"My family doctor wasn't available for an appointment today so I went to a physician in El Dorado Hills. But I wouldn't recommend him. His bedside manner was nonexistent."

"Really? I thought Dr. Radovich was quite personable when I interviewed him this afternoon."

I should have known this wasn't a social call. "Umm...he was probably in a better mood after lunch."

"I also had an interesting chat with Carol. She was surprised we hadn't spoken with Dr. Slater's girlfriend. She felt so sorry for the woman. According to her, poor Laurel didn't even have a photograph of Dr. Slater to remember him by." Tom's voice was measured indicating we were back in interrogation mode. "So tell me more about your relationship with Dr. Slater. I didn't realize it had progressed so far."

"Last night you encouraged me to see a doctor about my knee," I said, defending my actions. "Dr. Radovich was able to squeeze me in so I took advantage of the opportunity to talk to the staff. I might have exaggerated my relationship with Jeremy when I was talking to Carol. I thought I could find out something useful—you know, woman to woman."

Tom snorted. "And what did you find out from your ah, woman to woman discussion?"

Did I detect a hint of sarcasm in his voice? What did I find out? "Jeremy was well-liked by his staff," I said tentatively.

"Laurel, do I have to remind you that you are still a suspect? You *cannot* interfere with our investigation."

"I thought we moved past that little obstacle last night."

Dead silence.

"Okay, I'm sorry. I'll stay away from your investigation," I apologized. "But I really should attend Jeremy's funeral. When are they going to release the body?"

"The family scheduled the memorial service for Monday evening but I'm not allowing you to attend."

"Excuse me." My voice was as frosty as the inside of a Ben and Jerry's carton. "I don't believe you have the authority to do that, Detective Hunter."

A mild expletive sounded in my ear. "It's not safe. You can't just—"

I interrupted him. "May I remind you that I was the last person to see Jeremy alive. Except for his murderer. You know the killer always shows up at the victim's funeral."

Everyone knows that.

"That only happens in books." Tom's voice crackled with anger. "If you insist on attending the service, I'll be forced to lock you up."

"On what grounds?" I was infuriated by his tone and somewhat irrational at this point. He probably had more grounds than I had coffee grounds in my garbage can.

"Interfering with an investigation and...." His voice trailed off and I heard some voices in the background.

The next thing I heard was a muttered "Goodbye," followed by the sound of the dial tone.

The phone rang again seconds later. I assumed it was Tom calling back to apologize so I gave him the full brunt of my smart-ass repertoire. "Make sure you have plenty of hot coffee for me when you haul me in."

"Hot coffee, or cold chardonnay, your wish is my command," said an unfamiliar male voice.

"Who is this?"

"Peter Tyler, your mother's associate from the Centurion office. Ben's new playmate."

I laughed. "Oh, Peter, I'm sorry. I thought you were someone else."

"Someone you're not too happy with, I gather. Anything I can do to help?"

"No, although a glass of chardonnay sounds like a great idea right now." I crossed the room and opened the refrigerator. Nothing chilled except a gallon of two-percent milk.

"I'd deliver it personally if it wasn't so late. This may be short notice but I was wondering if you'd like to get together for dinner this Saturday."

I paused for a minute. After that last conversation with Tom, dinner with Peter might be just what the doctor, any doctor, ordered for me right now. And what better reference than my mother?

"I would enjoy getting together, but I have the kids this weekend. Does the offer hold for another time?" Was suggesting another evening a dating faux pas?

"Sure. How about the following Saturday? Have you been to the River Inn recently?"

My stomach churned. "My last time there wasn't a great experience."

"No problem. I'll come up with another restaurant."

We chatted for a few more minutes then hung up. The kids had given up on me and already gone to their respective rooms. I loaded their plates and glasses in the dishwasher and wondered what Tom Hunter would think of me going out with Peter.

Considering our recent phone call, it probably wouldn't bother him a bit. Except for concern about Peter's safety. Maybe I should drape an orange "Proceed with Caution" banner across my chest. I climbed the stairs then halted when I reached the landing.

Maybe Bradford was right. Could I be the common link?

It hadn't previously crossed my mind that these men had been murdered because they went out with me. Was someone interested in hurting the men I was dating? I plopped down on the carpeted step remembering Hank's comments the previous weekend. Was his recent ardor only because Nadine kicked him out? Or was he jealous of the guys I went out with?

All this detecting was driving me nuts. The thought of the father of my children committing murder was unthinkable. And the thought of him eliminating my dates in order to get me back was as likely as me dropping down to a size two.

The next morning I dressed in a navy suit, hoping Anne had rescheduled my interview. When I arrived at the office, my red voicemail light was blinking. My conservative suit would be wasted. The Human Resources department was booked solid with appointments all day, although Anne said she'd try to squeeze me in.

I called her back and left another voicemail thanking her for making an exception for me. By Monday, I wouldn't have to pretend my leg was still injured, so that was one less obstacle.

I was reviewing a file when I felt a tap on my shoulder. I spun my chair around, practically knocking Stan off his feet. He jumped back just in time. "How's your knee feeling? Were you were able to reschedule?"

"Anne postponed the interview until Monday. The doctor said it was just a strain so I'll be good as new by then."

"You never told me how you hurt it. Did you go out trick-or-treating?" He paused. "Or trip-or-treating?" He slapped his knee and howled at his wit.

Stan wandered back to his own cube and I returned to my loan file. Immersed in my work, I started when I felt a light tap on my shoulder. I swiveled slowly, a wise move, since this visitor was my boss. "Hey, Earl, what's new?"

My boss looked like he'd just lost his best friend. "Laurel, how could you do this to me?" he moaned.

What now? Did Dr. Radovich call and tell him I didn't need to miss work yesterday? Or did I make a mistake that cost the bank millions of dollars?

CHAPTER SEVENTEEN

I responded with my usual keen insight. "Huh?"

Earl's agitated hands ruffled the few remaining strands of hair strategically placed in his comb-over. "Anne said you want to leave me. I mean this department. I never thought you would apply for that position, even if it is a bigger salary."

"Earl, I have two growing children to feed. There isn't much opportunity for advancement here."

His mouth dropped open, reminding me to get him some Crest white strips for our Christmas gift exchange.

"No opportunity for advancement? I was planning on promoting you to Operations Manager." He laid his hand on my shoulder and winked. "We'd be a great team."

A wave of nausea followed his declaration. Did my boss have designs on me that were other than professional? Time to deflect the conversation. "Earl, did you ever meet Garrett Lindstrom, a local CPA? I think he might be a member of the Rotary. Aren't you a Rotarian?"

Earl jumped back. His face bore the same expression as Ben's, whenever I caught him sneaking cookies. "That guy is bad news," he yelled, shoving his hands in the pockets of his rumpled brown suit.

Huh?

"So you do know him. Have you seen him recently?"

"No, and I'm not planning on it." His face darkened, and he thrust his pudgy chin toward me. "Do you need more loans to underwrite?"

Nope. No shortage of loans on my desk. I shook my head and he strode down the corridor towards his office.

What was Earl's problem? One minute he was ogling me. The next minute he was yelling at me. Why couldn't I have a normal boss? Earl had been single for quite a while. Maybe he just needed to get laid. Although not by one of his "team" members.

My extension rang. I hoped it was Anne calling about a cancellation. It was time to get out of this department.

"Laurel, I met the most extraordinary person." My mother sounded breathless, quite unlike her usual self-possessed self.

"Are you trying to set me up with someone else? I already have a date with Peter next weekend." One fix-up was sufficient for this week.

"No, dear. A representative from the sheriff's department showed up at the office today. I've never met anyone quite like him."

That wasn't surprising. I had never met anyone as masculine and virile as Detective Hunter either. Or anyone so annoying. But showing up at her office without a prior phone call? That wasn't playing fair. He should have warned me he was going to interview my mother.

"What did he say?"

"Oh, he was so charming. We compared notes about raising our daughters, you know, what a trial they can be—especially when they make poor decisions about their relationships with the opposite sex."

My mother and the detective compared issues Kristy and I had with the opposite sex? What issues did Kristy have other than making sure she didn't squash any of the boys during her soccer games?

This conversation was not improving my bad mood. "Why were you and Tom talking about Kristy and me?"

"Who?"

"Detective Hunter. Isn't that who you met?" Was she showing early signs of senile dementia?

"No, his name isn't Hunter. It's Bradford, Detective Robert Bradford. Quite an unusual man." She emphasized the word *unusual*.

"You met Tall, Bald and Homely?" The thought of Detective Bradford interrogating my mother sent shivers from my bangs down to my bunions.

126

"Tall, Bald and Homely. That's funny." Mother giggled like a schoolgirl. "I'll have to tell Robert what you said the next time I see him."

See who? —Robert? This conversation was getting loonier and loonier. Was my mother consorting with the enemy?

"Why are you seeing Detective Bradford again? You realize he thinks I killed Jeremy. He's just using you to get incriminating evidence on me."

She giggled again. The last time I'd heard Barbara Bingham giggle was...well, I'd never heard my mother giggle. "Don't be silly. I told him there was no way you could have killed Dr. Slater. You're not organized enough to pull off a murder."

Thanks, Mother. Remind me never to call you as a witness for my defense.

"I appreciate your help, I think. But why are you meeting him again? Does he still think I'm guilty?"

This conversation was making me so crazy I'd turned an entire box of rainbow-colored paper clips into mangled metal squares. I shoved them into the wastebasket while I listened to her response.

"We're going to look at some houses next week on his day off. He just went through a painful divorce and has been living in an apartment for the last two years. I told him buying a house would help the healing process. Don't you agree?"

My mother is a firm believer that home ownership can solve all of life's problems. But if she could distract Detective Bradford from concentrating on yours truly as a murder suspect, she would help solve one of my current problems.

"Good luck selling him a house. But don't let him trick you into disclosing anything that would reflect badly on me. I don't trust him. At all."

"I have everything under control." She hung up, finally sounding more like the woman I had known for the last thirty-nine years than the giggling girl of the last five minutes.

I replaced my own receiver, stood and managed only two steps before it rang again. "What now, Mother?"

"Is this Laurel McKay?" said a slightly familiar male voice.

"Yes. Who is this?"

"It's Neil Schwarz from the *Mountain Democrat*. Please don't hang up again," he said with a rush. "I may have some information for you."

The reporter was either intuitive or accustomed to hang-ups, because that was my initial response. "Yes, Mr. Schwarz." I wasn't going to put my foot or even my little toe in my mouth if I could help it.

"I realize you may be reluctant to speak to a reporter." He chuckled. At least I thought it was a chuckle. It resembled the sound of Draino gurgling down the pipes, which didn't do anything to relieve my anxiety. He burbled on, "I would hate to write a story portraying you as a murder suspect, without presenting your point of view. We'll also want comments from your family."

No way. The last thing the *Mountain Democrat* needed was comments from my mother. I was still ticked off that she thought I was too disorganized to be a murderer.

Okay, getting a little off track here. What was the reporter saying?

".... and give us your side of the story," he said.

"Mr. Schwarz, I don't have a side to my story. Dr. Slater and I only had one date. Okay one dinner date plus a lunch date, but I don't think that counts—you might have to read *Cosmo* to find out—and I didn't actually get to eat dinner, because he drowned, but first he was hit, but of course I didn't know that because I was drunk, well, not really drunk, just mildly tipsy—have you ever had Dom Perignon?"

"Umm, no, I haven't. I'm not sure I got all of that, could you repeat what you just said?"

Not in a million years.

"I need to get back to work. You said you had information so it's your turn to share."

His phone clattered and the sound of raised voices filtered back to me. "Sorry," he said, "I have to call you back. A truck overturned on Highway 50 and I need to cover it. When I was researching your story, I came across something I thought you might find interesting. I'll call you as soon as I'm free."

Don't hurry on my account. I doubted the reporter had obtained any information I would find useful. It was probably a ploy to get me to spill my guts. Speaking of which, I hadn't had lunch yet. I managed to get to the break room without any further interruptions, bought a candy bar and a diet soda from the vending machines and headed back to my desk.

I arrived home in time to catch the six o'clock news. I was pleased to see that the overturned truck and closure of the main highway from Lake Tahoe was still the featured story. Not that I wanted to deprive anyone of a trip to the mountains, but it should keep Mr. Schwarz out of my hair for a while.

The three of us enjoyed an old family favorite, *National Lampoon's Family Vacation*. That movie almost made my life seem sane by comparison. Almost.

Rain pummeling my bedroom window Saturday morning woke me early. I knew nothing less than a flash flood would cancel a soccer game. I filled thermos bottles full of hot chocolate for the two of us. Ben wasn't any more excited than me about going out in the driving rain. With multiple turtlenecks under his soccer jersey, he looked more like a waddling duck than a speedy halfback, but I doubted any of the kids would be at their best.

I sat in my car and sipped hot chocolate from my thermos, waiting for the teams to head out on the field. Even the thought of bumping into Detective Hunter wasn't incentive enough to make me venture out of my toasty car into the pulsing rain.

I could hardly believe it had only been three weeks since I'd first met Tom. I smiled remembering our first meeting. What a grump he was then. And still was. My smile reversed into a frown as I recalled our last conversation when he forbade me to attend Jeremy's memorial service.

Although it might have been more than concern that I was messing up their investigation. He might care about me a little.

Whether it was the mini Niagara Falls pouring down my windshield or my eyes misting, it was impossible to discern any one on the field. I thought I saw Ben talking to one of the soccer players who had walked off the field. His friend wasn't recognizable since he was covered in brown muck from the top of his head to the spikes on his shoes.

As the kids drew closer, I recognized Ben's companion was Kristy. He pounded on my window so I rolled it down. "Hi, Kristy," I said, addressing the four-and-a-half-foot-tall glop of mud. "How was your game?"

Her eyes sparkled, shining through her mud-flecked face. "We won, and I scored a goal."

I smiled back. "That's terrific." I tried to think of a subtle way to ask if her father was around.

"They called my game off 'cause of the mud," Ben explained. "Three players on Kristy's team got hurt and they don't want no more injuries. Can she come to our house? Her grandpa brought her and he's waiting in that car over there."

Ben pointed to a large charcoal sedan parked five slots down from mine. "Go ask if she can come home with us, Mom. We'll wait in the car."

They clambered into the back seat before I could lay down some of the towels I'd brought. Oh, well, the back seat could use a good hosing anyway. I reluctantly stepped out of the car and hustled through the rain, now attacking me horizontally. I rapped on Mr. Hunter's car window.

He looked puzzled then his face cleared as he recognized me. "Hello there. You're that friend of Tom's we met at the River Inn last Saturday."

Was it only last weekend Jeremy had died? So much had happened in the interim, it felt like a month. "Yes, I'm Laurel McKay. Kristy is friends with my son, Ben, and she wondered if she could play at our house this afternoon. Is Tom working today?"

"Tom hated to miss out on Kristy's game, but some new evidence came up on a big murder case he's working on. I watched the game for a while then gave up and decided to wait it out in the car." He chuckled as he rubbed his gloved hands together. "My old bones can't take this cold like they used to."

New evidence. That sounded intriguing. I was curious to know what Tom was checking out but it was unlikely he had shared any information with his father. Still, it was worth a try.

"Did Tom say anything about the new evidence he discovered?"

"Nope, I only know that he's really frustrated with this particular case. Between you and me, I think the woman did it."

I stood in the downpour nodding at Mr. Hunter. There might be another case that involved a woman as a suspect but I doubted it. Would Kristy's grandfather have agreed to let her come to our house if he knew I was *the woman?*

We said goodbye and I sloshed back to the car. These soccer games were destroying my shoes. My water-soaked flats would be retired after today. Ben and Kristy were sharing knock-knock jokes ad nauseam. The smell of wet socks and sweat, combined with the aroma of hot chocolate added to my own nauseam.

As soon as we arrived home, both kids hit the showers. Kristy was too tall to wear Ben's sweats, so she donned a pair of mine and rolled up the cuffs. Her muddy soccer clothes went into the washing machine. If her father was chasing down a hot lead, the least I could do was relieve him of one domestic duty.

Kristy's grandfather had driven off so quickly I had no idea how long she would be at our house. The kids spent the afternoon teaching the kitten how to play soccer. They first threw the ball and she would run to it. Eventually Pumpkin learned how to bat the ball with her paws. Ben thought Pumpkin should be on television, but there was no way I was becoming an agent for a cat.

I stood in the laundry room folding Kristy's clean clothes when I heard the doorbell ring. It was probably her grandfather so I figured the kids could get the door. Seconds later Tom walked into the room.

His hair was wet, his face drawn and tired. He looked like he would welcome a comforting hug, but after our last conversation I had no idea where we stood. I clutched the laundry basket with a death grip. As Tom approached, I stepped back, bumping into the churning washing machine. He silently removed the basket from my arms and placed it on the dryer. Then he lifted me up on top of the washing machine.

Was the detective about to read me my rights?

CHAPTER EIGHTEEN

Tom gently placed his hand on the back of my neck and drew me close. My head spun, my heart palpitated and my body pulsated.

Okay, part of the pulsating might have been due to the spin cycle. The rest of my reaction was due to the close proximity of a man who could turn my body into a fiery inferno. A loud bell suddenly pierced the air. Tom jumped back three feet and I almost tumbled off the machine.

Jenna appeared in the doorway with an armful of dirty laundry. She narrowed her eyes at her mother perched on the washing machine. I could practically hear the thud of her eyes rolling. She turned around and retraced her steps down the hallway.

I hopped down and began moving the towels from the washer to the dryer. Tom remained silent as I completed the transfer.

"I guess you're here to pick up Kristy." I held the laundry basket containing her clean soccer clothes as I rambled on. "She was a mud pie after today's game."

He lifted the basket out of my arms and set it down on the dryer. "Kristy takes every opportunity to create as many loads of wash for me as she can. Thanks for doing her laundry and letting her come over here. My parents are wonderful about babysitting, but she usually wears them out within minutes."

"Your father said some new evidence came up today. Anything that will remove me from the list of suspects?"

Which as I recalled, was a list of one.

"It depends." He stuck his hands in his pockets and rocked back and forth. "How well did you know Garrett Lindstrom?"

"The only time I met him was that evening at Leonardo's. Why? What happened? Did any new evidence show up?"

Tom placed a finger on my lips then wrapped his muscular arms around me. I rested my head against his broad chest. It felt as if a grizzly bear was comforting me but I liked it. A lot.

"This might be the only way to stop you from asking questions," he said.

I smiled a sweet smile at him. My body might be occupied, but that didn't stop my brain from working, especially where murder was concerned.

Jenna appeared once again with her armload of clothes.

"Are you guys through doing whatever it is you're doing in here?" She tapped her left foot impatiently, her ponytail swinging to its rhythm. "Melissa is coming by in an hour and I don't have anything to wear."

"Well, excuse us," I said to my long-suffering teenager. "C'mon, Tom, let's go see what Ben and Kristy are up to. The house seems much too quiet." I worried the two seven-year-olds had been up to no good but both kids were sprawled asleep on the family room floor. A sleeping Pumpkin cuddled between them, a wiffle ball secured in her front paws.

Tom followed as I walked into the kitchen. Mr. Rooster clock said it wasn't too early for a glass of wine. "Do you want anything to eat or drink? I have wine, soda, peanut butter and jelly."

"A glass of merlot with a PB and J sounds particularly enticing." He settled into one of the oak chairs. "But I'll stick with a cola for now. I need to go back out with the crime scene techs."

I poured sodas for both of us then sat next to him, our toes within touching range. Tom's expression was reflective as he sipped his drink. I noticed threads of silver in his thick brown hair. Were those gray hairs there three weeks ago? Before I became a presence in his life?

Since he wasn't interrogating me for a change, I decided to switch roles. "What was the new evidence you mentioned? I gather it has something to do with Garrett."

133

He nodded. "I've been doing everything I can to find a motive for his murder. You wouldn't believe how many Love Club women I interviewed."

I hazarded a guess. "Twenty?"

"Lucky guess?" He frowned. "Or some amateur sleuthing?"

"Neither. Sunny mentioned it when I told her about our altercation. Were there any other assault victims?"

He sipped his soda. "Nope. No one else was stu...um...no one else was invited to sit in his car."

It didn't surprise me that no one else was stupid enough to get in Garrett's car. Or leave their keys in their ignition. Or phone in the charger. Or become a murder suspect.

"So I was the only woman dumb enough to get entangled in his front seat acrobatics. And to smack him. That still shouldn't qualify me a suspect."

"Did you ever go to his house?"

I shook my head.

"Let me rephrase that. Did you happen to drive past his house in a periwinkle Prius, license plate 'Laurel M,' on the day the body was discovered?"

My face colored. "It was just a drive-by. Sunny had just told me about Garrett's death. I needed to confirm it with my own eyes. There's no law against driving past a victim's house, is there?"

"No, but in your case there probably should be." He drained his glass. I stood up to refill it but he waved me back into my chair.

"Ever visit his office?" he asked.

Darn. Why didn't I think of that? I shook my head. "Why?"

"Due to the financial nature of his business, we wanted a forensic accountant to look through his files. We had to wait for someone to come up from Sacramento. They finally made it there yesterday. There were no files. Not a one. The place was empty except for some miscellaneous junk in his desk drawers."

"Someone broke in?" I asked.

He nodded. "It wouldn't have taken much. They could have used a credit card to unlock the office. Anyone could have done it."

"Even a lock-challenged mother of two?"

"Yep. The only thing left behind was one significant piece of evidence."

Our eyes locked. I had a feeling I wouldn't like his response.

"A business card from Hangtown Bank. For Laurel McKay, mortgage underwriter."

I opened the door of the pantry and grabbed a bag of Oreos. I ripped opened the bag, threw it on the table, grabbed a Double Stuf cookie and took a bite. Then another. My blood pressure dropped as the chocolate worked its magic.

Tom reached for a cookie. "You're awfully quiet."

"I'm thinking. I don't remember giving Garrett my card although it could have fallen out of my purse and landed in the backseat of his car. I have no idea how it ended up in his office. Jeremy asked me for my card when we met so he'd have my office number. But tons of people probably have my card."

Well, not tons. But more than the two victims.

I offered Tom more cookies. He grabbed a couple and put the bag on the table. We had something else in common besides dead bodies.

"Just because my business card is in his desk doesn't mean anything," I mumbled through chocolate-crumbed lips.

He sighed. "Let's just say it's highly suspicious that all of his files are gone. But your card in the drawer seems way too obvious to me. I told Bradford I think you're being set up by the real murderer."

"How did Tall, Bald and Homely respond to that?"

"Who?" He looked puzzled then chuckled. "Oh, Bradford. As far as he's concerned you're the one. Especially now that Garrett and Jeremy's deaths may be linked to the same murder weapon."

"What?"

I saw the "oops" flicker across his face.

"I hope I don't regret this. And you cannot share what I tell you with anyone, not your mother, not your best friend."

I lifted my right hand. "Scout's honor." Did you actually have to be a Girl Scout to utter those words?

"If you hadn't been with him when he died, it's unlikely Slater's death would have been pronounced anything more than an accidental drowning. There were lacerations and contusions all over his body, mainly from the battering he took from the rocks in the river. Since his lungs were full of water, the official cause of his death was drowning."

Okay, that made sense.

"Since both men were members of the Love Club and both dined with you shortly before they died, the medical examiner intentionally looked for similarities between the two deaths. Lindstrom had an unusual indentation on the back of his head, but the back of Slater's head was a mess.

I grimaced and pressed my hands against my stomach.

"Sorry, didn't mean to be so graphic. Let's just say that during the autopsy of both men, minute flecks of red paint were found embedded in their skulls."

"I watch *CSI* but what the heck does that mean?"

"It means both men could have been bludgeoned with the same instrument. It's just far more difficult to ascertain in Jeremy's situation. Fortunately, the water in the river isn't that deep this time of year, so the flecks weren't completely washed away. That's why I'm meeting with the crime techs later. They should have their analysis completed by then."

"What kind of weapon are you talking about?"

"It's hard to say at this point. Some kind of tool. A hammer or wrench with a red handle, assuming the paint flecks match."

"So just because the same weapon may have been used both times, Bradford is certain I'm responsible?" I wrinkled my nose in frustration. "It's not like I carry hammers and wrenches in my purse."

He grinned. "I've seen your purse. You could carry a chain saw in there."

"Well, I think the evidence is lame," I muttered.

Tom shook his head. "Opportunity, weapon. All he needs is a motive. And as far as Bradford is concerned he has a motive for both deaths."

My eyes opened wide and my lips opened wider as I stuffed another medicinal Oreo in my mouth.

"Here's the deal with Robert. His thirty-five-year marriage ended in an acrimonious divorce two years ago. A couple of months later he was forced to release a suspect accused of killing her husband because he didn't have enough evidence. She ended up murdering her in-laws a few days later."

I remembered that case. It was nasty.

Tom grabbed a cookie, rolling it around the table as he carefully selected his words. "It's not that Bradford is biased against women, but because of his history he may be overly suspicious of females in general. According to him, between the evidence we've discovered and his gut feeling, you're the killer."

We sat at the table eating cookies and contemplating one another. A detective and his suspect.

The sound of giggling children echoed from the family room. Tom walked into the family room then returned with his daughter. She rested her head on his broad chest as she settled in his lap.

"Daddy, did Laurel tell you I made a goal?"

Oops. I was so distracted by the murders and damaging new evidence I forgot to report on today's game.

Tom hugged her tight. "That's wonderful, honey."

"Are we going home now?"

"No I need to go back to work. You'll have to spend the night at Grandma and Grandpa's."

"Again?" She sighed with the gusto of a daughter trying to squeeze her father's tender heart.

She turned to me, her eyes hopeful. "Can I stay here tonight? Would that be okay?"

As far as I was concerned she could stay, but Tom shook his head. "Sorry, sweetie. I don't know when I'll be done and we don't want to disturb Ms. McKay in the middle of the night."

Why don't we ask Ms. McKay if she would like Detective Hunter to disturb her in the middle of the night? Heck, yes, but probably not with his young daughter in tow. I went into the laundry room, put Kristy's soccer clothing in a bag and met Tom in the foyer. He still held Kristy, her arms wrapped around his neck. No wonder his biceps were so well developed.

He lingered for a minute. "Thanks for watching Kristy."

"Any time. Provided I'm not in jail," I said dolefully.

"I'm doing everything I can," he promised.

"I know. Maybe I'll discover something at Jeremy's memorial service."

Tom's face closed up faster than the ticket window for a Rolling Stones concert.

"You're still planning on attending?" His eyes turned harder than granite and his voice dropped thirty decibels. How quickly he could revert to his official capacity.

"I don't have a choice. I was the last person to see..." My voice faltered when I realized Kristy was listening to our conversation.

Tom set her down and told her to play with Ben. She looked puzzled but evidently recognized his official tone. She was certainly better at obeying him than I was.

Tom waited until Kristy was out of the room before he lashed out. "Laurel, there is a *killer* out there." His face grew increasingly purple with each overly enunciated word. "He's already murdered two people. Do you want to be next?"

"No, but…"

"There are no buts. No buts whatsoever. Can't you see how dangerous this amateur detecting is? What about your kids?"

"What am I supposed to do? Sit here until Bradford arrests me? Then who will take care of my children?"

He didn't answer. How could he?

CHAPTER NINETEEN

The next morning the kids and I finally made it to church. With ten minutes to spare. My mother showed up shortly thereafter, a perfect Creamsicle confection in an orange knit suit.

Every time I belted out a "Hallelujah," my thoughts returned to my encounter in the laundry room the previous afternoon. It was difficult to keep a grin off my face. Thank you, Lord, for the health of my family, and for providing me with that very healthy specimen, Tom Hunter. Now if I could ask one tiny favor like providing the detectives with another suspect, I would be eternally grateful.

I reviewed the information Tom had shared about the murderer possibly using the same weapon on both men. Visions of murder weapons danced in my head. Suddenly I dropped the hymnal splat on the floor. That didn't get me any brownie points with my mother or Pastor Martin. His sweet blue eyes didn't look that sweet as he zeroed in on the source of the disruption.

I lowered my gaze and folded my hands while my brain considered various options. Hammers, wrenches—my ex-husband had all of those items on his tool belt. Although any normal male would have access to those tools.

Even I possessed a tool kit, albeit in plastic. In Ben's toy chest.

As soon as I arrived home, I changed into my navy blue sweats. My culinary skills are adequate but something inevitably spills when I cook. Mother arrived twenty minutes later.

"Laurel, you'll never guess who I was speaking with," she said as she entered the kitchen.

"Lay it on me." I bent down to reach inside the cupboard that held my baking pans. Success at last, one slightly bent and corroded baking dish. A bacon-scented kitchen was only minutes away. I caught the tail end of her sentence.

"...don't you agree with me?" Like I'd dare to disagree with my mother. Maybe by the time I turned sixty.

"Yes, absolutely." I would agree with anything if I could entice her to attend Jeremy's memorial service with me.

It turned out the wife of the new young couple from church was the granddaughter of one of my mother's former clients. The couple wanted to purchase a new house in the area and my mother was helping them. The real estate queen was never happier than when she had three generations of loyal customers.

The kids inhaled their bacon, avocado and mushroom omelets within seconds. They loaded their plates in the dishwasher and politely excused themselves, giving me an opportunity to discuss what had been foremost on my mind.

As I walked into the pantry to grab some more coffee beans, I tried to think of a scintillating lead into the conversation that would involve Jeremy. Before I could open my mouth, my mother brought him up.

"Have you heard anything further about Dr. Slater? I had no idea how well respected he was. Even though he practiced in El Dorado Hills, several of the agents in our office said he was their personal physician. Detective Bradford told me his memorial service would be held tomorrow."

"Really?" I attempted to look surprised. Unfortunately, the surprise was on me. The lid on the coffee grinder wasn't clamped shut and beans skittered across the tile counter. I glanced up to see if Mother noticed the wayward beans. She was in the pantry rearranging cans and boxes.

She popped out, arms laden with boxes. "These have all expired."

I had lived with the pantry queen's invasions for twenty years so her latest mission didn't faze me.

"Speaking of expired..."

"Yes, what a shame Dr. Slater died so suddenly." She proceeded to dump half my food staples in the trash. "He would have been quite a catch for you. Maybe you should attend the service since you were the last person to see him alive."

There are times when I love my mother, pantry expeditions and all.

"What a wonderful idea. I wish I'd thought of that. I'd feel funny going by myself so would you come with me? You might know some of the people there."

She patted my hand. "Of course I'll go with you, dear. You've had a tough few weeks and I'm sure attending this memorial service is the last thing you want to do."

Right.

"Do you think that intriguing Detective Bradford will go?" she mused out loud as she completed one more pantry sortie.

I almost gagged up my omelet thinking of a potential coupling of the ornery detective and my mother, but decided to keep mum for now. Mum was needed for a detecting expedition.

We agreed to meet at two-thirty at the Starbucks located a few blocks away from Fullers Memorial Home in El Dorado Hills. I don't know where people had meetings before Starbucks appeared on every corner.

Mother thanked me for brunch, but couldn't say farewell without some maternal advice. "Be sure to wear a nice dark suit for the service."

"I was planning on wearing a red polka-dot dress. I thought it would liven things up." Fortunately, looks can't kill. She shook her head and walked out the door.

The next morning I wore my best black wool suit to work. As I stored my purse under my desk, I glanced at the calendar to make sure I had no scheduled appointments. My agenda was clear. Earl probably wouldn't mind if I left a few hours early, especially when he was bent on enticing me to stay in this department.

The phone rang and I grabbed it. "Laurel speaking."

"It's Anne. We managed to squeeze in an opening for you today but it wasn't easy. Bill wanted to make a decision over the weekend because he needs to fill the position, but I talked him into waiting until he met with you. Your interview is scheduled for four."

Darn and double darn. How could I attend both the service and the interview at the same time? Talk about prioritizing.

"A dear friend passed away and I have to attend the memorial service at three. Is there any way you can squeeze me in this morning?"

"You are not making my job any easier," she responded in a clipped tone. "I doubt if Bill can change his plans again. Was this a very close friend?"

"Very close." I exhaled an Oscar-worthy sigh. "We were romantically involved and I'm completely devastated by his death."

"I'm so sorry," she apologized. "I didn't realize you had a boyfriend. What was his name?"

"Jeremy Slater," I blurted out.

"The doctor who drowned in the American river? I thought he was murdered by the woman he was dating."

A few seconds elapsed while Anne and I both contemplated her comment.

She cleared her throat. "Laurel, maybe this position isn't a good career move for you. There's a tremendous amount of customer service involved, plus considerable contact with the community. You wouldn't want the public worrying about your reputation."

"You aren't insinuating I had anything to do with Jeremy's death, are you?"

"Of course not. I'll get back to you if Bill says we can move up the interview." The phone slammed in my ear. Evidently being a murder suspect was not an ideal career path. But was it sufficient grounds for termination?

As I mulled over my future employment prospects, Stan slid into the chair in front of my desk. He was dressed in a conservative charcoal suit and subdued burgundy tie, quite unlike his normal fashion plate *Queer Eye* wardrobe.

"You look like you're going to a funeral," I commented.

"I am, sweetheart. We're going together, remember." Shoot. I'd forgotten Stan volunteered to attend the service with me.

"Thanks, but you don't need to go. Mother is coming with me now. You look very nice though." I hoped that would appease him.

"C'mon, you said I could help you look for the culprit." He pouted as only Stan could pout. "You know I watch *CSI* every week. I'm sure I'll discover some clues. Plus it can't hurt to have another set of eyes and ears."

"I hope you're not planning on climbing on top the casket looking for clues?"

"Puleeze. I have an intuitive sense when it comes to people."

He crossed his legs, pursed his lips and looked down his nose at me.

"It's a gay thing, you know."

I wasn't sure how useful Gaydar would be in finding a murderer, but I agreed he could come with us. As he walked out of my cubicle, the phone rang again. I thought it might be Anne calling back to reschedule my appointment, but I was greeted by a British accent.

"What's up, Liz?"

"Today's paper said Dr. Slater's memorial service is this afternoon. I thought we should go together and do some more investigating. Isn't that an excellent idea?"

Apparently, everyone I knew thought it was a great idea to attend the funeral. So much for discreetly sneaking into the service.

"I'm already going with Mother and Stan. There's no need for you to come."

"Are you sure? It never hurts to have another set of eyes and ears."

Great. Now my dysfunctional detective team was starting to sound alike. Liz agreed to meet us at Starbucks. If nothing else, that particular Starbucks would have a profitable afternoon.

I never heard back from Anne about rescheduling, but I decided to focus on the memorial service, and to paraphrase a few friends, keep my eyes and ears open.

Liz and my mother, dressed in nearly identical black pinstriped designer suits, were chatting over a couple of lattes when I arrived. I cast lustful eyes at the Frappuccino menu but decided to forego my favorite treat. Stan arrived right behind me. He and my mother argued over who would chauffeur our foursome. Even though Liz wanted to ride in Stan's new Beemer, we decided my mother's car was the largest and most suitable for our entourage.

When we arrived at Fullers Mortuary and Chapel, the parking lot was full of BMWs, Mercedes and Lexuses, or was it Lexi? It made sense since many of the mourners were probably doctors.

I pulled my team aside. "Remember, I hope to find that man I saw talking to Jeremy along the riverbank the night he died. He's tall and balding. If we sit in the rear of the chapel it'll be easier to notice someone with a bald spot."

All three agreed it was an excellent plan. We walked through the nine-foot double doors into a large foyer of wall-to-wall cream-colored carpeting. The overpowering floral mix of gardenias, gladioli and lilies made me gag. A gangly man with a prominent nose and an Adam's apple the size of a cantaloupe ushered us into the chapel. The place was packed but there were enough chairs in the next to last row to accommodate the four of us.

Perfect. I sat and looked around to see if I could find a man with a bald spot.

Whoa! The late afternoon sun slanting through the arched stained-glass windows of the chapel cast jewel-toned motes of light throughout the room. The sun glistened on the backs of the people seated in the twenty rows in front of us. A sea of shimmering balding heads, ranging from small, glowing bald spots to round, gleaming domes, greeted us.

I gasped and turned to Stan and Liz. They convulsed with silent laughter at my consternation. Shoot. We had at least sixty suspects with glow-in-the-dark bald spots.

Liz whispered to Stan and pointed toward the front of the room at a man with salt-and-pepper hair. No bald spot that I could see. When he shifted, I recognized Brian's profile. He must be here on behalf of the District Attorney's office. Brian said something to the man seated next to him. He nodded in response.

A big man with thick chestnut-brown hair. And very broad shoulders.

I slunk down, hoping Tom wouldn't turn around. Liz, who had no concept of the word "discreet," blew a kiss in Brian's direction. He looked surprised to see her and nudged Tom.

I couldn't make myself any smaller unless I crawled under my chair. Tom's stare burned through me. Fortunately, a tall man with a full head of wavy white hair walked up to the podium and began to address the crowd. Tom turned to face the speaker.

The service lasted well over an hour. The music and glowing oratory extolling the nurturing character of Dr. Jeremy Slater made me heavy-hearted. The sound of muffled weeping and sniffling almost drowned out the speakers.

How ironic that someone so health conscious should be cut down in the prime of his life. I began to feel it was completely my fault Jeremy had died. I'd lured him to dinner at the River Inn. The fact that he landed in the river without any help from me seemed irrelevant at this point.

Hushed sobs emanated from my right. Stan held a tissue pressed against his nose.

"What's wrong?" I whispered.

"Jeremy was such a wonderful man." A tear rolled down Stan's cheek. "His loss is so tragic."

I always knew Stan was compassionate, but the guy hadn't even met Jeremy.

The seemingly endless service finally ended. The minister announced that guests were invited to Mark Slater's house to mingle and mourn together.

Since we sat in the back of the chapel, we waited for the rows of mourners to leave. I held an impromptu consultation to decide if we should go to Mark Slater's house.

Stan was all for it. "I haven't had an opportunity to use my investigative prowess. Plus there are a couple of guys I'd like to meet."

My mother chimed in, "I recognized several of the physicians. I'd like to give them my business card. Doctors are excellent real estate prospects."

"I want to talk to Brian," Liz said. "I've barely seen him in the past two days."

Someone needed to talk to her team about priorities.

We moved into the foyer, now filled with wall-to-wall dark suits. The crush of people made mingling difficult and detecting impossible.

The crowd swallowed my friends. I was about to climb on one of the brocade Louis XV chairs to see if I could locate them when a hand gripped my elbow and hauled me back into the chapel.

CHAPTER TWENTY

The chapel was as dark as the inside of a coffin. The hand clasping mine was strong and I couldn't break away. Was my assailant the killer? Which bald man would it turn out to be?

No big bad baldies. Just one shaggy-haired angry detective.

"Tom," I said in relief. My heart still beat like a bongo drum on speed.

"I thought I ordered you not to come," he growled.

I yanked my hand from his and folded my arms over my chest. "Who do you think you are ordering me not to attend the memorial service of a man who was the kindest, most compassionate and intelligent man I've ever met, present company included. His loss is incredibly tragic and the least I can do is share memories of the last moments of his life with his family."

I turned on my heel. My dramatic exit was stymied because I couldn't locate the door in the dark. Suddenly both doors flung open. A familiar profile appeared in a beam of light.

Hank.

My ex rushed to my side, fist raised, ready to come to my rescue. Tom glared at him then stomped out without another word.

"What the hell are you doing here?" I asked, frustrated with all of the men in my life.

"I was talking to some friends when I saw that man grab you." Hank put his arm around my shoulder and drew me close. "Who was that guy? You know I'd do anything to keep you safe."

I took a long hard look at Hank. He seemed sincere, but an ex-husband's sincerity was questionable on the best of days. I brushed his arm away, opened the massive door and re-entered the lobby. "I didn't expect to see you here. How do you know Jeremy?"

"We ran into each other at a Sig Ep fraternity reunion last August," he replied. "Jeremy was a year ahead of me and we didn't hang out that much during college. He wasn't much of a partier."

Spoken by the Panty Raid Prince of Sigma Phi Epsilon.

"When I found out he was a doctor, I asked for his business card. Remember when I hurt my back a few months ago? I haven't had medical insurance since our divorce so he was willing to give me a break on his fees."

"Did you guys chat about anything other than your injury?" I asked.

"We talked about the construction business, how it's really been in the tank. I hinted maybe he'd like to hire me to build him a house. He's a doctor. He must have tons of cash."

I had visions of Hank running around the frat house wearing his tightie-whities over his head. Just the kind of guy I'd hire to build a custom home.

"Any luck with that?" I asked.

"Nah, he wasn't interested. He said he was having some loan issues and wondered if I could help him out. I told him that was your area of expertise. In fact, I gave him your card."

Hank moved closer, mere inches from me. "Is that how the two of you ended up dating?"

I moved back, stumbling as my foot caught in the carpet. Hank caught me. He was so close I could taste the onions on his breath. Before I could respond, Liz appeared at my side. "Bugger off, Hank," she said, with a look so scathing even my ex could get the hint. Liz had always intimidated Hank and apparently still did. He quickly melted into the crowd.

She curled an arm around my waist. "Are you okay, luv? Did Hank say something to upset you?"

"No, but I was surprised to see him. I didn't realize he knew Jeremy from college. Hank said he gave him my card but Jeremy didn't mention the connection when we first met."

"Jeremy probably thought you wouldn't go out with him if you knew he and Hank were acquainted."

"Good point. Did Brian complain about us being here? Tom went ballistic. I sort of intimated he couldn't touch Jeremy when it came to intelligence and compassion." I reached into my purse, grabbed a tissue, and blew my nose. "But he's absolutely right. We don't have any business being here."

"Bollocks. These men are all alike. Brian wasn't happy I was here, even after I told him your theory of finding the bald-headed guy. It would serve them right if we discover something."

"Absolutely. It's not like Tom's discovered the murderer. Look what happened when Anne in HR found out about my relationship with Jeremy. Now my career is on the line as well as my reputation."

"Let me say goodbye to Brian. I'm sure I'll get him to come around to my point of view tonight." She flicked her hand through her bronzed curls and sauntered over to Brian. Even in a suit, Liz's curvaceous hips swung seductively. The man didn't stand a chance.

I looked around for the rest of my retinue. Stan conversed with a thirtyish man of average height and build. I scrutinized the back of his head—at least one baldy was under investigation. Although, knowing Stan, he was trying to determine which team the guy was slugging for.

My mother was chatting with a heavyset woman wearing a tweed suit and a tall man with a full head of hair. As I walked up, I overheard her say, "Laurel thinks she saw the murderer. That's why we came here tonight. To see if she could recognize him."

Some detective. By the end of the evening, she'd probably tell every bald man in the room about our investigating. Fortunately, Mother was speaking with Peter Tyler. I recognized the woman as Penny, the receptionist from the Centurion office.

"Sssssh," I hissed in my mother's ear. She looked confused so I moved closer and whispered, "You're not supposed to tell everyone what we're doing. You might tip off the murderer."

"Don't be silly. They won't tell anyone about our detecting, will you?"

Penny's eyes sparkled as she responded. "Are you kidding? This is great stuff. I'm gonna get me a deerstalker hat and magnifying glass. Big bad bald-headed guys, ha, ha, ha." She whacked me on the back and strode off chuckling.

My mother looked miffed as she stared at the departing receptionist. I wagered Penny wouldn't be laughing in the morning. The last thing an employee wanted to do was get on the wrong side of Barbara Bingham's desk.

"I'll keep everything you've said confidential," Peter said. "But don't you think this could be dangerous?"

"Trust me. If we learn anything, we'll immediately share it with the police," I replied. "I don't want to be a hero. I just want my life to return to normal. I'm tired of being a suspect in two murders."

"You're involved in *two different* murders?" Peter's eyebrows jumped a couple of inches and his voice ratcheted up to a tenor.

I was trying to figure out how to respond when Liz and Stan appeared, rescuing me from having to go into any further detail. Peter said goodbye and departed without mentioning dinner the following week. Did that mean our date was off? A woman suspected of two murders probably wouldn't be a social asset in the top producer circle.

The four of us climbed in the car and headed for Mark Slater's house.

"This investigating is way more difficult than I thought it would be," Liz said. "I asked two couples what they were doing the Saturday night Jeremy was killed. They both walked away. Maybe I need to be a little more subtle."

"You think?" Stan mocked her. "The sheriff's department may be able to use the storm trooper approach, but we civilians need to be more discreet."

"So what did you find out, Mr. Discreet?" Liz punched Stan in the shoulder.

"Watch it. I found out one of Jeremy's neighbors is gay. We're meeting for a drink tomorrow night." Stan grinned. "His name is Barry and he's been single for a while also."

"Terrific." Liz said. "But what if he's the killer? Did he have a bald spot?"

"Practically every man at the service was balding somewhere on his cranium, including Jeremy's brother," Stan said. "We need to check him out too. You know, in ninety percent of murders, it's a close friend or relative."

"True," my mother replied. "They also say to follow the money."

"Exactly what we're going to do," I announced. Someone had to take charge of my merry band of investigators. "The one thing we know for certain is that Jeremy was about to buy a house in Lake Tahoe. But he had some concerns about the purchase."

"What kind of concerns?" Stan asked.

"He never had a chance to tell me. But if anybody can squeeze information out of a bereaved mourner, you guys can."

Liz and Stan exchanged glances. As pep talks went, it sort of sucked.

"Here we are." Mother expertly maneuvered the car into a parallel parking space. Parking skills are obviously not a genetic trait. The last time I'd parallel parked, my rear bumper became bosom buddies with a fire hydrant.

The Slaters' house was located on the country-club side of Serrano, an area of huge homes fronting the Robert Trent Jones-designed golf course. I stopped to confirm the address, but once we climbed the limestone steps of the imposing French Manor-style mansion, there was no doubt this was the Slater residence. Lights blazed from every gabled window.

It took the four of us to push open the massive paneled door. As we stepped on the ivory marble floor, my mother nudged my arm. She pointed to the enormous chandelier twenty feet above our heads, shooting Aurora Borealis rays of light.

"Waterford."

Wow. Knowing what one Waterford crystal wine glass cost, I couldn't imagine the dollars invested in that light fixture. I bet they didn't buy it at Home Depot.

We followed other dark suits into the living room, which was almost the size of my entire house. The two spotless ivory sofas flanking the fireplace would never survive a day around my kids. The perfectly coordinated yellow-and-blue chairs and matching draperies and rugs looked like something out of *Architectural Digest*. I was both impressed and disappointed. Mark Slater didn't need Jeremy's money, unless they were mortgaged to the hilt.

I glanced at the paintings hanging on the walls. Original works of art including some early twentieth-century artists. Definitely not the thirty-nine-dollar landscapes I've purchased at weekend sales at the Holiday Inn.

Many of the guests seemed acquainted with one another, probably relatives, or friends and neighbors. A petite woman with spiked platinum-blond hair, dressed in a clingy black Lycra spandex dress, more suitable for clubbing than mourning, waved at us. Liz waved back.

"Who's that?" I asked.

"Tara. The receptionist from Jeremy's office. With the acne issue."

Liz swirled her head to the left and the right. "Lots of good spa candidates here. I should have brought more business cards."

"You're going to market at a memorial service?"

My brash friend chuckled. "Hey, with my health and beauty tips these women can live ten years longer. Haven't you heard that collagen loss is approaching epidemic proportions?" She crossed the room and greeted Tara.

Stan noticed his new acquaintance, Barry, standing by the enormous limestone fireplace, so he wandered over. My mother drifted across the room, smiling animatedly at two elderly couples.

So much for my team.

My stomach gurgled. Even Nancy Drew didn't look for clues on an empty stomach and it had been eight hours since I'd eaten. The best place to start was wherever the food was.

I maneuvered through the crowd in the living room and across the entry into an equally enormous dining room. Plates of colorful pungent food covered the glossy mahogany table, which could have been Sheraton or Chippendale, but definitely not Ikea. The aromas of garlic, onion and chocolate perked up my salivary glands.

I contemplated getting two plates, to keep myself balanced, but decided it would be difficult to shake hands with potential suspects. There was only one other couple in the room. The man's bald dome was as bright as the highly polished table. He looked to be in his early seventies, tall and stooped. I couldn't imagine him knocking Jeremy into the river. But timing was everything. If he pushed Jeremy the right way, it might have worked.

I sidled closer and extended my right hand. "I'm Laurel McKay, a close friend of Jeremy's. Are you members of the family?"

The man set his wine glass down to shake my hand. "Jeremy is, or rather was, my nephew. I'm Henry Slater and this is my wife,

Bonnie." Bonnie nodded at me with red-rimmed eyes as she stared silently at her plate of hors d'oeuvres.

I always feel inept talking to relatives of the deceased. "I'm so sorry for your loss. I will truly miss Jeremy."

Henry Slater focused watery blue eyes on me. "How were you acquainted with my nephew, my dear?"

"We were friends." No point going into more detail. I tried to think of something relevant to ask them. Interrogating required far more tactical skills than I seemed to possess.

"This is a lovely home. Mark must be very successful in his line of work." I grabbed a piece of bruschetta and bit into it. Yum. Great caterer.

"Mark is an attorney." Henry answered my implied question. "He works in my law firm. In fact, the whole family consists of lawyers with the exception of Jeremy. I guess you could call him an ambulance receiver, not an ambulance chaser as my profession is often derided."

All attorneys. So money probably wouldn't be a motive among this family. Unless someone was a lousy lawyer.

My mouth and brain could have used some coordination as I crunched on the bruschetta and asked, "I wonder who Jeremy's beneficiaries are."

Henry seemed taken aback by my lack of tact. He stepped away and placed his arm around his wife's waist. "Let's go, Bonnie. It was nice meeting you, I suppose," he added under his breath. They left the room with disgusted looks on their faces.

I didn't blame them. I was disgusted with myself. I had zero skill in conducting a discreet inquiry. The senior Slaters had left their plates behind. They probably lost their appetite after speaking with me. I wished I had the same problem. My stomach was carrying on a conversation with itself and it didn't sound happy.

Maybe my questioning was so incompetent because my brain was carbohydrate deprived. I eyed the gold-rimmed platters of desserts, torn between the chocolate mousse and an apple crumble. Someone tapped my arm and I reluctantly transferred my gaze from the delectable pastries to the new arrival.

"Hey, Vivian. I didn't know you would be here."

"I felt like I had to come. Jeremy was very special to me." She looked wistful as she stared at the bountiful buffet spread in front of us. I couldn't tell if Vivian was contemplating the loss of her personal physician, or the array of dessert choices.

"So Stan told me you were dating Jeremy." Her chins bobbled in unison as she questioned me. "And now you're all trying to find the killer. Do you have any idea who did it?"

I shrugged. If only I knew.

"How about you? Can you think of anyone who would want to harm him?" I asked as I struggled to reach a chocolate-chip cookie from a plate situated in the center of the enormous table.

Success! I turned back to my co-worker, hoping she might possess some worthwhile information about her favorite doctor. Her somber brown eyes almost matched the shade of the chips in the cookie I'd snagged.

"Nope," she said curtly. "I'll let you and Stan play detective." Vivian walked out the door empty-handed. Amazing. I wished I had her fortitude and could abstain from the carbs lined up in front of me. Jeremy would have been so proud that his patient continued to adhere to his nutritional advice.

Vivian bumped into Peter on her way out. He apologized then joined me.

"I see you've found a few tempting items," he teased, as my gaze bounced between him and the chocolate petit four I'd snagged.

I chuckled as I eyed my overflowing plate. "You disappeared from the service so fast I assumed you weren't coming to the reception."

"Sorry," he said, looking sheepish. "I was a little freaked when you mentioned you're a suspect in two murders. But I thought it over and I've got to admit it takes guts to look for a killer."

Guts? Maybe. Stupidity? Far more likely.

I swallowed the last bite of the petit four then realized that Peter could be a useful ally from a real estate standpoint.

"When Jeremy and I were at dinner the other night, he seemed concerned about the purchase of a vacation home in Tahoe. Did you handle his real estate transactions?" I asked. "By the way, how did you know him?"

"Jeremy is, I mean, was my doctor." Peter looked thoughtful as he gnawed on a carrot stick. "A lot of Centurion agents were his patients, but I'm not sure whom he worked with in our office.

He never called me for any real estate advice if that's what you're asking." Peter pushed his plate away. "I still can't believe his drowning wasn't an accident. You're certain the sheriff's department thinks he was murdered?"

"Absolutely. I have it right from the horse's mouth." Although lately he'd been more like a horse's ass.

"So what's the next step in your investigation?" Peter asked.

"Yes, Nancy Drew, what is the next step?"

Busted.

CHAPTER TWENTY-ONE

"Hi Tom," I muttered. "Have you met Peter Tyler? He works at Centurion with my mother."

Tom shook Peter's hand. "Would you excuse us? I need to discuss something with Laurel."

"Certainly," Peter responded graciously. "I'll see you next week."

"Can't wait," I said.

Tom grabbed my elbow, and I relinquished my plate of goodies as he led me into the living room, which appeared even more crowded than before.

I scowled at him, not sure if I was more annoyed that he'd removed me from Peter's company, or that I'd left my desserts behind. A few people walked past giving us curious looks.

"Now what? Can't I have a conversation with a handsome, cultured man without you dragging me away?" I said.

"Why won't you let me do my job without interfering? Don't you realize any one of these people could be the killer?" Frustration lined his face as he worried about dead bodies, dangerous murderers and one stubborn female.

The hunk of my dreams stood in front of me. Begging me to stop meddling in his investigation. What indeed was my problem? Stubbornness? Stupidity? I didn't even know the answer. All I knew was this attractive and occasionally sensitive man was pleading with me to stop looking for a killer. Tom moved closer.

My antenna quivered but it wasn't due to his presence. My gang of detectives had surrounded us en masse.

"Laurel." Mother folded her arms across her pinstriped chest. "Would you care to introduce us?"

My cheeks flushed. "This is Detective Hunter. He's in charge of the investigation into Jeremy's death. Tom, this is my mother, Barbara Bingham."

"I'm pleased to meet you." Tom offered his hand and bestowed his high voltage smile on her.

My mother smiled and kept his hand clasped in her own. "How nice to meet you." She lowered her voice and I couldn't make out her next few words.

Tom shook his head. "I'm sorry but I'm not authorized to share that information. It's confidential police business."

She gave him the look that had terrified hundreds of her competitors. "Then I'll have to ask Detective Bradford. I'm sure he'll accommodate me. Let's go, Laurel."

With my team surrounding me there wasn't much I could say other than goodbye. Tom looked relieved that I was leaving. One less amateur detective to worry about.

I waved good-bye to Vivian who stood in the lobby chatting with someone else. Our group filed out the door and down the steps. Deep in thought, I lagged behind the others. When a heavyset man bolted out the front door and crashed into my shoulder, I lost my balance. I grabbed hold of the first thing I could find. His arm.

"Dr. Radovich!"

I wasn't sure if he would remember me from my brief visit to his office. He stared as if trying to recall my name. Recognition suddenly dawned.

"Ms. McKay." He spoke in that same brusque tone I remembered. "How is your leg feeling now?"

It felt fine before he crashed into me, but that didn't seem the most tactful response. "Much better. You seem in a hurry this evening." I jogged alongside attempting to match his brisk pace.

He raised his shaggy brows, muttered something under his breath and rushed down the street in the opposite direction from my mother's car. The chirp of a remote entry key signaled he'd reached his destination, a gas-guzzling black Hummer parked at the end of the block.

"Laurel, let's go," Liz called out, motioning to me. I hurried down the pavement.

"Follow that car."

My quick-witted detective trio responded in unison. "Huh?"

Luckily, my mother has excellent reflexes. She jumped in the driver's seat, turned the key, and had her right foot hovering over the accelerator by the time Liz, Stan and I belted ourselves in.

We briefly lost sight of our prey but caught up as he waited for the entrance gate to open.

"Don't get too close," I warned. Our front grille hovered a few inches from his rear bumper. My plan did not include plowing into the car of a murder suspect.

Liz peered over my mother's head. "Who are we following?"

"Dr. Radovich. He was acting in a suspicious manner."

"How do you know what's suspicious behavior for the doctor?" Stan asked.

"Um..."

We followed the SUV as it turned left on El Dorado Hills Blvd. The doctor drove up the Highway 50 on-ramp and headed east toward Placerville and the Sierras.

My mother sped up, remaining a few car lengths behind. "What should I do? Do you have any idea where he's going? Where does he live?"

Three excellent questions. Too bad I didn't have answers for any of them.

"His practice is nearby so he must live around here somewhere."

"I don't have time for a wild goose chase," she said.

Like I did?

Three exits later, the Hummer moved into the right lane. We followed directly behind him. He exited the freeway at an off-ramp that dead-ended at one location.

The Goldenwing Casino.

The doctor pulled the super-sized SUV into a parking stall and quickly jumped out, heading straight for the casino entrance. We parked in a stall a few cars down from his.

"It's somewhat unusual to go directly from your partner's memorial service to a casino, isn't it?" Mother asked.

Liz bounced in her seat. "I forgot to tell you. Tara, their receptionist, mentioned two creepy guys stopped in the office the day after we were there. That would have been Thursday. They didn't have an appointment but they insisted on speaking with Dr. Radovich. She said the guys could have starred in the Sopranos. After they left, Radovich canceled all his appointments for the rest of the week. He told her tonight that he's going on vacation for a couple of weeks."

"I bet the doctor owes the casino tons of markers and they sent their goons after him," Stan said.

I turned around and shot him my "puhleeze" look.

"It could happen. There's Mafiosi everywhere," he said.

"You have got to stop watching all those crime shows," I said.

"Hey, just cause I'm gay doesn't mean I spend my evenings watching the Home and Garden network," Stan replied. "Although did you see *Design on a Dime* last night?"

"Amazing ideas for staging houses," Mother said. "Did you see the one the week before—*Don't Break your Budget on your Bedroom?*"

"I really liked the segment they did on *Having Fun with your Futon*," Liz said.

"Guys," I said. "Can you switch from designing mode back to detective mode?"

"What do you suggest, Miss Drew?" Stan asked.

I shrugged. Ms. Drew was running out of clever ideas. Not that I'd actually had any to begin with.

"It's almost seven. I told Brian I'd meet him at seven-thirty," Liz said.

"I need to get home, too," I said. "There's probably nothing further we can do here anyway."

"Do you want me to come back and spy on the doc?" Stan asked. "See if he's a high roller?"

I hesitated. "Don't do anything that could be dangerous."

"Oh c'mon. Tonight's been the most fun I've had since we went shopping together. I need a little excitement in my life."

"Okay. Be careful. I don't want him to suspect anything."

"I'll go home and change into something more suitable. Maybe a tux—you know, the James Bond look. So I'll fit in at the casino."

I pictured my slight friend playing roulette, dressed in a black tuxedo, surrounded by senior citizens in pastel sweat suits, the mainstay of the Indian casino.

Mother spoke up. "It's hard to believe two men so different could be partners in a medical practice."

I compared the charming and kind Dr. Slater to his surly, somewhat scary partner. Not exactly two peas in a pod. I twisted around and looked at my two best friends. No one would put us in the same peapod either.

We pulled into the parking lot in front of the Starbucks. Liz climbed out of the backseat then stopped. "Laurel, you know that bald man you saw with Jeremy the night he was murdered? What if he left the River Inn after their conversation was over and someone else pushed Jeremy in the river?"

All eyes turned to me. Liz had a point. Did the suspect list just increase by thousands of people who weren't bald?

Stan shoved Liz out of the car. "C'mon sweetie, I've got a stakeout at the casino. Don't worry, Laurel. You'll figure it out."

Liz and Stan exchanged farewells and I hugged my mother good-bye. "You were a big help tonight."

"Of course I was, dear. You children would have been lost without me," she said. I eased my leg out of the car as she imparted her standard maternal reminder. "Don't forget your purse."

"I've never forgotten it. Yet. Good night." I slammed the door then stomped over to my own car. Mothers!

Speaking of which, it was time this mother checked on her offspring. The phone rang five times before Jenna picked up.

"Hi, honey, everything okay?"

"Yeah, we're fine. I'm on the phone with Katie. What time will you be home? Some guy called you three times but he won't leave his name."

That was odd. It seemed like every male I knew had been at the service this evening.

"I'll be home in twenty minutes." I heard my son hollering in the background. "Why is Ben yelling?"

"Oh, you know Ben, always whining. C'mon, Mom, Katie's holding for me."

"Tell her you'll call her back. Put your brother on the phone."

Ben's shrill voice blasted out of my cell. "Mom, when are you coming home? Jenna is making me play with my Legos. I don't want to play with my Legos, but she says I have to do whatever she says."

Honestly. I told Ben to put Jenna back on the line.

"What?"

"Ben said you're making him play with his Legos even though he doesn't want to."

"I'm in charge so he has to do what I tell him." I heard the implied "Duh" in her voice. It was obvious my daughter needed a few lessons in leadership training.

"You can't dictate what toys he plays with."

"Why not?"

I counted to five. "As long as he isn't doing anything wrong, he can play with whatever toy he wants."

"Fine, whatever. Can I go now? I promised to call Katie back." She sounded anxious to appease me and get on with her busy social life. I made a mental note to mentor her on her management skills.

The discussion about Legos reminded me that Garrett lived just a few blocks away. He was single and childless, so I had no idea who his beneficiaries were, but it was possible his home might be for sale. I couldn't remember his exact address but if I could get in the entrance gate, I was certain I could find it again and see if there was a for sale sign on the lawn.

Sneaking into the subdivision proved a simple task. Someone must have crashed into the gate because it was propped wide open. I missed Garrett's street on my first attempt. If the roads all looked alike in the daytime, the starless sky didn't help my evening tour. I finally located his street and residence. The crime scene tape had been removed and a green for-sale sign was posted on the front lawn. I grabbed a pen and paper and wrote down the agent's name and phone number. Mother could arrange for us to look inside.

I reached the entrance without any unwanted detours. I turned right, heading east on Serrano Parkway. Once the tree-lined parkway ended, I turned left on Bass Lake Road. It should take less than fifteen minutes to get home.

I drove down the two-lane road, my brain contemplating the tidbits of information we'd pulled together. None of which made much sense. Suddenly two beams of light behind me blinded me with their brilliance. The high beams of the truck or SUV flooded my car with enough megawatts to light up Arco Arena.

The vehicle moved closer and closer until it was inches from my bumper. I accelerated but it stuck to me like glue. I slammed the gas pedal to the floor. My car shimmied to the left. I yanked the steering wheel in the same direction and my tires skidded on the gravel alongside the road. We were approaching a ninety-degree curve with a posted speed of forty miles per hour. My eyes flashed to the speedometer.

Crap. I was doing seventy. If I didn't slow down, my car would never make the curve. I glanced in the rearview mirror to see how close my tailgater was.

I barely had time to scream before the tank riding my bumper slammed into me.

CHAPTER TWENTY-TWO

I always wondered what the phrase "your life flashing before your eyes" meant. In my case, it meant a whirling kaleidoscope composed of the faces of my loved ones, superimposed over the oak trees whizzing past the windows of my car.

Bam. The Prius landed on a rutted dirt track. My first thought was that if I survived this ordeal, I would finally break down and replace the shocks. My hands froze to the steering wheel, stuck in the official ten and two position, as I tried to hold on.

The screech of the brakes announced the end of our jarring journey. The car landed with a thud and a groan. The front bumper, face to face with the massive trunk of one of those great old dowagers—the California oak tree.

My air bag must be broken or it wasn't set to go off. I rested for a few minutes with my head pressed against the steering wheel. Headlights approached from the opposite direction. The noise of the engine indicated the car was slowing. I prayed the lunatic who rammed me wasn't coming back to finish the job.

Neither a lunatic nor a Good Samaritan. The car rounded the curve and proceeded on its way.

I opened my door and eased out. The midnight blue sky made it difficult to assess the damage but if there was any, it was minimal. I breathed in the pungent night air. A few deep breaths and I started to calm down. My chest felt like a small elephant had careened over me, but my back and neck seemed to have handled the impact okay.

This spot was too dark and isolated for me to hang around. I climbed into my sturdy little car, backed down the muddy path to the road, and headed north once again. My eyes remained super-glued to the rearview mirror all the way home. Once I was safely in my subdivision, I breathed a sigh of relief. I pulled into the garage, entered the house and to my amazement, found Ben engrossed in his Legos. Kids.

The next morning my chest still ached but that seemed to be the only residual side effect from the previous night's encounter. I examined the car in the garage under the fluorescent lighting. The rear bumper was dented and the front bumper had some scratches from the tree I'd nudged, but the Prius had proven surprisingly durable.

The big question was whether there was a connection between the SUV ramming my car and our detecting. Someone might have followed us from the casino. Or followed me home from Garrett's house. And that person could likely have been the killer.

The coffee I'd drunk earlier burned a hole in my stomach as I considered that a murderer might have targeted me.

On the other hand, it could have been a teenager out for a joyride. I debated whether to call Tom and tell him about the previous night's accident, but decided to wait until later in the day. It was too early in the morning for another one of his lectures.

I arrived at the office to an empty lobby. No Vivian in sight. Maybe she was still upset about Jeremy's death and decided not to come to the office today. I stopped to say hi to Stan but his cubicle was empty. No sign of him anywhere.

Where was everyone? Then I remembered Stan's undercover mission at the casino. All thoughts of my accident fled as I worried about my friend. I would never forgive myself if something happened to him.

I was about to file a report on a missing underwriting assistant when I walked by Earl's office. Stan sat in front of our boss's desk and he didn't look happy. Neither did Earl. I was relieved my pal was safe, but what was going on?

My phone rang and I picked up. "Laurel. Come to my office. Now." Earl's voice was curt. Not at all like the smitten boss who'd been hanging around my desk lately.

"Yes, sir." I grabbed a yellow legal pad, turned right, left then right again, arriving at Earl's office just as Stan rose. Stan averted his gaze from mine as he exited the office.

My chest constricted but I summoned up a fake smile. "Hi, Earl. I'm almost finished with yesterday's submissions."

Earl stood, walked to the door and closed it. Loudly. One might even suggest that he slammed it. I surmised this would not be a social visit. He lowered himself into his ergonomically correct leather chair, which groaned in response, then waved at me to sit in one of the visitor chairs.

"I'm not going to waste your time or mine. It appears you haven't been honest with me." Earl grabbed a forest-green Mont Blanc pen and rolled the slim cylinder back and forth over his desk blotter, the only uncluttered area on his desk.

"I don't know what you're talking about." I perched on the edge of my chair. That was no lie.

Earl lifted his head. He looked tense and...angry. "It's come to the bank's attention that you're being investigated by the sheriff's department for the murder of a respected member of our medical community."

My stomach clenched as my mind raced. I couldn't imagine Stan telling Earl about the investigation. Surely, Tom would forewarn me if they questioned anyone at the bank about me. Vivian knew that I'd dated Jeremy but she didn't know that I was a suspect. Did she?

I grabbed the arms of my chair for support. "I don't know where you could have received your information."

"From you—" He glared at me. "You told Anne Lewis about your involvement with Dr. Slater when you canceled your interview yesterday. She followed up by calling a friend of hers in the sheriff's department."

Rats. I squirmed in my seat, crossing and uncrossing my bare legs, trying to get comfortable. "Anne doesn't have all of the facts. Yes, I did go out on a date with Jeremy Slater. Yes, he did fall in the river. Yes, he did drown that evening. And yes, he was murdered."

Hmm. So far my defense was somewhat lacking. I decided to switch to the offensive. "I can't believe you would question my innocence. I barely knew Dr. Slater. Plus the sheriff's department doesn't consider me a suspect."

Or at least I didn't think Tom did. As far as Bradford, all bets were off. Actually all bets were probably on me.

"Even worse," Earl continued on, his expression morose, "a reporter from the *Mountain Democrat* has been hounding the president of the bank for a comment. Ask me how happy Mr. Chandler was about that."

I suspected Mr. Chandler, the bank president, wasn't too pleased to have a murder suspect working for the bank. Was the reporter that guy with the Draino chuckle? I had to get him off my back.

"You should have mentioned this situation to me. Not only is the bank's reputation at stake, but Dr. Slater was one of our best customers."

Great. Now I wasn't merely losing dates, I was also responsible for losing deposits.

"I'm sorry. Since I had nothing to do with Jeremy's death, I didn't think it was important for anyone at the bank to know about it. I promise to keep you informed about anything else I hear about the case."

"Make sure you do that."

His pen fidgeting was driving me crazy. I was about to grab it out of his hand when he dropped another bombshell. "If you hadn't joined the Love Club we wouldn't be in this predicament."

Interesting segue from death to dating. "I've only gone on two dates so far."

"Yes, but look what happened each time." His gaze started at my chest and drifted down to my crossed ankles. "There are eligible bachelors here in this office. Stick with people you know instead of this dating service."

Since I couldn't think of any bachelors at the bank that I personally considered eligible, I needed to direct the conversation elsewhere. "Did Anne mention rescheduling my interview?"

"The HR department decided they had sufficient candidates. Between missing your appointment and your involvement in a murder, they selected someone else."

My face fell at the news. This was turning out to be one crapola day.

"Looks like you're fated to stay in this department." Earl ran a hand over his balding pate, his smile so satisfied you'd think he'd won the lottery. "I promise to assign you additional responsibilities. It'll give us an opportunity to work closer together."

Oh goody. At least I was still employed although I would prefer a position where my boss wasn't hitting on me, harmless as Earl was.

I left his office and went straight, well, left, right, left, down to Stan's cube. I parked myself in the chair beside his desk. "Why the long face when you left Earl's office?"

Stan removed his glasses, rubbed his bloodshot eyes, then pushed the wire rims back on his pointed nose. "I should have told you before. When you applied for the branch manager posting, I assumed you would get it. I asked Earl if I could move up to a full underwriter. He said I could if they hired you for the manager position. I guess you didn't get it, right?"

I nodded glumly. "Evidently they prefer their branch managers not be murder suspects. I'm afraid if we don't solve these homicides, they'll fire me."

Stan's frown reversed into a grin. "Hey, wait until you hear what Stan Spade discovered last night."

"At the casino?"

He nodded. "It took me awhile to track Radovich down. That place is huge." Stan sent me a sheepish look. "And I got a little distracted by the dollar slots. But I won eighty bucks."

"Swell. So..."

"So after that I wandered around and finally spotted him in a private room in the back playing poker. Texas Hold 'em. Five thousand minimum."

"Five thousand dollars?"

"Yup, five thousand minimum just to get in the room. Only one table with six players. One guy had a ton of chips in front of him. Our doctor did not. He must have lost big and lost fast. I tell you, this guy definitely has a gambling problem."

"How long did you stay?"

"Not long. Once his chips disappeared, he walked away from the table so I left the casino. My eighty bucks was burning a hole in my pocket and I didn't want to lose it all in the slots."

"Excellent work. Are you ready for more?"

"Yeah, baby." He rubbed his palms together in the worst Austin Powers imitation I'd ever heard. I mentally rolled my eyes.

"Remember that first guy I went out with who was murdered?" I said.

"Sure. Garrett somebody. Why?"

"After we left the Slaters' house last night, I drove by his house. It's listed for sale so if my mother can get us in, we might find something the detectives missed. What do you think?"

"Are you kidding?" He flashed me a brilliant smile. "I'm in."

I called my mother's office. Penny said she was on a call and asked me to hold. The receptionist also asked if I'd eliminated any more dates.

Everyone's a comedian.

As I waited, I tried to recall my conversation with Earl. Something he'd mentioned didn't make sense. Mother's abrupt greeting interrupted my thought process. "What do you want, Laurel?"

"Oh, hi. I wondered if you could get me into Garrett Lindstrom's house in Serrano. I drove by last night, and it's listed for sale. Can you show it to Stan and me this afternoon?"

There was a slight delay and I heard her punching some device. "I'm booked almost all day, but I could squeeze you in between one and three. I need to call the listing agent but the house should be vacant so I can use my lockbox key."

"Perfect. We'll meet you there at two."

My observant mother would no doubt notice my crumpled hybrid. If she suspected my crash was due to our investigating, Garrett's key would be back in the lockbox faster than I could say Prius. I told Stan about the accident and asked if he could drive.

"You were rammed from behind? After we split up?" His jaw dropped so low it almost touched his loafers.

I nodded. "I'm amazed the car got away with only some scratches. Probably kids driving too fast and afraid to stop."

The freckles on his nose popped out as his face paled a few shades. "I think we may be asking the right questions. Someone is scared and they tried to stop you. Permanently."

My hand trembled and the pen I was holding slipped through my fingers and landed on the floor. I bent over to retrieve it. "You're probably right, but I have too much at stake. We just need to be more cautious from now on."

We both concurred with that decision. A few hours later, we left in Stan's car for our personal open house tour. We arrived at Garrett's a couple of minutes late due to two wrong turns, both of which Stan blamed on my poor directions. Gay men don't appear to have any better navigational skills than straight men.

Mother's gleaming Chrysler was parked in front of the garage. She stood on the front porch, arms crossed over her chest, the right foot of her Prada pump tapping her noticeable displeasure.

"You're late and you have lettuce on your blouse." She picked the offensive piece of foliage off my chest and flicked it on the front lawn.

"At least I'm wearing healthy food these days." I took a deep breath and tried to maintain my cool.

"The agent won't be meeting us so we can go inside." She inserted the key in the lock "I hope this isn't another wild goose chase."

Geez. Here we'd been collecting clues by the dozens. Not to mention the high probability someone had attempted to murder me last night. Although I probably shouldn't share that with the woman who brought me into this world.

The three of us entered the great room. All leather and glass-topped tables. Garrett was one of those white freaks. White leather sofa and carpet. A few abstract paintings in shades of white and gray.

Mother and Stan wandered down a long hallway to the left. I went the opposite direction into the kitchen, which followed the same theme, white cabinets with uncluttered black granite countertops. Stainless steel appliances. I opened a few doors but except for one cabinet, filled with plates and glasses, the shelves were empty.

Laughter radiated from the other end of the house. I followed the sound of their voices into the master suite, entering a replica of Hugh Hefner's bedroom straight out of the Playboy mansion. A leopard-printed furry thing covered the king-size bed. Mirrors lined most of the walls.

They both chuckled at the ceiling where an enormous oval mirror hung directly over the bed. Yuck.

Stereo equipment and a huge flat-screen television comprised the rest of the furnishings. Garrett probably had a collection of porn for late night screenings. I assumed the police had removed personal items of any significance. Calling Tom to find out was not an option.

Stan opened a drawer in the black lacquer dresser before I could stop him. After looking at the décor, I had no desire to learn anything further about Garrett. Like the style of his underwear. Or size. Ick. Too late. Stan held up a teeny-weeny zebra print thong.

I peeked in the bathroom, which continued the jungle theme with leopard-print wallpaper and matching towels. Where on earth did he find this stuff? There was a large Jacuzzi tub, an enormous dual-head shower stall, and an oversized brown wicker hamper. My mother and Stan walked up and peered over my shoulder.

"I would kill for a bathtub that size," I mused. My companions stared at me. Guess I could have phrased that better.

The room down the hall from the master bedroom was probably a guest room, very plain and furnished in beige on beige decor. The last room appeared to be Garrett's office. Now this was more like it. Garrett had a multitude of golfing souvenirs decorating the top of a glossy ebony desk. It sure beat the animal safari theme in his bedroom. Framed prints of what I gathered were famous golf courses hung next to a wall lined with polished black bookcases and file cabinets. Stan wandered over to examine the prints.

I opened a few of the file drawers but as I suspected, they were empty. Either cleaned out by Garrett or the sheriff's department.

"Anything in there?" Mother asked.

I sighed and slammed another drawer shut. "Nope. I don't know what I was thinking. I guess I'm just desperate to find something that would point to a suspect other than me."

"If you'd only listened to me," she complained, "and not joined that stupid Love Club."

"Hey, what's done is done. You don't need to air our dirty laundry in front of Stan."

His face lit up. "Dirty laundry. *CSI* always goes through the laundry hamper."

"Ick." My mother and I responded in unison. At least we agreed on something.

Stan wandered off to emulate his favorite investigators. I opened the rest of the desk drawers. Nada.

"Oh girls," my buddy trilled.

After accidentally viewing Garrett's zebra-print thong, I really didn't need to learn anything further about his personal habits, but his office wasn't providing anything useful. We returned to the master bath.

"*Voila*." Stan pointed to the opened wicker hamper with the panache of Vanna White. The hamper was stuffed with teeny animal print bikinis, T-shirts and dirty socks. No vowels or consonants that I could see.

"Stick your hand all the way to the bottom," he instructed.

It was a very big hamper full of dirty laundry. Double Ick.

"Stan, you have five seconds to reveal the secret in the bottom."

He smirked.

"Wait a minute. That's the secret, right? A false bottom?"

"That's my girl detective."

I knocked the hamper over. Not subtle but effective. Dirty disgusting smelly underwear, tube socks, T-shirts and ...

Tax returns?

CHAPTER TWENTY-THREE

I grabbed the stapled returns off the floor. "Interesting choice of filing cabinet."

"He must have been afraid someone would go through his files in the office and the house. Who would think to look in his dirty laundry?" Stan's smile was as wide as the double-sink vanity.

Underwriters review tax returns all day long so it only took me a few minutes to rifle through the pages. Nothing jumped out other than the intriguing fact that all six returns showed excellent income, in the hundreds of thousands. Maybe Garrett kept them in a special place because they were his best clients. He was definitely a weirdo. Just because the returns were filed with his dirty laundry didn't mean there was anything dirty about them.

We debated what to do with the documents. Since I was a prime suspect, I couldn't keep them. My mother wanted nothing to do with the returns. I reluctantly turned them over to Stan Spade's safekeeping until I figured out a way to tell Tom. We locked the house. Stan and I hurried back to the office hoping Earl wouldn't notice we'd been gone over an hour.

I plowed through my loan files to make up for the time I'd been away, then left shortly after five to pick up my son. I'd planned on cooking a homemade meal for a change, but soccer practice went into overtime. The unhappy duet of Ben's and my growling stomachs left me no choice. I was forced to buy a home-cooked Chinese dinner from Lotus Garden, the closest takeout to our house.

The phone rang as I cleared the dishes—okay the cartons—from the table. Jenna grabbed it. She spoke briefly then handed it to me. Who is it? I mouthed. She shrugged and walked out of the kitchen.

"Hello," I said, my voice husky.

"Hi Laurel. It's Peter."

"Oh, hi." My heart rate slowed from its initial take-off when I thought Tom was calling me.

"We're still on for this weekend, I hope. I thought we'd try a new restaurant in Placerville called The Sequoia. It's received some excellent reviews."

"Sounds good."

We agreed he would pick me up at seven on Friday. We chatted for a few minutes until I begged off saying I had to help Ben with his homework. After my car crash, I was beginning to have reservations about going out with Peter. What if something happened to my mother's colleague while he was out with me?

Was it time to start doling out pepper spray to my dates?

The phone startled me. Probably my mother ensuring I hadn't screwed up her matchmaking efforts.

"Yes, Mother, Peter and I are still going out Friday night." I grabbed a sponge and started wiping the kitchen counters.

"Well, that's disappointing news," said a deep familiar voice. Startled, I knocked over Ben's unfinished glass of milk. White liquid spurted across my lactose-intolerant silk blouse.

"You are so lame," I muttered. I dabbed at the spots with a wet towel.

"Excuse me?"

I apologized for my lame remark and hoped Tom wouldn't remember my earlier comment.

"So, about this dinner date Friday night," he said. I swear the man has a memory like an elephant. Of course that could be the reason he made detective.

"Just dinner at The Sequoia with a friend of my mother's. You know how that goes."

"Sure. My parents have fixed me up a few times. They feel I've been a grieving widower long enough. They think Kristy needs a mother."

172

"A little feminine influence couldn't hurt," I agreed, envisioning the muddy tomboy as she attacked the boys on the soccer field. "It's hard to be both a mother and father at the same time. I guess you can relate to that firsthand."

"Definitely." There was a lull in the conversation. Should I tell him about our discovery today, my accident last night, or wait and find out why he called?

"Laurel, I've been thinking I was sort of off base last night, you know, at the memorial service. I realize you and your friends are only trying to clear your name and since you don't know what you're doing, you can't really interfere with our investigation."

Humph. If this was Tom's definition of an apology, it wasn't working.

"Great. I've managed to put my size twelve in it again."

I flopped into the nearest chair. This could be a lengthy phone call. "Would you like to start over?"

"First, I want to apologize for my behavior the other night. It was inexcusable." He paused. "By the way, do you really think it's safe to go to dinner Friday?"

"Safe for me, or my date? My mother would kill me if I canceled."

"Okay, but try to stay out of trouble."

"Trouble? Me?" I laughed. "I don't suppose there's anything new with *my* case."

"One dead end after another. No pun intended. Add to that a fatal motorcycle accident near Salmon Falls Road late last night. You didn't crash into any bikes on your way home, did you?"

"No, but something crashed into me," I mumbled.

"What?" His shout was so loud I thought my receiver would explode.

"I was rear-ended last night. I just missed colliding with a tree."

"Are you okay? Did you report it?"

"No. I mean, I'm okay but I didn't report it. The car or truck that hit me just kept on going."

"Jesus H.," he swore. "Why didn't you call me? Where did it happen?"

"On Bass Lake Road. I was on my way home after driving by Garrett's house."

Uh oh. TMI. Too much information for a homicide detective.

"You just happened to drive by Lindstrom's house last night?" His voice had switched from warm concern into frostbite territory.

"Kind of. I wanted to see if the house was listed for sale."

"And?"

"It is. So Stan, Mother and I sort of looked at it today."

His voice softened, something I'd noticed didn't usually bode well for me.

"So now your fingerprints are all over the house, correct?"

Fingerprints. That was dumb. Next time I'd bring latex gloves with me.

"Well, sure, but my mother and Stan's prints are there too," I replied.

"Your mother and Stan are not murder suspects."

Right. "We found some clues." Surely he'd be happy about that.

"Clues we missed." His sigh was so forceful I felt it through my receiver.

"Did your guys find the tax returns in the laundry hamper?"

"What?"

I spent the next five minutes explaining Stan's unusual, but effective foray into Garrett's dirty laundry.

"I'll get someone over to his house right away," he said.

"Um, there's a strong possibility the returns aren't there anymore."

I held the phone away from my ear while he ranted. When the decibels diminished to a moderate level, I jumped back in.

"We were afraid the killer might come back to the house and discover them. There has to be a reason why Garrett hid the returns in the hamper. I assumed you wouldn't want me to hang on to them since I'm your number one suspect, so Stan took them home. He'll bring them to the office tomorrow."

"Fine, just fine," he replied.

Funny, he didn't sound fine.

"Would you like to know what we discovered when we followed Dr. Radovich?" Maybe that would put him in a better mood.

"You followed Dr. Radovich?" He yelled in my ear. "When?"

"We accidentally ended up behind his car after Jeremy's memorial service," I muttered.

The sound of garbled conversation in the background drifted over the phone.

"I need to go. I'll be at the bank tomorrow to pick up those tax papers. But listen to me, Laurel. No more following suspects, no more attending memorial services, no more visiting dead guy's houses. My job is difficult enough without worrying about you all the time."

"But—"

"Goodbye." The phone slammed in my ear.

Alrighty then.

CHAPTER TWENTY-FOUR

I had barely settled into my office routine the next morning when the phone rang.

"Guess what I discovered?" Liz said.

"What?"

"Something dodgy is going on at Slater and Radovich's medical practice."

I closed my loan file. Detecting definitely trumped underwriting. Even though it meant putting aside the credit file of a well-known Hollywood personality buying a mansion in Lake Tahoe. Yes, a little glamour occasionally wanders into the life of a mortgage underwriter.

"What did you find out?" I asked.

"I stopped at their office yesterday to drop off some brochures for Tara. That kid may dress like a bimbo, but she's a brainy bimbo. After we chatted at the memorial service, she decided to do a little investigating herself. Neither she nor Carol have anything to do with the books, so she had to wade through a ton of clutter in Radovich's office before she found something."

Liz paused for effect. Why did my detectives have to be so dramatic?

"Tara eventually found the checkbook for the practice in his miscellaneous file. She has no idea how much money they normally keep in the account, but Dr. Radovich has been writing checks to himself every week for several months. For thousands of dollars."

"Wow. That ties in to the losses Stan noticed at the casino. I wonder if Jeremy realized what Radovich was doing."

"Should we follow him again?"

"No, we're supposed to leave that to the sheriff's department. When I spoke with Tom last night he was adamant we stay away from the doctor."

"Any new developments I should know about?" She giggled. "Either from a criminal or a sexual perspective?"

"Very funny. Most of our conversation consisted of him yelling. Although he did say he was worried about me."

"Worried about you getting hurt? Or worried he might have to arrest you?"

"Gee, Liz. You really know how to boost a girl's spirits." I looked up and almost fell out of my chair. "Stan Spade just appeared with our latest evidence. Call you later."

I hung up to greet my assistant. Clad in a belted beige trench coat and plaid fedora, Stan looked more like a pervert than a detective.

"Nice duds," I remarked.

He tipped his hat before he plunked it down on my desk. He held the tax returns clasped to his chest. "I swear I couldn't sleep a wink last night worrying someone might break in and steal these. I made an extra copy just to be on the safe side." He thrust the originals and the copies into my waiting arms.

"Did you look at them?" I asked.

"Nah. I figured my job was to discover the evidence. Your job is to evaluate it." At the sound of approaching footsteps, Stan grabbed his hat and slunk away. I quickly stashed the purloined papers in a drawer.

Carl King, manager of the loan-servicing department, paused in front of my desk. He was dressed in his standard navy blue suit, crisp white shirt and red-and-navy-striped tie. He handed two fat manila files to me. "I'd like you to review these delinquent loans. They're ready to go into foreclosure."

I grabbed the files and blinked at him in surprise. Despite other banks' issues, conservative Hangtown Bank hadn't foreclosed on a property in over twenty-five years.

"Did I approve them?"

"No. Mary Lou underwrote them and Earl countersigned since both loans are over a million. That's why I want you to examine them. Just to make sure..." he hesitated, obviously not wanting to cast aspersions on my co-workers. "Let's just say I'd like another set of eyes to check over the paperwork."

"Sure. I'll get right on it."

Carl smiled in appreciation. "Then I'll leave them in your capable hands."

I appreciated Carl's confidence and opened up the first file. The Carters, a wealthy couple, had purchased a two-million dollar house. The six-thousand-square-foot Tuscan style home was situated on a two-acre lot with magnificent views of Folsom Lake. The underwriter had approved a loan for 1.4 million, 70 percent of the sale price. According to the notes from the loan-servicing clerk, the borrowers had not returned any phone calls.

I flipped through the file. Just because our bank hadn't previously encountered any fraud didn't mean it was impossible. Technology provided creative tools for those with a criminal bent. It didn't take much brainpower to produce false documentation.

The monthly bank statements appeared authentic though. Our funding clerk had contacted their banks and verified their assets. The Carters' tax return, which showed sufficient dividends, interest and pension income to make the house payment looked legit. I compared the borrowers' signatures on page two of the tax return to the loan documents. Everything looked okay.

Wait a minute. Whose signature was in the spot reserved for the tax preparer?

Garrett Lindstrom, CPA.

Interesting. But not particularly relevant. Garrett had owned his CPA practice for almost ten years. He probably did taxes for tons of our bank customers. Was the Carters' return included in the group we had taken from Garrett's house last night?

I reached into my drawer and removed the stashed returns. Herman and Glenda Carter. Would I find the other delinquent borrowers' return in there as well?

Bingo. Darren and Margie Andrews. Their return was also in the pile. I flipped open their loan file with increased interest. Another well-to-do retired couple buying a 2.2 million dollar home, this time with a 1.5 million loan.

Two delinquent borrowers who used the same CPA.

A clue? Or a coincidence?

My deductive processes needed a caffeine infusion. I headed toward the break room stopping at Stan's cube on the way. I was relieved to see he'd hung up his trench coat and fedora.

"Any luck with the returns?" he asked.

"I'm not sure, come grab a cup of coffee with me." The smell of scorched popcorn filtered into the hallway. "Hey, who burnt the..." My voice faltered when I saw Earl removing a blackened bag of popcorn from the microwave. He turned around with a sheepish look.

"Guess I stunk up the office, huh? I can never get the hang of this microwave popcorn. I thought I would have time to take a phone call but ..." His voice trailed off as he ruefully looked at the charred mess in his hand.

My brain did a quick calculation. Four, maybe five minutes to microwave one of the large bags of popcorn I store in the cupboard. That would occupy Earl while I checked out his office. Since Earl had full signing authority, he and Garrett could have been involved in some type of scam. It was a lot easier to commit fraud when you have an inside source.

"You know, that popcorn is really unreliable so I use this brand." I bent down and grabbed some of the stash I'd hidden in the back of the cupboard. When I straightened, I noticed Earl's eyes glued to the back of my thighs. He had a hungry look on his face but I couldn't tell if it was directed at the popcorn or at me.

I handed the canary-yellow bag to my boss. "Make sure you don't leave the break room while it's cooking or you'll burn it. Stan, tell Earl about that problem file we were working on."

Stan started to protest, but I stared him down. If anyone could drag out five minutes with useless chatter, Stan could. I zipped down the hallway, checking out the other cubicles to make sure a gallery full of viewers wasn't watching. Most of the staff appeared to be out to lunch. Or rather, out at lunch. Only a few of them were really out to lunch.

I slipped into Earl's office and plunked down in his chair, keeping an eye out for any employees passing by the door. I peeked through the mess on the desk. A few candy wrappers. A bowl of dried-up instant oatmeal and a half-eaten granola bar. A stack of loan files with familiar borrower names waiting for his review. As an underwriter, I had the authority to approve or reject a loan, but all rejected loans must have a second review by management. In this office, that was Earl.

I opened the top drawer. Messy, messy boy. Earl's desk made my cubicle look like Martha Stewart's by comparison. Napkins dotted with multicolored stains of dubious origin were interspersed with the usual office supplies. A trillion paper clips in every shade of the rainbow were scattered everywhere. I poked through the debris with a pencil—no telling what viral germs lurked in his desk.

My attention shifted to Earl's credenza. I squatted with my knees locked together, slid open the doors and shuffled through the folders. I glanced through a couple of files before I struck gold— Slater, Jeremy, typed on the label.

Male voices reverberated from outside the office. I thrust the files back in the credenza and ducked down. I peeked over the desk. Stan was attempting to block Earl from entering the office. I lowered my head just as a muffled crash sounded, followed by a loud expletive.

I couldn't resist looking. Stan must have run out of stalling tactics and decided to knock over the bowl of popcorn. White kernels, mixed with blue ceramic shards, covered the floor. Both guys had disappeared.

I grabbed the Slater file, stood and stretched, both knees creaking in harmony. I definitely needed to get to the gym. A tiny scrap of paper, the size of a fortune from a cookie, flipped out of the folder. I shoved it in my jacket pocket and streaked through the door. Seconds later the men returned, a broom and dustpan held in Stan's hands.

"Do you want me to clean that up for you?" Normally I balk at performing the menial tasks assigned to women for the past couple hundred years, but in this case, it would provide an excellent distraction.

"Here." Stan handed the broom to me. I grabbed it, tucking the pilfered file under my arm.

"Thanks, Laurel." Earl smiled slyly. "Like I said, I don't know what I would do without you. You don't mind if I have some more of that popcorn, do you?" Without waiting for an affirmative from me, he ambled in the direction of the break room.

"What were you doing in there?" Stan asked.

"I wanted to go through Earl's files and figured this might be my only opportunity. I found a file with 'Slater' written on the label. Unfortunately, you guys showed up and I didn't get to finish going through the stuff in his credenza."

Out of frustration, I walloped one of Stan's Ferragamo loafers with the broom then shoved it into his more than capable hands. I headed to my cubicle to review my purloined file.

Mary Lou popped her head over our adjoining wall. Today her attire included a lime-green suede jacket, matching turtleneck and black leather miniskirt. It didn't take much analysis to deduce another meet and greet with a member of the opposite sex must be scheduled.

"Did you go out to lunch?" she asked.

"Nope. Just the break room. Why?"

"Some big guy stopped by your cubicle. I told him you were probably at lunch." She giggled nervously. "He was kind of scary looking."

So was she, in her glow-in-the-dark outfit, but who was I to hand out fashion tips?

Was he one of those goons who visited Dr. Radovich's office? Or worse. Detective Bradford coming to arrest me. That man could frighten the Sopranos into becoming model citizens.

Her eyes veered in the direction of the reception area. "He's back. Good luck." She ducked back down.

I took a sip of cold coffee and turned to meet the big scary-looking guy.

CHAPTER TWENTY-FIVE

With an expression so stern he could scare the panties off a suspect, an angry Tom towered over my desk. "Hand them over."

I didn't waste time pretending I didn't know what he was talking about. I grabbed the original returns and handed them to him.

"Is this all of them? Did you make any copies?"

Did I personally make any copies? I chose to go with a literal translation and shook my head.

He thumped the pages against his hand. "Anything new in *your* investigation?"

Hey, that was my line. Did I detect a hint of sarcasm?

"Nope. No investigating. Just underwriting." The fact that two of the six sets of tax returns we found in Garrett's laundry hamper belonged to two of the bank's delinquent borrowers was curious, but at this point, it was a foreclosure problem for the bank, not a homicide issue.

"Good. I'll call you at home tonight. I expect you to be there."

He strode down the hallway leaving me alone with his ultimatum. This detective was starting to tick me off. It's a good thing we hadn't become involved. He was bossier than my mother.

Time to review the Jeremy Slater file that I'd grabbed from Earl's credenza before he noticed its absence. The loan file was for property on Ski Run Boulevard in South Lake Tahoe. Since the sales contract I'd discovered on Radovich's desk was for a condo located on Ski Run, this must be the same purchase. Jeremy's application indicated he owned only one piece of property, his residence in El Dorado Hills. It was valued at $700,000 with a mortgage of $300,000. His assets included several substantial bank accounts. He earned over $350,000 from his medical practice.

I glanced at his credit report. Two credit cards with small balances. He had a mortgage with our bank with a balance under $300,000 and another mortgage with Worldwide Bank for $1.2 million.

Where did that come from?

I went through his file again. His application clearly stated he owned only one property, his home. So why did the credit report show an additional 1.2 million loan? That's not a dollar amount someone forgets to mention.

According to the credit report, the jumbo mortgage was originated in June, only five months earlier, so there wouldn't be a record of it on his tax return. Even worse. The loan was ninety days delinquent. Jeremy was the last person I would expect to be behind on mortgage payments. Just out of curiosity, I looked to see if he did his own taxes.

Son of a CPA. Garrett Lindstrom had prepared the return.

We had a dead accountant who stored tax returns in his dirty laundry and a dead doctor with a delinquent loan. If I were Colombo I'd be in detecting heaven.

Me. I was just confused. Why was this file in Earl's credenza?

Time to use my detecting skills for my job. I went on the internet and within seconds, I was searching an El Dorado County Assessor's website. I typed in Jeremy's last name and the site immediately listed all El Dorado county properties owned by a Jeremy Slater. According to the tax rolls, Jeremy Slater owned two properties, both in El Dorado Hills.

The first property was the residence he listed on his loan application. The other property had an assessed value of $1.8 million sold to Jeremy Slater on June 22. That meant that the $1.2 million dollar loan must be on this property.

Big house. Big loan. Big problem if he couldn't make the payments. Was he delinquent because Dr. Radovich cleaned out the funds in their business account?

Using the parcel number, I was able to retrieve the street address from another web site, 124 Via del Lago. Builders in El Dorado

Hills are big on using Italian names for their subdivisions. I had to admit Via del Lago sounded way better than Street by the Lake.

I looked at my watch. Much as I hated to halt my investigation, it would have to wait until tomorrow. Time for this detective to morph into a mom. Since the school district had scheduled teacher meetings for the Friday before the Veterans weekend, Hank had informed me he would take the kids to Tahoe all four days. The weather in November could be iffy, meaning two feet of snow was as likely as sixty-degree temps.

The odds of Hank planning for inclement weather were as likely as the Easter Bunny showing up on Thanksgiving. That meant I needed to make sure Ben had snow gear that fit.

Supposedly, they were staying at some big fancy resort. Knowing Hank's ability to wheel and deal, he'd probably lined up a free stay that would involve sitting through a ninety-minute timeshare presentation. Jenna couldn't wait to use her empirical skills to calculate the most likely candidates to win horse races. With her assistance, Hank could clean up at the Sports Book. Why couldn't I have a normal daughter who wanted to shop and go to the spa?

I picked up Ben from soccer practice then drove to Budget Mart, the area big box store. Two hours and one hundred dollars later, Ben owned the latest in waterproof snow gear in a mottled green-and-brown camouflage pattern. The good news was that it was affordable. By the time he grew out of it, his taste in clothing hopefully would have improved.

The phone rang seconds after we walked into the house. My arms were loaded with parcels so Ben raced into the kitchen to answer the call. I plopped the packages on a chair and waited for him to hand the receiver to me.

Strange. He wandered into the living room chatting away. Must be his father on the line. A few minutes later, he ambled into the kitchen, his rounded cheeks as rosy as if he'd been playing in the snow.

He handed the phone to me. "It's for you."

"What do you want?" I asked Hank, annoyed that I was a hundred dollars poorer due to his winter expedition.

"I want to talk to the most beautiful murder suspect in the county," said my favorite baritone.

I flushed. "Oh, I thought Ben was talking to his dad. How did you get on the line?"

"Kristy called Ben so I thought I'd touch base with you after they finished."

So that was the reason for my son's inflamed cheeks. I hoped he was more successful with his budding romance than I'd been so far.

"I'm trying to decide if being called the most beautiful murder suspect in the county is a compliment. Although I suppose it's better than being known as the hottie in the Hangtown hoosegaw." My attempt at frontier humor ended in a whimper.

"I've tried to be brave," I blubbered, "but you guys don't seem to be getting anywhere. Anytime now Bradford is going to show up on my doorstep, arrest warrant in hand. I don't want to be Miranda-ized."

Tom waited patiently until my outburst was over and my sniffling had subsided.

I sighed. "Are you checking to make sure I'm staying out of trouble?"

"Is that possible?"

I wasn't in the mood for sarcasm. "Did you make any progress with those tax returns?"

"We reached a couple of his clients, but all we've learned so far is that Garrett had been their CPA for years. None of them had any complaints about his tax work. Why he chose to store those particular returns in a clothes hamper is beyond me. Do you have any ideas?"

"*Moi?* My job is to provide the evidence, not evaluate it."

He grunted. "Well in case you happen to run across an extra copy of those returns and happen to discover something we've missed, you will report back to me, right?"

Did I hear him correctly? Did Tom officially promote me to underwriting detective?

"Of course. Don't I always?"

"Yeah." He didn't bother to hide the sarcasm in his voice. "Listen, I'm about to share some critical information with you. Remember that motorcycle accident I mentioned last night? The one off Salmon Falls Road?"

"What about it?"

185

"The victim was a guy named Mike Clark. Does the name ring any bells?"

"No. Should it?"

"Not necessarily." He sounded relieved for some reason. "He's a part-time real estate appraiser. That's why I thought you might know him."

"Are you kidding? Every Tom, Dick and Mike became licensed appraisers in that last refinance boom. They made a fortune doing eight to ten appraisals a day. Half the time they didn't even bother getting out of their cars."

"Interesting, but not relevant," he replied.

"So what exactly is relevant?"

"Give me a minute. Originally we thought the victim took the curve too fast and then crashed down into this steep canyon. The bike was bashed in the rear, which could have occurred when it rolled down the hill. His body probably wouldn't have been discovered for days if some teenagers hadn't been wandering around looking for a private spot to do something they shouldn't be doing."

I chuckled. "You'll have to give them a medal."

"Yeah. Anyway when the guys examined the body, they found an unusual indentation on the back of his head that seemed inconsistent with the fact he was wearing a helmet. We think someone rammed his bike then went back and finished the job."

"What does that have to do with me?"

"The crime scene guys think there may be a similarity between Lindstrom's head injury and this one."

"Tom. You can't possibly think I had anything to do with this incident. Just because the guy is an appraiser."

His sigh reverberated over the phone line. "Let's just say I'm not the detective you need to convince. But as far as I'm concerned you're still the most beautiful murder suspect in the county."

CHAPTER TWENTY-SIX

Being assured that I was the most beautiful murder suspect in El Dorado County may have boosted my self-esteem, but it certainly did nothing for my peace of mind. Tom's remark just reinforced my belief that I would have to solve these murders before they hauled me off to jail.

Four new loans requiring a rush underwriting decision perched on the corner of my desk when I arrived at work the next morning. It wasn't until late afternoon that I finally had time to open both delinquent files and compare them, line item by line item.

The Carters were moving from a half-million-dollar house to the two-million-dollar residence on Vista del Monte. The Andrews lived in Placerville and planned to move down the hill to their multimillion-dollar purchase.

After reviewing both files, I couldn't fault Mary Lou for approving the loans. The borrowers appeared strong from both an income and asset standpoint. Everything looked in order. The loans funded a month apart from one another. So far, the only commonality was that Garrett had prepared both tax returns.

I flipped to the appraisals. Both of the Mediterranean style houses were gorgeous. For two million plus, they should be. I drooled over the photos, which revealed one mouthwatering custom feature after another. Granite counters, slate floors, Brazilian cherry built-in cabinets throughout the house, shower stalls as big as my bedroom.

I would kill to...

I would love to own a house like that.

Reading down the second page of the appraisal, I finally had an A-ha moment.

It's standard procedure for an appraiser to use at least three recent sales to determine the value of a property. Each of these appraisals used identical comparable sales. It could be a coincidence, or there were limited sales in the two-million-plus range the appraiser could use. The distance between the properties was less than a quarter of a mile so they were probably all from the same subdivision.

My eyes dropped to the signature line.

Get out of town.

The appraiser was Mike Clark. I pulled open the other loan file and flipped to the back page. Mike Clark again.

The man who prepared the tax returns for the Andrews and Carter loans had been murdered.

The man who appraised both properties was dead. Possibly murdered.

The woman who underwrote both loan files was alive and—

I screamed and dropped one of the files on the floor as Mary Lou popped her over-permed blond curls over our adjoining wall. She shot me a curious look. "Laurel, are you okay?"

"Yeah, fine, just immersed in some loans." I bent over and rescued the file before glancing up at my cubicle mate. Could the beautiful blue-eyed blonde be a killer?

We must have been sharing the same wavelength. "Have you heard anything new about those murders?" she asked.

I dropped the folder again but this time it landed on my desk. "Nothing recent," I replied, wondering if she was making small talk or had a specific reason for asking.

"Do you have any more Love Club dates this weekend?" she asked. "I'm still waiting to see how that works out for you."

At the rate the bodies were piling up, it would be a very long wait.

"No dates in the near future. Say, I wondered if you've ever met Mike Clark? One of the bank's approved appraisers."

Her left eye twitched and her smile turned into a snarl. "He's no one you want to know." She grabbed her purse and sailed out of her cube.

What did she mean by that remark? I looked at my watch. Darn. Clues galore but no time to pursue them. The delinquent loans would have to wait until tomorrow. I needed to sneak out a few minutes early myself, so I could say goodbye to the kids before they disappeared for four days.

When I arrived home, Hank's black Ford truck sat in the driveway. Two battered navy suitcases, two backpacks, and a shopping bag full of boy's toys were scattered on the oak-planked entry. The squeak of a faulty piece of plywood resonated, as one, two, then three bodies clambered down the stairs.

"Mom," hollered both kids making me feel as welcome as Norm when he entered the bar in *Cheers*.

"Hi, honey," greeted Hank. The warm, fuzzy feeling vanished when I realized my ex had been wandering through my home. For some reason, maybe because he designed and built the house himself, Hank still felt ownership. As far as I was concerned, the only ownership he possessed was providing the child support for me to make the mortgage payments.

I scowled at him. "What were you doing upstairs?"

"It's okay, Mom." Jenna laid her palm on my arm in an attempt to placate me. "The upstairs sink was dripping and I asked Dad to repair it."

Hank smiled. "If it needs fixing then I'm your man."

Okay. I could be a grown up, too. "Thanks. Are you guys ready to go?"

Ben threw his arms around my waist. "Dad says we can go sledding if it gets cold enough."

I raised my eyebrows at their father.

"Yep. If it drops below freezing, they're going to make snow at Sugar Bowl."

Brr. Snow in November wasn't my cup of hot chocolate, but I knew they'd have fun whatever they did. I hugged the kids until they complained I was squeezing them to death. Hank was halfway out the door when I had a thought.

"Hank, you know a lot of appraisers, don't you?"

"Yeah, I've bumped into quite a few of them when they were making their final inspections of the houses I've built. Why?"

"Do you know a guy named Mike Clark?"

That Mike Clark sure didn't have much of a fan base. Hank's face became darker than snow clouds over the Sierra. He clenched and unclenched his jaw then shook his head. "Nope."

I was stunned by his reaction, and so stupefied by his obvious lie that I stood there while he kissed my cheek and sauntered out to the truck.

I mulled over Hank's surprising response as I waved goodbye to the kids. He backed the truck down the driveway, turned right, and passed a car approaching from the opposite direction. A mud-speckled white sedan with big brown letters on its side and a bar of red, white and blue on its roof. The phone rang and I slammed the front door, racing into the kitchen before the caller could hang up.

"Laurel, it's Tom."

"Hi. Hey do you..." The pealing of the doorbell interrupted me. "Someone's at the door. Can you wait a minute?"

"Yeah, about that. I'll call you later." He hung up on me.

He hung up on me?

I was not in the mood to greet whatever maniac was ringing the bell so incessantly. I peered through the narrow window next to the front door. Why was Tall, Bald and Homely here this time of night? A nervous deputy shifted restlessly by his side. I flung open the door to be greeted by an official-looking document covered with the tiniest font I'd ever attempted to read.

"Ms. McKay, I have a warrant to search your house." Not waiting for a reply, Detective Bradford strode through the entry, followed by the deputy who bore a strong resemblance to a sad-eyed spaniel trotting after a St. Bernard.

Make that a Rottweiler. A St. Bernard would at least have brought me a keg of brandy.

CHAPTER TWENTY-SEVEN

"You can't do this," I stuttered.

Bradford blasted me with his razor-like gaze. The burly detective might be old, crotchety and biased against women, but I had a feeling his mental agility had not diminished.

"We most certainly can," he sneered. "It will be less painful if you cooperate with us."

Who me? Just call me Miss Cooperation.

"Fine." I said. "May I ask what you're looking for?"

"Let's start with where you keep your tools."

They must be looking for the murder weapon. It certainly wasn't in my house so I didn't have anything to worry about. Except I had no idea where my tools were hiding. I vaguely remembered Jenna using the hammer to hang a picture in her room. Years ago, my screwdriver had grown legs, occasionally appearing in the most unlikely places.

Tall and Bald noticed my hesitation. He smiled, looking like a cat, after he'd feasted on a canary for dinner. "If you can't direct us to your tool drawer or tool chest, we'll have to examine every inch of your house." He looked around the cluttered room. "Inch by inch."

"Hey," I protested. "I'm not reluctant to help but I don't know where all my tools are. It's not like I'm a contractor. Or a guy. Just do whatever you need to do, but please make as little mess as possible."

Detective Bradford and Deputy Spaniel—I still didn't know his name—conferred for a minute then split up. The younger deputy headed toward the kitchen and Bradford went into the garage. Good luck finding anything in there. The garage would probably look better after he scavenged through it.

I settled into the sofa and switched on the early evening news. The TV camera zeroed in on a reporter from Channel Two reporting live from the side of some road. He pointed down a rocky, treed hillside to a spot far below. I hit the volume button on the remote.

"I'm standing at the site on Salmon Falls Road where a deadly accident occurred three nights ago," announced the reporter. "Or was it murder?"

Uh-oh.

"The sheriff has been unavailable for comment. It's difficult to believe that three murders have occurred in this small county in less than a month. Our sources claim there are distinct similarities in each incident. Can these lovely Sierra foothills be harboring a serial murderer?"

The reporter shivered. I shivered along with him.

"This is Chuck Basso, reporting live from…"

Bang. The door into the kitchen slammed shut and I missed the last thing the reporter said. I leaped up from the sofa as Bradford entered the room. He grunted but didn't stop. The sound of his heavy feet clumping up the stairs alerted me to his current mission. I saw no reason to stay behind so I followed him. He crossed the threshold into Ben's room and hesitated. I was directly behind him and plowed into his back. Ouch. He was solid.

Ben's room already looked like it had been ransacked, but that was due to my son's packing technique, which consisted of emptying every drawer on his bed. It was one way of ensuring he didn't forget anything. Bradford shrugged his shoulders and moved on to the next room. My bedroom.

He walked over to my armoire then yanked on the handles of the top drawer.

I screamed and slammed the drawer shut, nicking the raised surface of the detective's hairy knuckles. His eyebrows drew together in one furry unattractive line. "So this is where you hide your tools."

No. This is where I hide my white cotton granny panties. I did not want that getting back to Tom Hunter. That mental image could be tough to erase.

We were in the middle of a glaring duel when the squeak of footsteps on the stairs got my attention. The young deputy stepped into the bedroom. He shifted from one foot to the next.

"Get on with it, Mengelkoch," Bradford barked.

He hesitated then asked me, "Would you mind if I use your bathroom?" He blushed as he looked at his superior officer.

"Of course not." I smiled sweetly at Deputy Mengelkoch as I reverted into Miss Cooperation. "The kids' bathroom is right across the hall."

He ducked his head then disappeared. Bradford and I returned to exchanging baleful glances. I was wondering if our stalemate would ever end when Bradford looked over my shoulder. He growled again.

"What now, Matt?"

I turned to see Deputy Mengelkoch beckoning to Bradford. The senior officer rolled his eyes then followed the deputy. I was tempted to use the opportunity to relocate my undesirable underwear, but I was also curious to see what the deputy had discovered. I followed the curmudgeonly detective across the hall and into the bathroom.

Matching schisms appeared on both sides of Bradford's craggy face as he broke into a broad grin. Was he admiring the rainbow-colored tropical fish décor, which dated back to Jenna's toddler days?

Or was he looking at...

What was that strange thing sitting on the vanity? It was almost a foot long. Funny-shaped metal on the top with a chipped red wood handle.

"Ms. McKay, thank you for making our job so easy," he said. "I never expected the murder weapon to be out in full view."

"Look, I don't know what that, that..." I waved my hand at the offending tool, "that doohickey is."

Bradford snickered. "You know I was beginning to think you were one of the smartest criminals I'd ever encountered. But it looks like Detective Hunter was finally successful in getting you to let your guard down. Imagine having the nerve to use the same pipe wrench not only as a murder weapon, but to fix a leaky pipe."

He pointed to the wet spot under the sink. The leak my ex-husband had fixed minutes before.

CHAPTER TWENTY-EIGHT

Two hours later, I was curled in a fetal position on the sofa, dressed in my red Betty Boop flannel pajamas and fleece robe. Multicolored candy wrappers littered the coffee table as I attempted to distract myself by watching a mindless reality show.

The detective and his deputy packaged the evidence, Hank's pipe wrench, which they were rushing to the crime lab to determine if the red paint on the handle matched the paint flecks discovered in the victims' wounds.

I expected Bradford to cuff me and take me down to headquarters. Luckily, my fingerprints weren't on the tool or I would have received an official invitation to a sleepover at the jail. With my luck, I'd be bunking with Burly Bertha, one of the Hangtown jailhouse locals.

Bradford repeated his previous warning not to leave town, then he and Mengelkoch pulled out of my driveway, tires squealing. I called Tom on his cell and we conversed briefly.

I accused him of pretending to fall for me in order to get me to confess to a crime I didn't commit. I waited for his response but he didn't deny anything.

So I hung up on him.

As far as the pipe wrench, what could I say? It was Hank's. But did that make him the murderer? I clutched the remote to my chest, massive hiccupping sobs wracking my body as I contemplated the duplicity of the men in my life. A bundle of fur jumped on my lap. A pair of sympathetic green eyes stared into mine as a tiny sandpaper tongue licked salty tears from my cheeks.

Pumpkin and I cuddled together watching TV until the late news came on. The two anchors greeted their audience and immediately launched into the lead story: the unsolved murders of El Dorado County.

I bolted up, disturbing the sleeping kitten. Pumpkin squawked as she tumbled off the sofa, landing on all fours. I grabbed my furry friend and she settled next to me. Two pairs of eyes glued to the news.

Camera shots veered from the River Inn to the hilly shot they'd shown on the earlier broadcast. Someone in the sheriff's department had leaked the surprising fact that the same weapon might have been responsible for the deaths of three prominent residents of El Dorado County—a CPA, a doctor, and a real estate appraiser.

The reporter interviewed several locals, all of them demanding additional resources be brought in to solve these horrible crimes. The camera switched back to the reporter on his hillside perch. His expression was grave as he spoke into the mike, "Chuck Basso, signing off from El Dorado County."

With this kind of media publicity, it could be mere hours before they hauled me in. What would I use for my defense? Tell them the father of my children owned the pipe wrench?

"Pumpkin, what should I do?" I moaned to the kitten. She stared at me with unblinking eyes then proceeded to clean her privates.

We all have different ways of dealing with stress.

I dealt with my own stress by watching *I Love Lucy* reruns into the wee hours of the morning. I woke at six, bleary eyed, bushy haired, and with a crick in my neck, but bound and determined to prove my innocence. Without the kids to slow me down, I arrived at the office a half hour early, beating Vivian twice in one week.

I vaguely recalled reading about a famous philosopher who declared there were only six degrees of separation between each person and everyone else on the planet.

Or maybe it was Kevin Bacon.

Regardless, in our small foothills community, the number must be even less. Just how many degrees separated my field of suspects from the victims?

Dr. Radovich—He had massive gambling losses and was stealing money from his partner. Was Garrett his CPA? If so, he might have killed both Jeremy and Garrett to cover up the theft.

195

Earl Fisher —Jeremy's loan file was in Earl's credenza. Mike Clark did appraisals for the bank. Earl knew Garrett Lindstrom even though he wouldn't admit how. Was Earl getting paid under the table to approve fraudulent loans?

Mary Lou—She underwrote both delinquent loans. She didn't like Mike. Was Mary Lou part of a financial scheme involving Mike, Garrett and Jeremy?

Hank—Jeremy was his doctor. He disliked Mike Clark. He hated the thought I was dating again. He owned a pipe wrench. Did he own *the* pipe wrench?

Detective Bradford—He suspected me of killing off my dates. I suspected him of trying to date my mother. That was a crime in itself.

Okay, Bradford wasn't a suspect, but any of the other four could have committed the murders. Would my ex-husband intentionally plan the trip to Tahoe, leaving behind the weapon that would implicate me in the murders he committed?

Omigod. Were my children at risk? I dialed Jenna's cell. No answer. I started to freak then remembered cell service in Tahoe was erratic. I hated to involve my mother but I needed maternal advice. I phoned her office.

"Centurion Real Estate, Peter Tyler speaking."

"Peter, it's Laurel. Is my mother in yet?"

"No, amazingly enough. Sometimes I think she lives here."

His comment made me laugh. "Yeah, there's a reason why she's the top producer."

"Well I'm going to give her a run for the money this month. I'm glad you called though. I'm looking forward to dinner tonight."

Oh, yeah. It's amazing how murder can distract a person from their social engagements. I doubted if I would be an entertaining dinner companion, but with Peter's knowledge of the local real estate market, I might get some of the bank's questions answered.

Tom was definitely out of the picture now that his underhanded scheme had been revealed. I still couldn't believe how he'd lured me into believing he cared about me.

Peter and I agreed he would pick me up at my house at seven. Mary Lou approached my cubicle so I said goodbye and hung up. "Sorry I jumped all over you when you mentioned Mike Clark

DYING FOR A DATE

yesterday," she apologized. "I would have stayed to explain but I'd promised to take Vivian to the body shop to pick up her SUV." When I raised my eyebrows, Mary Lou replied. "She hit a deer. Or, according to Vivian, it hit her."

"Poor dear," I said. Mary Lou sniggered when she realized I was referring to the doe-eyed version and not the crabby receptionist.

I flapped my hand at her. "Speaking of accidents that didn't end well, did you hear about Mike Clark?"

She nodded as she slumped in the guest chair. "I read about it in the paper this morning." Her baby blues widened as she met my gaze. "You don't think I had anything to do with it, do you?"

I shrugged and attempted to look non-accusatory. She contemplated the ceiling for a minute. "Okay, promise not to tell anyone what I'm about to tell you."

I wasn't sure I should promise in case she revealed anything criminal, but I nodded.

"Five years ago, Mike and I lived together briefly. At the time, I worked at another bank. One day I was underwriting a loan and the information on the appraisal didn't make sense. Mike was the appraiser so I asked him about it at dinner that night. It turned out the builder had bribed him to falsify some information. Mike stated the house was worth more than it really was. He promised me it only happened the one time and he'd never do anything like that again. When I told him I would still have to report it to my boss at the bank, he hit me. I chickened out and never told my boss." Tears welled in her eyes. "I moved out the next day."

Her face had turned a sickly shade of green, which did not blend well with the tangerine angora sweater and skirt ensemble she was wearing. She rubbed her palm over her forehead. "I feel a migraine coming on. I think I better go home."

She grabbed her purse and raced down the hallway in her four-inch stilettos. I stared after her, mulling over her rapid departure as well as her comments about the fraudulent appraisal Mike had produced five years ago. Could there be an issue with the appraised values of the two delinquent files?

In most fraud situations, the borrowers are the beneficiaries. In this case, if the loans went into foreclosure the borrowers would lose their custom homes. Plus their big down payments. It was odd they would purchase such huge houses and not make any payments, unless both families had encountered some recent financial reverses.

I flipped opened the preliminary title reports for the name of the seller. The owner of record for both houses was TLC Partners.

According to the legal description, both lots were part of a subdivision called Bella Lago. The words evoked images of a beautiful lake setting.

I lifted Jeremy Slater's loan file from my three-tiered tray and placed it on my desk. The 1.2 million dollar loan that appeared delinquent on his credit report was on a property located on Via del Lago, the same property used as a comparable sale for the Andrews and Carter files. I Googled the address. Just as the appraisal stated, the property was within a quarter mile of the Andrews and Carter houses.

Which proved nothing.

I tried Jenna on her cell. Nothing.

I called Liz. Voicemail.

I wandered down to Stan's cube. It was trench coat and fedora free. Where was my team when I needed them? I passed Earl's office. My boss sat behind his desk reading the funnies. He read the *Dilbert* comic strip daily, assuming it was a guide to good management skills. I heard him chuckling. If he was in a good mood, it might be an excellent time to ask about Jeremy's loan.

"Hi, Earl."

His face creased into a welcoming leer but at least it appeared friendly. He waved me into the office.

I settled into a chair and leaned forward. "You remember Jeremy Slater, right?"

He nodded. "Of course, one of the bank's best clients who died on your watch."

I wished people would stop thinking it was *my* responsibility to keep my dates alive. I was never going out with a large depositor again.

"Yeah, about that. Jeremy mentioned he was concerned about a mortgage he was trying to get on a vacation home in Tahoe. Did you help him with a loan?"

He reached into a jar of miniature candies, unwrapped the gold paper and stuffed the candy into his mouth. No invitation for me to do the same. I tapped my foot and counted to ten while he chewed.

"We started processing an application for him on a condo," he said at last. "When we ran his credit, it showed a ninety-day delinquency on a mortgage with another bank. We denied his loan but he claimed the delinquent loan didn't belong to him. Since he is, or was, such a good client of the bank, I told him I would research it. Once he died, there didn't seem to be much point in pursuing it."

Earl swiveled around and opened the credenza. He sifted through a stack of files, looking perplexed. It wasn't that easy maintaining an innocent expression when I knew the missing Slater file was currently in my possession.

"I must have mislaid the file." He reached for another shiny gold-wrapped candy. "So how's that Love Club thing going for you?"

The last thing I wanted to do was discuss my social life with Earl. "I've given up on the Love Club."

He cocked his finger at me. "Wise decision."

I agreed. No more men from the agency. No more detectives from the sheriff's department. I was sticking with referrals from now on. Speaking of which, I needed to see if my mother had returned my call.

I returned to my desk, checked both my office phone and my cell. No messages from Liz, my mother, or Jenna. I dialed Stan's cell. "Where are you?" I whined.

"I'm home sick," he sniffled, sounding equally whiny. "What do you want?"

"I need you. Are you on your death bed or just lying in bed watching your soaps?" Stan was a *Days of Our Lives* addict, recording the program daily and catching up on the weekends.

He sneezed in response. "Don't you have anyone else to pester?"

Not really. Everyone had disappeared. Stan was it.

"I have some detecting for you." That would be the true measure of determining how sick Stan really was.

"Can it wait? I've hung up my trench coat this week."

Okay, he definitely was ill. "I suppose, but..."

He sighed, sniffled, wheezed then sneezed. "Tell me what you want me to do."

I proceeded to explain about the multimillion-dollar delinquent loans and the coincidence they were all located in the same subdivision. Stan also lived in El Dorado Hills so he could drive by the houses, see if the borrowers were home, and perhaps find out why they never made any payments. He reluctantly agreed to complete the task sometime over the weekend.

By Monday, I hoped we'd discover something that would help the bank. Plus make them appreciate what a great employee I am. In case, they doubted the wisdom of employing a murder suspect.

I left the office promptly at five. Vivian was right behind me.

"You seem to be in a hurry. Hot date?" She smirked. "Hope this guy lasts longer than your last two."

I whipped my head around. "Hey, it's not my fault those other two guys died." At least, I didn't think it was. Unfortunately, I needed to prove my theory to the sheriff's department and I needed to do it fast.

"Yeah, that's what they all say," Vivian replied. "Have a nice weekend." Her door opener chirped and she entered her black Infinity. I glanced at her SUV. The body shop had done a great job of repairing whatever damage the deer had done. Maybe I should take my own car in there and see if they could sand down those dents on my Prius before my mother noticed.

As Vivian roared out of the parking lot, I stared at her, my face clouding up even more than the sky above me. Three accidents had occurred on Monday night. Was it a coincidence or not?

CHAPTER TWENTY-NINE

The phone rang as I zipped up my date night black skirt. I grabbed the extension by my bed.

"May I please speak with Laurel," said a familiar masculine voice, but one I couldn't place.

I ran through my database of male callers. It wasn't that large of a database.

"This is she."

"Um, Laurel, it's Earl, you know Earl Fisher—from the office," he added, as if there could be more than one Earl Fisher.

"Hi Earl, what's up?" My boss had never called me at home. Did he discover the missing Slater file in my desk drawer? I knew I should have put it back in his credenza.

He cleared his throat. "I wondered if you'd like to go to dinner with me tonight."

Over my dead body was my first thought as I attempted to jab my pearl earring stud into place.

"I don't think that would be appropriate. Besides I already have a date tonight."

"Oh? You gave me the impression you were done with the Love Club. Wouldn't you be more comfortable going out with someone from the office? Someone safe?"

Safe? I wasn't sure Earl qualified for that category. But this was the perfect opportunity to grill him.

"Before I could even think of going out with you, I need to know more about your relationship with Garrett Lindstrom. Were you and he involved in a scheme to defraud the bank?"

"What?" he yelled. "Are you drunk?"

Not yet, but the way my week was going it sounded tempting. I looked at the clock. Peter would arrive shortly. Time to play hardball.

"My contacts at the sheriff's department informed me you're the number one suspect in Garrett's death."

Okay, I was stretching the truth a little. But that comment might shake him up and get him talking.

I must have sounded more threatening than I intended. A crash followed by a scream assaulted my ear.

"Earl, are you all right? What happened?"

"I let go of my glass." Earl's voice quivered. "What do you mean I'm a suspect in Garrett's death? He's dead?"

"He died a few weeks ago. You didn't know that?"

"No. I haven't seen him in several years. He used to live a couple of blocks away from us. Garrett and my wife became romantically involved after they both joined the neighborhood watch committee. I guess they decided it was more fun to watch each other."

"I'm so sorry. I had no idea." Poor guy. I could certainly empathize with the torment of a wayward spouse.

"The four years since our divorce haven't been easy. I know you probably can't tell, but I don't date much."

I didn't have the heart to tell Earl it was fairly obvious.

"You didn't hear about Garrett's death on the news last night?" I asked. "Or read about it in the obituaries?"

"I don't watch the news. Too depressing. And who reads the obituaries?"

A few of my single girlfriends read them daily hoping to find eligible widowers, but that probably wasn't relevant to our current conversation.

"I had no idea he was dead." Earl paused and his voice reflected his terror. "Oh, jeez, you killed him, didn't you?"

"Me?"

"Yeah, I heard you telling the staff you whacked him with a cell phone," he shouted. "You're a murderer. I'm calling the cops."

"I didn't kill—"

The dial tone buzzed simultaneously with the doorbell pealing.

Great. Now Earl and I suspected each other of murder. That reminded me. I'd never gotten around to reading that slip of paper that had fallen out of Jeremy's file when I removed it from Earl's credenza. It must still be in my jacket pocket.

The doorbell continued its relentless ringing. Too many suspects. Too little time. The scrap of paper would have to wait until I returned home. I ran down the stairs and opened the front door. Peter greeted me, dressed in a black turtleneck, charcoal blazer and slacks. He held out a spray of multicolored fall flowers. The last bouquet I'd received was from Hank on our first wedding anniversary. Seventeen years ago.

I was touched by Peter's thoughtfulness. Knowing my interfering mother, she'd probably supplied him with a list of the top ten ways to woo her daughter. Peter followed me into the kitchen. His six-foot-two inches came in handy retrieving my one and only crystal vase from the top shelf of a cabinet.

"How long have you lived here?" he asked, while I attempted to arrange the yellow, orange and purple flowers. I vaguely remembered learning how to do this at some point in my life, but had never had any occasion to practice.

"Since Jenna was a toddler, almost fourteen years now." I finally gave up my power struggle with the flowers and jammed the stalks in the vase.

"That's right. Ben said he had an older sister." Peter chuckled. "I bet he keeps you on your toes. Are Ben and I going to have a Matchbox matchup before we go?"

"No, he won't be smashing any miniature cars into your wingtips this time." I smiled remembering the two of them playing on the floor at the real estate office. "Both kids are spending the weekend with their father in Tahoe. So you have me all to yourself."

Peter took my hand in his. "I'm looking forward to that."

I pulled my hand free. I liked Peter but I wasn't ready for any kind of intimacy just yet. I grabbed my black leather coat, and he courteously helped me with it. We were almost out the door when the phone rang.

"I'd better answer it. I've been trying to get hold of the kids all day." I ran into the kitchen and lifted up the receiver before the answering machine could kick in.

"Hi Laurel," said that familiar husky voice.

"Oh, it's you."

"Am I interrupting anything?" Tom Hunter asked.

"A dinner date, so if you'll excuse me." I waved at Peter, leaning against the door.

"Where are you going?"

"Why. Are you joining us? Bringing some matching metal jewelry for my wrists?"

"That's not necessary, Laurel. Besides..."

I heard voices shouting in the background. I glanced over at Peter. He frowned and pointed at his watch.

"Let me call you back in a few."

The dial tone came on and I banged the phone down. Peter gave me a curious look. "That conversation sounded intriguing," he said. "Was that one of your amateur detective buddies?"

"No. Just some jerk."

We'd almost made it to the front door when the phone trilled again. I flashed Peter an apologetic look and raced back into the kitchen skidding across the wood floor. "Hello," I gasped, winded from my twenty-foot run. No doubt about it. Time to enroll in a gym.

"Ms. McKay, Neil Schwartz from the *Mountain Democrat*," gurgled the Draino voice. "I'm glad I caught you. We never finished our conversation the other day."

"Mr. Schwartz, I have a dinner date. Can't you find someone else to annoy?" I wanted to hang up but was afraid if I upset the reporter I would end up as a headline on the front page of the paper. *Murder suspect seeking new victims to date.*

"Trust me, I have information you'll want to hear. Did you know the sheriff's department has identified the murder weapon? The killer used a pipe wrench."

Peter cleared his throat from the doorway. So far this conversation had yielded nothing I hadn't already learned from my own official sources. "Yes, I'm aware of the weapon that was used. I really need to leave now."

"How about giving us a statement regarding the fact your ex-husband has been hired by the largest plumbing company in Sacramento?" No comment other than the fact that maybe now I would receive my child support payments on time.

The reporter zeroed in for the kill. "Your ex has been reported as saying he would kill any man that got near you. Any comment now?"

CHAPTER THIRTY

I hung up on the nosy reporter and we made it out the front door without any further interruptions. Peter held on to my elbow as he guided me to his luxurious British racing-green Jaguar. Two more things in his favor—well-mannered and financially stable.

I was seething over the reporter's remarks. It took more than motive and a weapon to make a murderer. It took planning as well as guts, both of which Hank had in short supply. But he did have a temper. Did the breakup with Nadine send him over the edge?

Although Peter attempted to entertain me by sharing humorous real estate anecdotes during the ten-minute trip into Placerville, I couldn't stop replaying the reporter's implied accusation in my head. I'd read too many stories about husbands cracking up and killing their wives and children.

I fumbled in my purse for my cell. Shoot. We were in one of the hilly no-service zones. I'd try again after we reached the restaurant.

The Sequoia House had been renovated from a decaying clapboard Victorian mansion into a spectacular first-class restaurant. We pulled into the last vacant parking space. The massive stained-glass embossed doors opened into the beautifully remodeled entry. I stepped onto a gorgeous carpet, either Aubusson or Chinese, I never could keep them straight. Rose velvet chairs lined the wall for guests who had to wait for a table. Tonight that did not include us. We were immediately ushered into the Verandah dining room.

With its stained-glass windows, patterned-tin ceiling and plantation fans, I felt transported to a more tranquil time–the

Victorian era. A nice respite from the crazy life I called my own. The maître d' led us past a room full of antiques to our table. Once we'd been seated, I realized the velvet chairs had been designed for the sole purpose of promoting good posture. Our silver-haired waiter approached, brandishing two dinner menus along with a wine list.

"Would you prefer a white or red wine?" Peter peered at me over the large gold-embossed menu. "Maybe some champagne to celebrate our first date?"

My face colored slightly at the thought of my last date when I swigged almost an entire bottle of champagne.

"I think I'll stick to water for now."

He returned the wine list to the waiter with his request. "We'll have a bottle of the house Syrah. I might be able to talk her into sharing some of it later on."

After the waiter poured the wine and we ordered our dinners, rare steak and a baked potato for Peter, and blackened salmon accompanied by pesto mashed potatoes and *haricots verts*—AKA teeny-weeny green beans—for me, we settled back in our chairs.

Peter rested his elbows on the table and leaned in. "You look so stressed. I hoped this would be a nice break from your troubles."

"That's very sweet of you. I wish I could forget my problems, but I'm worried about my kids and concerned my ex-husband is involved in the murders."

Peter looked puzzled. "Why would you suspect your ex?"

"Well, for one thing, he's jealous of the men I've dated. I think that gives him a motive."

Peter smiled. "I'd be jealous if my beautiful ex-wife were dating other men." His compliment bolstered my spirits.

The waiter chose that moment to deliver our entrees. My cell buzzed just as he set down my plate. I rifled through my purse and located my phone. The call had come from Jenna.

"Would you excuse me? I need to call my daughter." I streaked out of the dining room before he could respond. The lobby was packed and noisy so I went into the ladies' room, which was surprisingly empty.

It turned out I had two voicemails. The first was from Jenna, bubbly and joyful, the result of picking five out of six winners at the Sports Book. She and Ben were having a wonderful time but would I please stop leaving so many messages and being such a worrywart. I didn't know whether to be relieved the kids were having a great time with Hank or annoyed that I'd been reclassified as a smothering mother. The second message was from Stan. It was unintelligible and incomprehensible. According to Stan, he'd gone door knocking, but there were no doors to knock on. I dialed his number.

"Ah-choo."

"Hey, it's Laurel. Are you okay?"

"Go away and leave me alone in sneezy peace."

"I'm sorry, but your message didn't make any sense. What do you mean there weren't any doors to knock on."

His next sneeze exploded into my eardrum. "I drove around and around those streets but there were no houses at any of the addresses you gave me. There's only one huge home with a for sale sign on it, and a sales trailer located on a knoll at the top of the subdivision."

"Are you sure you drove through the right subdivision?"

He honked again. "Hey, I may be on my death bed but I'm not delirious. Yet. Bella Lago. Off of Salmon Falls Road. I'm going back to bed."

The dial tone buzzed in my ear while a gazillion questions buzzed inside my brain. None of which would be answered in the rest room. Something fishy was going on and I was beginning to have an inkling where the stench was coming from.

I returned to the table and apologized for my absence. Peter was empathetic about my maternal concerns. "I can understand why you'd be concerned about your children's safety. When are they due home?"

"Not until Monday night. I think I may have worried over nothing. My daughter left a message and it sounds like both kids are having a great time."

Peter looked thoughtful as he sipped his wine. "So no more doubts about the ex."

I shrugged as I took a bite of my pesto mashed potatoes, which tasted far better than they looked. I had many doubts about my ex, but I seriously couldn't imagine him as a murderer.

In the meantime, a million questions milled around in my brain.

"My mother mentioned you're a developer. How are sales going in this market?"

"It's been kind of slow. But we think things will pick up again soon." Peter ran a finger around the rim of his wine glass. "The lots have the most incredible views of Folsom Lake. Nothing else like it in the area."

"What's the name of your subdivision again?" I snagged a bite of salmon as I waited for his answer.

"Bella Lago."

The salmon landed with a sick thud in my stomach.

Peter latched on to my free hand. "I'd love to show you the property sometime. The view of the lake from the top is spectacular." He ran his finger lightly down my palm. "And romantic."

His touch made me tremble. But not in a good way.

"Do you have any partners?"

"I do." He drained his wine glass and smacked it down on the table.

Peter's reticence was most unusual. Was it due to the typically competitive nature of real estate agents or something else entirely? I felt like a dog with a bone and I intended to keep gnawing until I got all of my answers. It was time to find out whose names the "L" and "C" stood for in the TLC partnership.

"How many houses have been built so far?"

He dropped his fork and knife on his plate. "Would you excuse me for a minute?" He stood and walked away from the table heading, I assumed, to the men's room.

I stared at the mound of pale green potatoes on my plate. They resembled miniature hills. I thought about the subdivision Peter had developed. And the three delinquent loans I'd uncovered. The empty lots Stan had driven by. What would it mean if Mike Clark had prepared appraisals on multimillion-dollar homes that did not exist? Who would benefit from the fraudulent sales?

Our eyes locked as Peter returned to the table.

I had the answer to my question.

CHAPTER THIRTY-ONE

Peter rested his hand on top of mine. "Sorry if I seemed a little testy. Bella Lago has become a real sore point. One problem after another. First, there were huge excavation costs because of more bedrock than the engineers anticipated. Then the county made us realign some of the water lines, another unexpected expense. " He reached for the bottle of Syrah and poured the remainder in his glass. "But I've taken care of all my issues. Finally."

The waiter arrived to clear our plates, producing dessert menus for each. Peter snatched my menu and returned it to the server. "Sorry to end our evening so quickly, but I received a call when I was away. A problem transaction." He turned to the waiter. "We'll take the check."

Fine with me. I needed time to evaluate the information Peter had divulged. And the information he'd been reluctant to disclose. We both remained silent as we entered his luxury sedan and headed back to my house.

I had no idea what Peter was thinking, but I hoped he didn't have the ability to read minds. Because my cerebral cortex was processing the information that it was quite likely I was sitting next to a murderer. And the murderer was about to deliver me to an empty house.

My heart pounded so hard I wondered if Peter could hear it. There had to be a safe place he could drop me. Somewhere I could call the cops.

I was mulling over a variety of safe havens when Peter interrupted my thought process. "Do you mind if we stop at the Centurion office before I take you home? It's right on the way."

I nodded. Perfect. Peter wouldn't expect me to run and there was a gas station around the corner from the building.

In less than ten minutes, we were at the Cameron Park office. Peter parked in front of the Centurion building and turned off the ignition. I was almost afraid to make eye contact with him, but he grinned, his left hand resting on the polished wood steering wheel.

I wondered if my imagination was getting out of control. Maybe I had read too many mysteries. An hour ago my ex-husband had been my number-one suspect. Now my date had moved into the first-place ranking.

I rummaged through my purse making sure my cell phone was accessible. One of Ben's leftover cherry gummy bears fell onto the immaculate floor of the car. I picked it up and dumped it in the side pocket.

Peter pushed open one of the frosted-glass doors and I followed him inside. I desperately needed to use the bathroom and a full bladder would not be conducive to a speedy getaway. Plus the bathroom would provide a convenient excuse to disappear for a few minutes.

"Peter, I'm going to use the ladies' room."

He nodded and headed to his own office. The overhead lights above the large brass-plated Centurion Realty sign barely lit the space. The empty desks shape-shifted into distorted monsters, ready to jump at me from the shadows.

By the time I reached the rear of the building my nerves were shot. I pushed on the bathroom door. The floor behind me creaked and I whirled around to a terrifying sight. One I'd read about in many a murder mystery but never expected to experience myself.

CHAPTER THIRTY-TWO

Boy, those mystery novels had it all wrong. When faced with a gun, I didn't want to flee.

I wanted to pee.

Peter grabbed my shoulder and spun me around, the hard end of the gun digging into the small of my back. He prodded me down the corridor into his office then shoved me into one of the chairs. My purse fell and some of the contents rolled onto the navy tweed carpet.

"You killed Garrett," I blurted out. "And Jeremy."

Peter laughed. Not a pleasant sound. He walked around the uncluttered desk and sat down. "Laurel, I swear you are as nosy as your mother. I thought if I took you to dinner, I could find out what you'd discovered. But you just wouldn't stop asking questions."

"I am not as nosy as my mother." Nobody is as nosy as my mother. I looked at the weapon pointed at me. My nosiness wasn't the real issue right now.

"Whatever. You've been poking around and I could tell at dinner you were close to figuring it all out. My plans have been screwed up ever since you joined that stupid Love Club. What are the odds you would be on a date with each of the men I killed on the night they died? If it weren't for you, no one would have tied Garrett and Jeremy's deaths together."

He cocked the gun right at my heart. It felt like an invisible bulls-eye was emblazoned over my left breast.

"But then the detectives decided you were the primary suspect which worked in my favor. The only hitch was Mike Clark. Mike was under the impression you'd accidentally killed Garrett with the cell phone. One day I slipped up and mentioned Garrett and I had fought. Mike figured out that I'd killed him. Eventually he realized I'd murdered Jeremy too. He tried to blackmail me. His partner. Can you believe it?"

Peter looked hurt that one of his gang of fraud fugitives had tried to extort money from him.

"So you killed Mike," I stated in a voice far calmer than I felt.

He smirked. "Right again. We agreed to meet at the Bella Lago sales office at midnight so I could pay him off. Once he left, I jumped in the company truck and followed his motorcycle out of the subdivision and down Salmon Falls Road. You know how windy that road is?"

He looked at me for confirmation.

"It's a dangerous strip of road. What did you do? Ram him in the back of his motorcycle?"

He nodded. "Yep. Just as he rounded a curve I smashed into his bike and it crashed down into the canyon. I was positive he was a goner, but I climbed down the hillside to make sure. He was still breathing. I grabbed the money then hit him on the back of his head with the pipe wrench. You can see I had no other choice, can't you?"

I bobbed my head in agreement. I wasn't sure Mike's blackmail was a perfect rationale for murdering him, but nodding seemed the most expedient response with a gun pointed at me.

"I was worried about using the same weapon I'd used on both Garrett and Jeremy, but I figured the buzzards would have him for dinner long before his body was discovered. I didn't expect those two teenagers to find him so quickly. Don't kids have curfews anymore?"

The subject of curfews was a continuing debate in my house but not a top priority right now. I balanced on the edge of the chair, my hands clasped together.

"I guess you were the one who rammed my Prius on Bass Lake Road, weren't you?" I said.

He nodded. "A lesser female would have been scared off by that accident. But not you."

I couldn't tell if Peter was annoyed with me or if he admired my tenacity. Considering my current situation, I wished I'd been a little less tenacious myself. Unable to resist, I asked the obvious. "The murders are all tied to Bella Lago, aren't they?"

He hesitated. I didn't know if it was the bottle of wine he'd downed at dinner or the fact he had nothing to lose by sharing his confession with me.

"You were right on target about the sales at Bella Lago. We had expectations for huge profits. Moving the water lines delayed the grand opening by six months."

"By then the market changed," I said, "and the economy was heading downhill fast."

"You got it. When we finally started selling lots, home prices were decreasing. Foreclosures were mounting. Not a lot of folks were looking to buy expensive lots to build multimillion-dollar homes.

"That subdivision drained me with all the cost overruns. We couldn't even sell the spec home we built. Everything I'd worked so hard for. We still had bills to pay to the bank, the subcontractors. There was only one thing we could do."

"Speaking of 'we,' does TLC stand for Tyler, Lindstrom and Clark?" I asked.

"Your mother was right. You are smart." He leered at me. "As well as hot."

My mother said I was smart? Peter thought I was hot?

I looked at the muzzle of the revolver and shivered. Regardless of how smart and hot I was, the gun was still pointed in my direction.

"So who came up with the idea? Garrett?"

He nodded. Of course. Garrett had tons of wealthy clients. As their CPA, his files contained not only their tax returns but copies of their W-2 forms, 1099 statements, and complete bank and investment company year-end statements.

"He could create an entire loan package with authentic documents." He smiled wickedly. "No one could tell they were fakes."

He was right. Neither Mary Lou, a senior underwriter, nor Earl had noticed anything amiss.

Peter continued to gloat over the deviousness of their scheme. "Garrett forged their signatures on the loan application and the closing documents. I'm a notary so that wasn't a problem. Mike produced fake appraisals with photos of other million-dollar homes in the area. All these Tuscan style houses look alike anyway. And no one ever inspected the houses."

That was true. Banks used to rely on their approved appraisers to protect them from fraud. It was only recently the government decided they needed to regulate that aspect of the lending business.

"How could you make sure the borrowers wouldn't catch on?"

He smacked the desk with the palm of his free hand. I curled back in my chair.

"Garrett was supposed to pick wealthy retirees, people who were set financially and who wouldn't be buying another house or applying for a new loan. We planned to make the mortgage payments for a couple of months and then pay off the fake loans when lots sold and we had the extra cash. We figured if they ran their credit report someday, it would just look like a bank error, a loan that was on the books for a brief period of time then paid off."

"But what about the collection letters the servicing department sends out?" My analytical mind kept looking for the flaws in his scheme.

"Not a problem. We used different fake post office boxes for each of the borrowers."

Peter eyes reproached me. "It was an excellent concept. Those big view parcels would have brought in profits of at least half a million each. It wasn't our fault the lots didn't sell and we couldn't pay off the fake loans. It was all due to the crappy economy."

Of course it wasn't his fault the fraudulent loans became delinquent. Totally due to the economy, which meant the list of people he could blame was endless.

"Okay, I understand your financial problems. And though I don't agree with what you did..." Peter glared at me. "I understand you needed cash."

Fear was temporarily replaced by curiosity. "But why did you have to kill three men?"

So maybe I am a little nosy.

My captor rummaged through his desk with his free hand, managing to keep the gun pointed at me with the other one. "One of Garrett's clients, Jeremy Slater, fit our profile: successful doctor with a nice home in Serrano. He had tons of money in the bank and no reason to apply for an equity line. We didn't think he would need to run a credit report."

"Then Jeremy decided to buy the vacation home in Tahoe," I said. "When his application was declined by the bank, he discovered a jumbo loan in his name on property he didn't own."

Peter nodded. He slammed the first drawer shut and opened another one. "Right again. We put that loan through Worldwide Bank. Jeremy contacted them and discovered they had a full file on him, tax returns, verified assets. At first, he thought his partner had committed the fraud because that bozo was siphoning cash from the practice to cover gambling losses. When his partner assured him he had nothing to do with the fake loan, Jeremy realized no one else had access to that information other than his personal CPA. Jeremy accused Garrett of creating a fraudulent loan and the dummy confessed."

That dummy Garrett.

"Jeremy and Garrett argued about it just hours before you and Garrett went out to dinner. He called me after he got home. He was not in a good mood."

Good.

"Garrett was drinking heavily to ease the pain from you hitting him..." Peter looked at me with admiration. "You really are quite a woman, Laurel."

Much as I appreciated the compliment, I was still terrified.

And I still had to pee.

"Anyway, when Garrett admitted he'd confessed the entire scheme to Jeremy that afternoon, I drove to his house to see if we could come up with some type of damage control. Garrett was freaking out. He picked up the phone to call the police. Said we needed to come clean. I had to stop him. That pipe wrench was lying on the kitchen counter by the sink—when Garrett turned away, I grabbed it, swung, and it was over."

His lip curled in satisfaction. "Just like that. My problem fixed in an instant. Your little encounter made you the perfect suspect so I stuffed him back in his car, threw the wrench in my trunk, and took off."

"So you killed Garrett with the pipe wrench. A red-handled wrench?" I guessed.

He nodded. "Craftsmen. The finest tools money can buy."

Yup. Craftsmen produced excellent tools. For contractors like my ex-husband. And killers like the man sitting across from me.

"Did Jeremy figure out you were also involved in the scam with Garrett? Is that why you killed him?"

He smirked, the fluorescent lights in the office making his emerald eyes glitter. "I had no choice. I told Jeremy I would take care of everything but he kept nagging me. He casually mentioned he was having dinner at the River Inn that evening although I had no idea you were his date. I realized that would be the perfect place to remove him from the picture. All I had to do was lure him out of the restaurant."

"So Jeremy responded to your text and met you outside."

"Yep. We walked over to the bluff to talk. The wrench had been so effective on Garrett that I stuffed it in the pocket of my cargo pants just in case. I distracted Jeremy and hit him on the head. It stunned him. Then I shoved him into the river. I figured the rocks and the water would take care of him. Everyone would think it was an accident. There was just one little complication."

"Always the complication, aren't you, Laurel?"

I was about to defend myself when lights flickered on throughout the outer office.

My heart dropped all the way to my flat feet as the sound of a familiar voice echoed from the hallway.

CHAPTER THIRTY-THREE

Centurion Real Estate's top producer strolled into Peter's office. "And here I thought I was the only one who stopped in on Saturday nights," Mother said. "You shouldn't be working when you're out with my daughter, Peter. Are you trying to snatch that number one spot from me?"

Peter and I looked at each other. I didn't know what to say.

He did. "Barbara, you and your daughter will be the end of me yet."

Or vice versa.

Her eyes widened as she zeroed in on the gun. "I thought you two were on a date. I realize Laurel can be a little difficult at times, but you don't have to point a gun at her."

"Mother, Peter killed Jeremy. And Garrett. And Mike, the appraiser."

"Mike who?" As usual, she focused on the most irrelevant part of the conversation.

"Never mind. It doesn't matter. What does matter is that Peter is a murderer and he's holding a gun. On both of us."

Her face paled and she slumped into the chair next to me. For once, she looked all of her sixty-two years. Peter drummed the fingers of his left hand on the desk although his gun hand remained steady. Was he trying to figure out what to do with us? Maybe I could give him some ideas.

"Please let us go," I pleaded. "You've got the money, Peter. Why don't you leave the country?"

"Wonderful idea," Mother chimed in. "I'd be happy to service your listings for you while you're gone."

One would think that when one's mother is facing a gun, she would *not* be tabulating real estate commissions in her head.

"Right. I'm sure neither of you would inform the sheriff's department. But I can't leave until Monday. Two more fake loans are recording at eight a.m. Once the sales proceeds are wired into the partnership account I'll transfer the money into my personal account."

He shifted the gun to his left hand and opened another drawer. "I've already booked a flight. By Monday afternoon, I'm off to Rio. All I need to figure out is the best way to dispatch you two."

I didn't care for the way he used the word *dispatch*. Who would know if we were missing? Hank and the kids wouldn't be home from Tahoe until Monday night. Tom knew I was on a dinner date so the earliest he might check on me would be tomorrow. And my mother, who wouldn't hesitate to intervene, had already done so.

"Wait a minute. The guy I saw with Jeremy had a bald spot on the back of his head."

"Just in case anyone saw me from a distance I chose to go *au naturel* that evening." Peter lifted the top of his thick blond hair. Damn. That was a great looking hairpiece. If we'd ever reached the kissing stage I guess I would have realized it.

The thought of kissing a murderer made my pesto potato-filled stomach lurch.

Peter pulled something out of the drawer and smiled in satisfaction as he waved a plane ticket at us. He motioned for both of us to stand.

I rose slowly, racking my brain for a way to extricate us from this mess. How could I get the gun away from Peter without either of us getting shot?

What would a kick-ass female detective do in this situation? And wouldn't it be great if one of those kick-ass women were here right now?

Peter herded us out of the office, turning off the lights as we walked ahead of him. No evidence of any midnight-oil-burning real estate agents left behind. He hesitated as we stood in front of the cars then reached into the pocket of his slacks for his keys.

Peter beeped open the trunk of the Jag indicating we should throw our purses inside. Darn, that eliminated any chance of us using our cell phones. He motioned to my mother to get behind the wheel. He ordered me to climb in the front passenger seat then he slid into the back seat.

"Barbara, if you try anything funny I won't think twice about putting a bullet in the back of your daughter's head."

Multiple shivers slithered down my spine as he stroked my cheek with the gun. I didn't doubt him for a minute. The man had already killed three people.

I thought about my children. At least I no longer had to worry about their father being guilty of murder and removed from their life. Now all I had to do was figure out how to keep them from losing their mother and grandmother.

CHAPTER THIRTY-FOUR

We drove out of the parking lot then took the entrance ramp heading west on Highway 50, exiting five minutes later on El Dorado Hills Boulevard. Once we crossed Green Valley Road and headed north on Salmon Falls Road, I realized where Peter was taking us.

Bella Lago.

After a silent and tortuously short drive, we arrived at the massive stone entrance.

"Barbara, hit the red button to the right of the visitor phone. That will open the gate. Then drive to the top of the hill."

The driver's window noiselessly rolled down and Mother stretched her left arm toward the intercom. Her knuckles gleamed white in the moonlight as she punched a round red button on the control panel.

The gate creaked an eerie greeting as we drove through. The large car silently glided up into sheer dark nothingness. The roads were steep and during the day, I imagined there would be beautiful vista points.

I shifted slightly and felt the cold metal caressing my neck. Moments later, we arrived at the summit. The hilltop had been leveled to make room for a small modular trailer that served as the sales office. As in most El Dorado Hills subdivisions, there were no streetlights. A smattering of stars sprinkled the dark velvet sky.

I felt as if I were in a dream. No, make that a nightmare. What good was all that mystery reading to me now? Nothing less than a miracle could get us out of this alive.

Mother parked next to a lone black truck. One that I imagined had acquired a few dents in the front bumper. She turned off the ignition and we sat in silence. Peter seemed lost in thought. I wasn't sure if I should interrupt him but that didn't stop Barbara Bingham. She twisted her head and looked directly at Peter. "If you harm us they'll hunt you down."

"No one will connect me with the two of you."

"But Peter," I objected, "I told several of my friends I was going out with you. And Mother probably told everyone about our date."

"Of course I did. I thought you two made a great couple. You have so much in common."

Yeah. I dated the men Peter murdered—*some* common denominator.

Peter nudged the back of my neck with the gun. "Get out of the car, both of you. No sudden moves."

We eased the car doors open. I wasn't planning on doing anything to upset Peter. Not while he was holding that gun.

Even though I wore my black leather coat, the gusts of wind chilled me on the inside. My mother shuffled forward, slowly rounding the front of the car. I reached out and clasped her slender frame to mine.

"Stop that!" Peter hollered. "Stay at least three feet away from each other."

We pulled apart and followed Peter up a makeshift wooden staircase to the sales office. Our captor turned away to fumble with his key ring. I looked around for a possible weapon. Off to the side of the trailer was a small pile of lumber.

As Peter attempted to open the door, I winked at my mother, placed my finger against my lips, and tiptoed back down the steps.

Creak.

Never try to make a stealthy getaway treading on cheap plywood.

Peter wheeled around. Mother's eyes bulged with fear as he shoved the gun into her side.

"Try that again and your mother is history. Now open the door." The keys clanged together as he threw them at my feet. Her eyes implored me to do as he instructed. I picked up the key ring from the foot of the stairs and trudged back up.

Darn. My first choice opened the door instantly. I hesitated but Peter pushed me into the trailer. He punched a light switch illuminating the office, then shoved my mother against a battered beige metal desk.

The sales office wasn't much to look at but that wasn't unusual for the early stages of a building project. Peter motioned for us to sit. I fell into one of the dark green plastic chairs and scanned the scratched surface of the desk. The desk was sadly lacking in potential weapons. I found a staple remover—which would be useful if Peter shot us with staples—and a glue stick.

Maybe I could glue his hands together.

Peter banged desk drawers open and shut. He finally held up a large black metal flashlight. "All right ladies, this will make your hike a little easier."

I pleaded with him one more time. "My ex and the kids will be trying to get hold of me. If I don't answer, I'm sure they'll call the police."

He smirked. "Didn't you say they weren't coming home until Monday evening?"

Lucky me. I finally met a man who listened to my babbling.

"I'm supposed to have dinner with Detective Bradford tomorrow," Mother said. "Certainly he'll wonder what happened to me."

I sensed my eyes bulging out of their sockets. "You have a date with Bradford? How could you? The guy thinks I'm a murderer."

She stiffened in her chair. "Robert is a very capable detective. Eventually he would have determined you were innocent."

"Well, I wish he'd discovered it a little quicker," I responded, nodding in Peter's direction.

"Laurel, dear, I—"

"Focus, ladies!" Peter waved the flashlight in one hand and the gun in the other. He grabbed my mother's arm and shoved her out the door. "It's time to take care of a few loose ends."

I didn't need to be clobbered over the head to know we were the loose ends. We were quickly running out of options. All that wine Peter had drunk should befuddle his thinking but he hadn't missed a thing so far.

Mother was right. Peter would be the chief suspect if I vanished. But how long would it take before anyone realized we were gone? Would Bradford be concerned when my mother didn't show up for their dinner date? Would Tom wonder where I was? Would he even care? By the time the sheriff's department put everything together, Peter would be thousands of miles away.

On a beach in Rio, clasping a delicious mojito in his murderous hands.

Peter handed the flashlight to me. The three of us hiked down the road away from the trailer. Peter walked behind us, the gun aimed at my back. The moon was a toothpick-sized sliver of light and the few stars didn't provide much illumination. The subdivision was supposed to have fabulous view lots, but the lake was invisible to my naked eye.

Massive shapes loomed alongside the road. The huge machines used for site development.

I increased the length of my stride; my mother followed my lead. I gradually veered to the right, hoping Peter wouldn't notice. As we reached the enormous vehicles, I directed the flashlight to the opposite side of the road and screamed. "Rattlesnake!"

Peter turned and pointed the gun in that direction. I took advantage of his momentary lapse of attention and bonked him with the jumbo-sized flashlight.

A gunshot rang out.

I clicked off the flashlight and grabbed my mother's hand. We raced to the earthmover closest to the road and hid behind one of its gigantic rubber tires.

I peeked out. Peter was still upright although rubbing the back of his head. I calculated how many bullets remained. In the old westerns, there were only six bullets in each gun. What was the norm these days? Next time I read a mystery, I would pay better attention to weaponry.

Assuming I would ever have the opportunity to read again.

We crouched behind the earthmover. It was so cold we could see our breath. Ice coursed through my veins but I didn't know if it was from the cold or my fear.

"C'mon ladies. You know I wouldn't hurt you. I just wanted a place to detain you until I left town."

Yeah, right. Shove our bodies in a shallow grave in the beautiful Bella Lago subdivision. That would detain us for a lifetime.

I edged away from the earthmover. Could we make a run for it and escape back to the sales office? I remembered seeing a phone on the desk. How long would it take 911 to get someone out here? And how would we keep Peter from shooting out the lock? And us.

Distracted, I slipped on a piece of gravel. The noise sounded as deafening as a boulder rolling down a mountainside.

Crack!

A bullet whizzed past my cheek. I picked up a fist-sized rock and threw it across the road.

Peter turned and fired in the direction the rock landed.

With his attention temporarily diverted, I grabbed my mother's arm and we darted over to one of the mammoth backhoes. Mother quickly clambered up the metal ladder and entered the small glass-enclosed cab. I scrambled up and squeezed into the enclosure. The tiny space was a tight fit and I vowed that if I survived this ordeal I would drop another ten pounds.

My mother looked perplexed as she gazed at the controls. Did we need a key to operate this thing?

"There's no ignition. I wonder how it starts?" she asked.

I pointed to a square numbered keypad on the console. What combination should I try?

I pressed 123 and the engine roared. Would we be able to escape and reach the safe haven of the sales office?

A shot rang out. The window exploded.

CHAPTER THIRTY-FIVE

The glass window of the backhoe disintegrated into a spider web of cracks.

"That SOB isn't going to hurt my baby." Mother yanked on some type of lever and we started moving forward. I couldn't decide if I was more stunned by the bullet hitting the window or my mother swearing. We rumbled onto the road. If I hadn't been so terrified I might have enjoyed the ride.

Peter stood in the middle of the pavement, his mouth gaping. Good thing he'd drunk all that wine. Otherwise his brain might have relayed a message to his legs to react more quickly. We were on the verge of mowing him down when he came to his senses. He ran to the side of the road and scaled the ladder of another big machine. No wonder his development costs were so high. Half the heavy equipment in the county resided in his subdivision. Our own backhoe careened downhill, away from the sales office—not the direction we needed to go.

"How do we turn this thing around?" I asked over the roar of our machine.

Mother looked for some type of braking mechanism. She must have found something because we jerked to a stop. She looked for a lever that would allow us to switch directions.

Bam. The grinding sound of metal hitting metal resounded through the night. My head hit the roof of the cab. The evening sky glimmered with the brilliance of a zillion stars before I blacked out.

When I came to, my head felt like it had partied in a trash compacter. The ringing in my ears sounded like a chorus of sirens.

"What happened?" I gingerly prodded a rapidly expanding lump on the top of my head.

"Peter rammed us." Tears ran down her lined cheeks. "I was so worried about you."

Wham. Another enormous jolt threw us into each other.

"I can't believe we're being rear-ended by a backhoe." I shook my head in disbelief. Bad idea. I almost blacked out again. The sirens grew louder. Accompanied by a hundred chain saws buzzing in unison. Suddenly an enormous beam of light pierced the dark sky. Was I losing consciousness again? Was that cosmic shaft of light radiating from heaven?

I peeked out the side window. Neither.

A helicopter from the California Highway Patrol hovered overhead, its searchlight focused on both vehicles. The clang of a bullet bouncing off metal resounded through the night.

The searchlight had turned us into sitting ducks—target practice for Peter. I swiveled in my seat. There must be a way to outfox him. Peter stood in the door of his cab, his left arm clasped around the metal frame, his right hand holding the gun leveled in our direction.

"Mom, do something."

She looked flummoxed by the array of levers. Technology has never been my forté but one of the joysticks had a drawing of a claw on it. It reminded me of the helpful drawings on my computer keyboard. When in doubt, go for it.

I pressed the button.

Bingo.

The immense claw-like attachment on the rear of our backhoe telescoped out and crashed through the front windshield of Peter's machine. The impact knocked him from his precarious perch. He fell and landed in a flurry of gravel on the side of the road.

"Those sirens are getting closer," Mother said. "I see headlights coming up the main road."

"Thank goodness. I thought I had permanent ringing in my ears."

The spotlight illuminated the killer, his face eggplant purple with anger and pain, as he rocked back and forth clutching his ankle.

I was petrified he still had possession of the gun. Peter crawled across the asphalt surface, his leg dragging behind him, in a desperate attempt to retrieve his weapon, which must have landed across the road.

Mother maneuvered the throttle and before you could say "Bella Lago," the huge front bucket lowered. She expertly scooped Peter up. Within seconds, he was trapped nine feet above the ground.

Flashing beacons of lights crested the hill. The noise of the sirens diminished as the cars screeched to a halt. The helicopter briefly touched down in an open area and an officer jumped out racing in our direction. Sheriff's deputies, their guns drawn, surrounded the backhoe. One of them bellowed through a megaphone. "Put your weapons down. Leave the vehicle. Now."

Okay with me. My entire body trembled from PTDMSS—post-traumatic dating a murderer stress syndrome. Mother opened the door and gracefully descended the ladder. Of course, she's taller and slimmer, and was dressed in a pair of slacks and flat-heeled shoes. I slipped on the second step, losing one high heel in the process. I almost landed on my well-padded posterior. Fortunately someone caught me before my legs were exposed up to my bikini wax.

Engulfed against a broad chest, my heart rate went into overdrive as Tom's arms wrapped around me.

"Uh, what should we do with this guy?" One of the deputies pointed to the backhoe bucket where Peter peered over the edge. Tom reluctantly released me.

"I'll take care of him," Mother said. With the agility of a teenager, she climbed into the machine. We applauded as she slowly lowered the bucket. Two of the deputies grabbed Peter and handcuffed his hands behind his back.

As the officers marched the prisoner past Tom and me, Peter's face contorted in anger. He spat at me, his spittle landing on my bare foot. "You stupid cow."

Stupid cow?

That was the last straw. I limped over and kicked Peter in the balls. The deputies couldn't stifle their grins as he bent over from the impact of my one remaining pointy-toed stiletto.

Tom drew me close and whispered in my ear. "Laurel McKay, you are one hell of a woman."

227

I was still in a state of shock, but it didn't keep me from asking, "How did you find us?"

"Brian called Liz to tell her he'd be working late. He suggested you girls go to dinner. When she told him you were on a date with Peter Tyler, he came unglued. Brian knew we were trying to put together a case against Tyler."

I shot an accusing look at him. "You never told me that."

He matched my look with one of his own. "You never gave me a chance."

Oh.

"We were suspicious Tyler had something to do with Mike Clark's death. He claimed he didn't know him, but Clark's fingerprints were in the sales trailer. It took a while to follow the paper trail, but we finally ascertained that TLC was a partnership between Tyler, Lindstrom, and Clark. With Tyler the last man standing, we knew he had to be our guy. We just didn't know why."

Good thing Tom knew an amateur bank detective. I'd fill him in on the details of the loan fraud case later.

"The minute Brian heard you were out with Peter, he called me and we raced to Placerville. I couldn't remember whom you were dining with, but I remembered last week you said you were going to The Sequoia."

After a lifetime of being ignored, I'd met two men who actually listened to me. Of course, one of them also tried to kill me.

"When we arrived at the restaurant you'd already departed. We sent deputies to Peter's house and the real estate office. The deputy who checked out the Centurion office noticed a red gummy bear on the recently vacuumed carpet in Tyler's office. That locked it up for me."

Good thing I hadn't gotten around to cleaning out my messy tote. Next time I'd leave a trail of colorful gummy bears. Although hopefully there wouldn't be a next time.

"How did you think of looking in Bella Lago?"

"What better place to stash a body than a beautiful but deserted lakeside setting? I hopped in the copter and we kept in touch with the other units. I didn't care how long it took. I was going to search every ravine in this county if I had to." His hand trembled as he lightly traced his fingers down my face. I sensed he wanted to kiss me but not with an audience of El Dorado County's finest watching us.

We stood next to each other. The heat radiating from the burly detective warmed me up as we watched Mother climb down from the backhoe. She picked up the shoe I'd lost, and ambled over to where we waited.

"Well, that was quite an adventure." Her eyes gleamed as she handed me my shoe. I merely stared at her, this woman who never failed to amaze me.

"When did you learn to operate a backhoe, and why didn't you tell me you could drive one?"

"I don't recall you ever asking me, dear. For your information, your father worked construction during the summer while he attended college." A wistful look passed across her face. "Sometimes I'd come out at night and we'd..." she hesitated and blushed, "we would fool around with the machines."

Fool around with the machines? Hey, I was her thirty-nine-year-old daughter. I'll bet they were fooling around *on* the machines.

"Ladies, I hate to make you do this but we need you to come to headquarters." Tom put his arm around me and squeezed. "I know you both must be exhausted but this can't wait. We want this guy locked up for good."

"That's fine," I said. "There's just one urgent thing I have to do first."

"Retrieving some evidence?"

I shook my head and raced into the sales office in search of the bathroom.

After we took care of that tactical maneuver, we walked over to Peter's car. Tom located the trunk release button on the Jaguar's console and we collected our purses. My hero had to coordinate the enormous force that had rescued us, so we climbed into the back of one of the squad cars. Deputy Sam would take us to headquarters where the sheriff waited to interview us.

The back of the patrol car wasn't the most aromatic place to be but I couldn't have cared less. I leaned my head against the leather seat and shut my eyes. My mother slid in and grabbed my hand in hers. We held on tight, exchanging weary smiles.

This was a Mother and Daughter outing we would never forget.

CHAPTER THIRTY-SIX

The next few hours were a blur. Once Peter sobered up, he lawyered up. He refused to say anything until his attorney was present. Because Peter had divulged his motive to me, I had to repeat my story numerous times before the sheriff was finally satisfied. My voice occasionally broke when I realized how close my children came to losing both their mother and their grandmother.

Detective Bradford sat next to my mother during my entire recital. He remained silent, gnawing away at a toothpick, with an occasional glance at her profile. When I got to the part where she lowered the backhoe bucket to scoop up Peter, he threw his head back and guffawed.

I wasn't too tired to miss the wink she gave him. Was she planning a romantic backhoe assignation with him? There was only one question yet to be resolved, at least, one question relating to this case. I had a ton of questions about this budding relationship between Mother and Detective Tall and Bald.

"What's the deal with Dr. Radovich and his gambling losses?" I asked.

"I'm happy to say we caught up with the doctor at a facility designed to help those with gambling addictions. For whatever reason, I think Jeremy's murder made him realize he needed help."

Or maybe Dr. Radovich had a little encouragement from the Sopranos duo. Either way, I was glad he was on the road to recovery.

At two-thirty, my mother and I were finally released. Tom arranged for one of the deputies to drop us at our respective houses. He promised to call me first thing in the morning.

Mother and I were exhausted and spent the drive in silence.

The deputy pulled into my driveway. I opened the car door then leaned over and hugged my mother. "I don't know what to say. You were completely amazing tonight."

"Honey, I wasn't half as incredible as you. You were the one who figured out Peter was the murderer." Her eyes started to tear as she clutched me close. "I am so very proud of you."

I frowned at her. "I still can't believe you set me up with a killer."

She chuckled. "Hey, every good real estate agent has to have a killer instinct."

I decided to ignore her and eased my tired body out of the squad car.

"Don't forget your purse." At last count, my mother had reminded me not to forget my purse approximately 4,580 times. After tonight's adventure, she could remind me as often as she wanted.

I grabbed my tote. "Thanks, Mom."

I let myself in the house and walked to the kitchen. Miniature tremors coursed through my body as I realized that only a few hours earlier, I'd stood in this room with a murderer.

Food, I needed food. No, make that carbs. I needed lots and lots of carbs. I opened the freezer and smiled. A gallon of brownie chunk ice cream beamed back at me.

I slid into a chair, dug my spoon into the chocolate delight and raised it to my lips. A blur of fur landed next to me, her reproachful green eyes meeting mine. I couldn't tell if Pumpkin wanted a snack, or if she was my reminder that I had vowed to lose weight if I came out of this ordeal alive. I sighed and put the tub back in the freezer.

Pumpkin was right on my heels as I climbed up the stairs. Fine with me. I could use a cuddle tonight, although I'd prefer to cuddle with a handsome detective. One who thought I was a helluva woman.

I walked into the bedroom and undressed, hanging my leather coat next to my red blazer. Suddenly I remembered the slip of paper I'd retrieved from Earl's office. The one I'd stuck in my jacket pocket then forgotten.

I reached inside, grabbed the minuscule piece of paper with its microscopic print and held it up to the light. Would the tiny fortune end up being a clue?

I read the words aloud.

The love of your life is right outside your door.

The doorbell pealed. I chuckled, tucked the tiny slip of paper into my pocket, and went to answer the door.

The End

AUTHOR'S NOTE

I hope you enjoyed reading this book as much as I enjoyed writing it. If so, please consider leaving a review. Favorable reviews help an author more than you can imagine.

All the Laurel McKay Mysteries are listed below.

Dying for a Date
Dying for a Dance
Dying for a Daiquiri
Dying for a Dude
Dying for a Donut
Dying for a Diamond

To find out about new books, upcoming events and contests, please sign up for my newsletter:

http://cindysamplebooks.com/mailing-list/

ACKNOWLEDGEMENTS

There are so many readers to thank– friends who loved the book, even in its early stages. Thanks to Barb, Cathy, CJ, Diana, Judy, Karen, Lisa, Lois, Lynne, Madelyn, Marci, Matt, Maxx, Michelle, Nancy, Nora, Penny, Robin, Sandi, Sunny, Sharon B, Sharon W, Tracy, Val and Vicki. Your positive remarks kept me going. I can't thank my critique group enough for their unwavering support and excellent suggestions (Kathy Asay, Norma Lehr, Pat Foulk, Rae James). Special thanks to the Cindy Sample fan club (Jaci, Jana, Liz, Nina, and Terri). They read, critiqued and reread some more.

Huge thanks to the professionals who ensured that my murderous schemes were accurate: Lt. Kevin House of the El Dorado County Sheriff's Department, and medical examiner/author D. P. Lyle, M.D.

I'd like to give a shout-out to Capitol Crimes, the Sacramento chapter of Sisters in Crime, the Sacramento Valley Rose and the Northern California Publishers & Authors for their support. Thanks also to Cindy Davis, Linda Houle and Lisa Smith, the Dream Team, who gave me the opportunity to follow my dream. Thanks to my new editor, Kathy Asay and my cover artist, Karen Phillips who have been a huge help in my new journey.

**Keep reading for an excerpt from Cindy Sample's
next Laurel McKay Mystery**
Dying for a Dance

CHAPTER ONE

I didn't think my night could get any worse. But when I stumbled on a dead man with my broken shoe heel stuffed in his mouth, I realized it definitely could.

I was valiantly attempting to learn the choreography for my best friend's New Year's Eve wedding. Liz envisioned a bridal party version of *Dancing with the Stars*. After I tripped my instructor for the third time in ten minutes, I decided the routine looked more like *Dancing with the Dorks*.

My twenty-one-year-old Vietnamese instructor, Bobby Nguyen, epitomized a ballroom dancer—tall and slender, graceful and flexible. Despite his attentive coaching, I remained cardboard stiff and clueless.

"C'mon, Laurel, remember what I told you," he said. "Bend your knees and make your thighs do the work."

I glanced down at my thighs. Obviously, work wasn't included in their job description.

The mirror-lined walls of the Golden Hills Dance Studio reflected my image multiple times. Shoulder length reddish-brown hair grazed my aqua V-neck sweater. Black tummy-tuck jeans provided much needed slenderizing, and my brand new silver shoes almost made me look like a dancer. Presentation is everything, especially when you have no clue what you're doing.

Frank Sinatra's version of "It Had to Be You," wafted from the speakers. Dimitri and Anya, a pair of instructors, glided by us, their synchronized movements mesmerizing to watch. I eyed them with envy. If I wanted to look as graceful as a gazelle, I had to stop charging around like a rhino on roller blades.

Bobby positioned himself with his head held high, shoulders down, right arm resting in the middle of my back. Per his instructions, I thrust out my chest, sucked in my stomach and tightened my butt.

"Let's do it," I said.

Bobby's soft tenor intoned the foxtrot count in my ear. "Slow, slow, quick, quick."

I repeated it to myself...slow, slow, quick, quick... ACK!

The heel of my right shoe slipped out from under me. With the grace of a defensive linebacker, I slid across the waxed floor and crashed into Dimitri and Anya. Bobby rushed over to assist me as I attempted to extricate myself from the tangle of arms and legs.

"Sorry." I shot an apologetic smile to the instructors.

As they rose to their feet, I overheard Dimitri refer to me as a "*klutzsky*." I had a feeling the words Anya muttered in Russian didn't translate into "nice dancing." The couple disappeared from the dance floor, probably in search of safer terrain.

My thirty-nine-year-old body hadn't performed the splits in at least thirty-six years. With Bobby's assistance, I struggled to my feet.

"Are you okay?" My teacher's eyes darkened with concern. Dance protocol recommends that you keep your partner upright, at least most of the time. I swayed to the right and discovered my heel was no longer connected to my right shoe. My one-hundred-fifty-dollar investment in sexy silver shoes had just gone down the proverbial drain.

"I'm okay, but my shoe isn't." I glared at the detached heel lying a few inches away. "Bobby, this incident confirms I'm not meant to dance the wedding routine."

"No, it only means we need to practice more. You've been dancing for less than three weeks. Do you have other shoes you can wear to finish our lesson?"

I nodded. "I came right from work so I'll change into my black heels."

Bobby gave me a sympathetic hug and I waltzed—okay, I still didn't know how to waltz—so I clumped through the enormous dance studio toward the back of the building where the cloakroom and studio owner's offices were located. As I walked past the office, I heard raised voices from behind the closed door.

Crack! The sound of a slap reverberated from the room.

Dimitri, the dance teacher I'd crashed into earlier, stormed out of the office. He slammed the door behind him. His elegant hand didn't quite cover the scarlet mark on his high Slavic cheekbone. He scowled at me then rushed away.

This studio was proving to be more drama-filled than the daytime soaps.

I entered the cloakroom and drumped my broken overpriced shoes into one of the small cubicles assigned to footwear. I slipped into my black faux leather pumps and headed back to the main dance floor for more foxtrot torture.

Forty uncomfortable minutes later, my private lesson with Bobby was over. My bunions ached and my toes hurt from being stomped on multiple times—by me.

I entered the cloakroom and exchanged smiles with an attractive dark-skinned student named Samantha. She zipped her jacket, picked up her shoe tote, and exited the room. I buttoned my black leather jacket and grabbed my purse. That's when I discovered my dismembered shoes had disappeared. I looked inside every one of the tiny cubicles, and pawed through the oversized gray wastebasket outside the door, in case someone had accidentally thrown them away. *Nada.*

My silver shoes had danced off without me.

I couldn't believe someone stole them. Liz's wedding was only three weeks away. Now I'd have to buy a new pair instead of merely repairing one shoe. At this rate, I would need a second job to pay for the honor of serving as matron of honor.

As I left the studio and walked through the parking lot, my mind rapidly calculated my additional wedding expenses.

I barely noticed the pink and lavender cotton candy clouds stretched across the twilight sky.

I did notice the man lying on the ground, a pool of blood under his head.

My silver heel jammed into his mouth.

I definitely noticed him.

ABOUT THE AUTHOR

Cindy Sample is a former mortgage banking CEO who decided plotting murder was more entertaining than plodding through paperwork. She retired to follow her lifelong dream of becoming a mystery author.

Her experiences with online dating sites fueled the concept for *Dying for a Date*, the first in her national bestselling Laurel McKay mysteries. The sequel, *Dying for a Dance*, winner of the 2011 NCPA Fiction Award, is based on her adventures in the glamorous world of ballroom dancing. Cindy thought her protagonist, Laurel McKay, needed a vacation in Hawaii, which resulted in *Dying for a Daiquiri*, a finalist for the 2014 Silver Falchion Award for Best Traditional Mystery.

Laurel returned to Placerville for her wildest ride yet in *Dying for a Dude*. The West will never be the same. *Dying for a Dude* was also a 2014 Next Generation Indie Award Finalist in both mystery and humor. Then on to *Dying for a Donut*, the most lip-smacking mystery of them all.

Cindy is a four-time finalist for the LEFTY Award for best humorous mystery and a past president of the Sacramento chapter of Sisters in Crime. She has served on the boards of the Sacramento Opera and YWCA. She is a member of Mystery Writers of America and Romance Writers of America. Cindy has two wonderful adult children who live too far away. She loves chatting with readers so feel free to contact her on any forum.

Sign up for her newsletter to find out about upcoming events and contests. http://cindysamplebooks.com/mailing-list/

Check out www.cindysamplebooks.com for contests
and other events.

Connect with Cindy on Facebook and Twitter
http://facebook.com/cindysampleauthor
http://twitter.com/cindysample1
Email Cindy at cindy@cindysamplebooks.com

38779771R10151

Made in the USA
Middletown, DE
12 March 2019